I0524862

This book is a work of fiction. Any resemblance to persons, locales, or organizations, whether real or imaginary, is purely coincidental

Blood Child

ISBN-13: 979-8-9850602-4-9

Library of Congress Control Number: 2025908715

A One Tempest Book

For the goobers Hannah, Sarah and James.

Acknowledgements

This work could never have been made possible without the generous help of others willing to share their thoughts, ideas and time in order to make this book a success. A big thank you to Carolyn Labrie, Alex Roy, Corinne Cohen, James Davis, Josh Rivera, Skip Pepin and of course mom and dad for all their help!

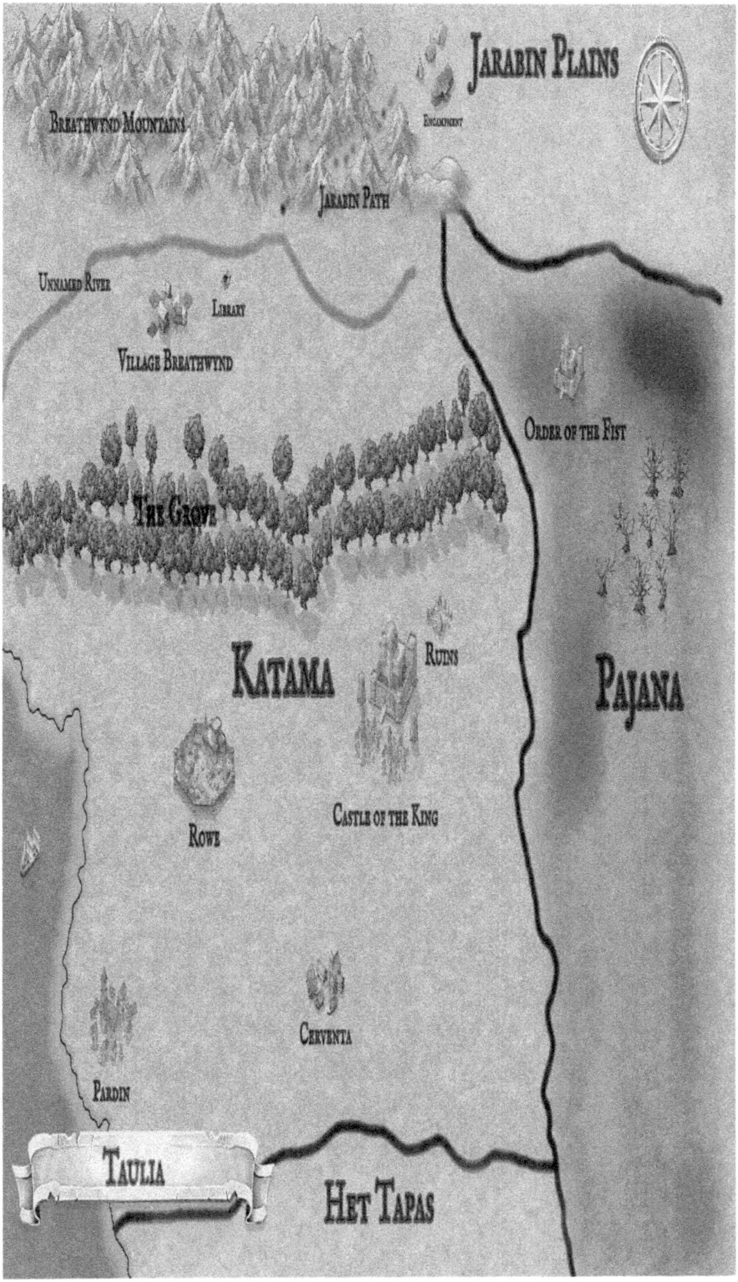
Jarabin Plains
Breathwynd Mountains
Encampment
Jarabin Path
Unnamed River
Library
Village Breathwynd
Order of the Fist
The Grove
Katama
Ruins
Pajana
Rowe
Castle of the King
Cerventa
Pardin
Taulia
Het Tapas

Blood Child

Volume III of the Dragonsouled Chronicles

Prologue

Corly screamed. A primal howl of rage, grief and anger building in the pit of her stomach and surging up the back of her throat before releasing every ounce of emotion the human condition allowed. Breathing heavily, the rawness in her throat matched the rawness of her shattered soul as she stared across the dim room at the person warily scrutinizing her.

Her face ached where she had been slashed and she could feel blood slowly seeping down her nose to mix with the tears flowing from her eyes. She had lost her Makavai, the ritual headdress marking the wearer as a Bloodsetter, when she had been slashed across the face. Lord Regam would be angry about that, but she had far more important things to worry about. Like this person she had to kill.

She had once loved him with all her heart, but after what he did to the people of their village she would never forgive nor forget until she had taken revenge. The deceased villagers he had left in his wake would never be able to rest unless she settled things here and only the Godlings above knew what horrors he would inflict upon further innocents should she fail. The memories of the night her village had been massacred felt like a lifetime ago, but the mental scars were still just as fresh as the night she had almost died. Ever since discovering the truth, she had never let her anger ebb or focus falter as she sought the one person she had dedicated herself to killing. Finally, *finally* she had found him.

Gripping her shortened blade, made exclusively for her diminutive frame, with sweaty palms she gritted her teeth against the throbbing ache in her face. Corly knew this might be her only chance to kill the creature her former friend had become and failing to do so would have far reaching consequences that she didn't want to think about.

He was more than just a friend. Much more. Shuddering, she forcibly suppressed the happier memories the two of them once had shared. Things had drastically changed in the course of a single night when her village had been razed to the ground by whatever *thing* the one standing across from her had become. She had been obsessively pursuing her vengeance ever since and had been taught extensively by her saviors where her efforts should be focused to be most effective. As soon as she encountered him and looked into his malformed eyes, she knew the person she had once loved no longer existed and that it was her responsibility alone to end things here before she lost her nerve.

Despite her best efforts to control her emotions, memories of the night Village Breathwynd was massacred kept pressing on her mind and she no longer tried to control her tears.

It had been right before dusk. Oltan and Darien had just left the bakery where she was assisting the village baker Mistress Wavely. Darien had gotten a good scolding earlier in the day when he had tried to pilfer some sweet rolls from right under Mistress Wavely's watchful eye. He should have known better, but sometimes Darien wasn't so bright despite all that studying he did. Mistress Wavely always took whatever chance she could to tell Oltan, the man raising Darien, he focused far too much on making Darien study and not enough time on learning some common sense. Corly had always found that side of Darien endearing since it was just part of who he was, even if it did often frustrate her.

After Oltan and Darien left she had been told to start cleaning the large ovens the village blacksmith, Master Beldhar, had built as a favor for the Mistress. The ovens and their ventilation system, built with some helpful information given by Oltan and the books from his library, were a marvel to the people of the village. Master Beldhar had spent so much time, effort and supplies forging, testing, re-forging and retesting the system until completion that he swore he would never make anything so complex ever again. The end product was so magnificent and structurally awe-inspiring that Corly doubted *anyone* could replicate the Master Smith's work. Each oven had a pump attached to its base that caused several blades inside the oven to rotate while they baked. Supposedly this moved the hot air around so things baked faster and increased the quality, but it didn't do her legs any favors after spending so much time stamping on the things! Not to mention how large each of them was and how long they took to clean afterwards!

"Not doing anything like that ever again! But you can bet the behind of any Godling ya fancy that they ain't coming down no matter what happens!" he had loudly proclaimed when pressed about his work by curious minds.

Corly did count it a bonus that she, Darien and the few others their age in the village had picked up some interesting curse words just by hanging around the bakery while the ovens were being worked on and installed. Johnder, Master Beldhar's apprentice and step-son who was slightly older than the rest of them, had been especially helpful in teaching them all they had wanted to know.

She pulled over the small wooden stool she needed to reach the upper handle and pulled herself up to crawl inside one of the three large ovens now that it had cooled and started happily humming to herself as she worked. Earlier she had walked down to the bakery with Darien after dropping off a delivery and having had breakfast together when she worked up the courage to quickly kiss him. She had been trying for quite some time to find the perfect opportunity to make her intentions clear since he was always so oblivious and she had finally found the right moment. She wondered if that morning was an indication of what mornings being married to Darien might be like. Corly giggled; she was in a decidedly good mood.

She giggled again at how surprised and embarrassed Darien had been. She had never seen him turn such a deep shade of crimson before.

I shouldn't have waited so long if I knew he was going to react that way!

She occupied her thoughts with other ways to elicit a similar reaction as she scrubbed away. For once the smell of burnt wood, ash and wheat didn't bother her a single bit. She heard Marsa, Mistress Wavely's other assistant, ask what was wrong with her since Corly was never this happy when tasked with the tedious chore of scrubbing the ovens.

"You can head on home dear. Don't worry about little miss Corly, she must have had a very good day today," Corly heard Mistress Wavely tell her senior assistant. "And I can think of a *very* good reason why!" she added loud enough that Corly was sure she was meant to hear.

Corly could feel her ears burning, but decided she didn't really mind the teasing. After all, she was finally getting things with Darien on track to where she had wanted them to be for a while now.

"I wonder what that reason could be? I'm suuuuure you'll tell me tomorrow, right?" Marsa whispered as stuck her head in to say her goodbyes. "By the way, I already turned the dampers on the main flues for you since you always forget so you owe me some gossip!"

Corly grumbled a bit, but Marsa did have a point. The senior assistant laughed merrily at her discomfort before departing. Corly sighed. *Great. Now I have to tell her everything that happened today.* Her and Darien's burgeoning relationship was a rather hot topic among the older people of the village so she was sure most everyone would know within a day or two if Marsa got all the details. She most certainly wasn't going to tell her about the kiss though, that's for sure!

With her determination set to keep the more intimate details a secret from Marsa, Corly continued her work. That was when she heard Oltan's familiar rasp again. She paused in her scrubbing at the unexpected interruption. *That's odd. We're closed now and Oltan should know that. Plus, Mistress Wavely gets up super early to start the day so why come back so late and after he had already been here?*

"I don't hear any cleaning happening in there dear!" Mistress Wavely called in a loud voice.

Corly jumped at the volume of the large woman's voice and almost bashed her head against the ceiling. Scrubbing in earnest, she tried her best to eavesdrop on what Oltan and Mistress Wavely were talking about. The sound of her cleaning drowned out most of the low voices and Corly frowned. Mistress Wavely never spoke in a low tone unless the conversation was about something serious, but then she heard the baker laugh loudly and say something about Oltan being "far too much of a worrier." and that she was sure that "everything will be just fine."

Her frown deepened. *What are they talking about?*

She slowed and almost stopped scrubbing again, but a loud and pointed "Harumph!" from Mistress Wavely got her moving double time. At this rate she'd never get the ovens clean enough to get Mistress Wavely's approval before she could leave, but her curiosity was getting the better of her.

She could still hear Oltan faintly protesting whatever the problem was and was surprised that he would continue after the Mistress had already given her opinion. He had never persisted so much in any matter before that she could remember outside of his giving lessons. *Something's not right. Maybe I should stop by after I'm done and make sure everything is ok.*

She knew it was just an excuse to see Darien again, but she decided she would go even though her parents would be furious with her for staying out so late. Plus, Darien would undoubtedly have to walk her home afterwards and a small smile curled at the corners of her lips at the thought of how surprised he would be when she dropped by unexpectedly twice in the same day.

He probably won't know what to say and get all flustered again. She had to admit she loved eliciting that kind of reaction from him.

Picking up humming another nameless tune, she scrubbed the first oven clean. Wiping the sweat from her brow she wrinkled her nose at the smell. *Maybe it wouldn't be such a good idea.*

Gathering up her supplies and inching backwards out of the large oven, her feet touched the top of her stool and she coughed lightly at the minor amount of ash covering her smock. She sneezed loudly and almost banged her head against the upper lip of the large oven door.

"Bless you dear. And please be careful. I don't want your parents complaining to me that you didn't arrive home in the same condition you left," Mistress Wavely boomed.

"Mmhmm," Corly sniffled before lifting her cleaning supplies into the next oven and dragging over the little wooden stool Oltan had made for her so she could climb up into the cavernous opening.

Hauling herself up into the second oven Corly thought she could hear what sounded like someone yelling out on the village commons, but shrugged it off and chose not to ask Mistress Wavely about it. "I don't want to get yelled at any more than I already have," she softly grumbled.

She sat up inside the oven and sighed at the amount of work she still had ahead of her. Mistress Wavely never let either her or Marsa leave unless their cleaning efforts met her strict specifications and there had been more than one occasion when she had had her ear twisted and admonished to do it again.

The painful thought got her moving as she began clearing and cleaning the second oven's insides. If Master Beldhar wasn't such a kind person she might have cursed his name for building something that was such a monstrosity to clean. Not that she ever would, but the thought did cross her mind.

Sighing at the tedious task of scrubbing another oven, she lightly hummed to herself once more. She always tried to distract herself in some way so that she wouldn't get overwhelmed by the amount of work ahead of her and humming or lightly singing was always her preferred method. It was something she always found relaxing and made her task more tolerable.

She became so engrossed in her work that she didn't notice the increase in volume and number of voices coming from the commons until Mistress Wavely suddenly poked her head inside the oven door.

"Stop what you're doing and open the emergency vent in the back! Stay put and be absolutely silent until I say otherwise!" she said with an urgency Corly had never heard before.

"What?" Corly jumped at the sudden intrusion and this time succeeded in banging her head on the ceiling of the oven. Rubbing her head, she managed to half turn around to get a look at Mistress Wavely, who had turned to look out the bakery door facing the village commons. She had never seen such a look of panic and concern on Mistress Wavely's face and it scared her near to death.

"Just do it child!" Mistress Wavely hissed before slamming the heavy oven door shut with a loud clang. A moment later Corly heard the locking lever sliding into place and loud voices mixing in with Mistress Wavely's own booming voice.

Corly stared at the inside of the oven door for a few moments in stunned silence.

Did she just lock me in here? Corly started to tremble slightly and felt her chest tighten. She crawled to the door and tested it to make sure that she really was locked in. She opened her mouth to call out in a panic, but quickly closed it. Mistress Wavely would never do something so reckless or so dangerous without good reason, but what was it? She tried to think about what was happening as she crawled to the back and unlatched the emergency ventilation hatch that connected to the building's exterior. It was a good thing Master Beldhar had the foresight to install such a thing 'just in case' as he had put it. At the time Mistress Wavely had chastised him for being too worrisome, but right now Corly was thankful for the prudent man's foresight.

Sitting in terrified silence she hugged her knees to her chest and tried to control her breathing. The slight inrushing of air from the small vent was minor consolation for her worry. Faint voices still filtered in from the outside, but she couldn't quite make out what they were saying. All that she could glean was whatever was happening on the green was causing commotion and panic. Taking slow, measured breaths Corly tried to think things through like Oltan had taught her and Darien to do in situations where nothing was clear.

She often joined Darien in his lessons beginning some number of years ago and took Oltan's teachings seriously, even if Darien himself often spent half his time daydreaming or trying to grasp things that went over his head. Because of Oltan she could read, write and do basic numbers, but she felt the most important thing she had learned was how to rationally think and assess, especially when things seemed odd or outside her normal experience. She took this aspect of his teachings most seriously because she noticed Darien often ignored the thinking part and tried to barrel straight ahead and charge through any problem. It was one of his habits that absolutely infuriated her, especially the times when the answer to a problem was painfully obvious.

Thinking of Darien was only serving to further her worry and distract her so she pushed aside her concern so she could focus while sitting in silence.

Oltan should be with him so he's probably fine.

She began to nibble on her thumbnail as she thought about what might be happening outside and hoping Darien was ok. Obviously something was very wrong, but she couldn't think of anything that would cause such worry and panic in the normally boisterous baker.

Biting her nails was a bad habit she had for whenever she got worried. Both her parents and Mistress Wavely had chastised her countless times over the years, but nothing they had done or said had been able to break her of the habit. There was something about it that always felt cathartic.

Her distracted thoughts continued until a familiar scent tickled her nostrils and she sneezed. Corly frowned. The smell was much like one she was used to having worked for so long in the bakery, but somehow felt...off. It was the scent of burning wood. Unlike when the bakery was in full operation, the scent lacked the familiar warm, comforting tinge of wheat bread and slowly burning embers that normally accompanied it. The smell was far more acrid and foul.

She couldn't figure out why she smelled something like this locked inside the oven since nothing had been baked in quite some time and everything had cooled off. After a few more worried moments she cocked her head to the side and put her small ear to the vent in the hopes of maybe catching something from outside. The faint rush of air tickled her ear as she strained her hearing and tried to keep her breathing steady.

Pushing her hearing to the limit she tried to ignore the sound of her heart pounding in her ears. She was able to pick up a jumbled mess of voices, but couldn't decipher what any of them were actually saying.

Whatever is happening, it must be pretty crazy.

She gnawed her thumbnail all the way down to the point where she drew blood and she unconsciously switched to the other one. She was able to pick out Mistress Wavely's voice among the rest, but the only word she could hear clearly was 'Oltan'.

Oltan? What in the name of all the Godlings is going on?

She debated as to what she should do. Mistress Wavely had told her to stay put, but she had always had problems sitting still for too long. Her choices were obviously limited as to what she could do locked inside as she was, but she was getting warmer and warmer by the moment. Sweat was beginning to drip in rivulets into all sorts of uncomfortable places and an overwhelming sense of claustrophobia washed over her. She opened her mouth in an attempt to call out to Mistress Wavely or anyone else that might be able to hear her when she was interrupted by angry shouts and a bloodcurdling scream that abruptly cut off.

Corly's stomach sank. Tears formed at the corners of her eyes as she tried to keep from panicking. She still didn't know what was happening, but instinctively felt like her life was in danger. Inside the oven kept getting hotter and hotter and now she understood why.

She sniffed back her tears as smoke began to slowly seep through the locked door. *The bakery is on fire!*

If she didn't find a way out quickly she would either burn or choke to death and neither was an option she desired. Her terror intensified and she screamed out for anyone who might be able to hear her as she began to hyperventilate.

"Mistress Wavely? Master Beldhar? Anyone!? Can you hear me? I'm still in here!" she yelled in a shrill voice. She scraped up her knees and elbows as she hurriedly crawled to the door and began banging on it in earnest with a small balled fist in near hysteria.

"Darien! Help!" she screamed as she continued to pummel the door with her diminutive fist.

Choking back a sob, more and more smoke entered her lungs. Corly crawled back to the emergency vent gagging and choking the entire way until she could get a small lungful of air. She gasped at the burning in her lungs as she inhaled.

The buildings outside must be on fire too!

Tears flowed from a face dirtied and streaked with soot as she tried to take another breath and stumble back towards the oven door in the desperate hope that someone, anyone, would come to her rescue. Her throat was so raw she could barely swallow and when she sniffled and wiped her nose her hand came away with no small amount of blood.

She was so hot that she felt like her skin was about to blister and her hands were swollen from their insistent hammering on the door. The smoke stung her eyes and filled her lungs as she fell back gagging for air. Corly weakly pulled herself back towards the vent again, hoping that the small amount of tainted air would be enough to keep her alive. Her breathing started to slow and her chest tightened even further as she continued to desperately gasp for air. Nearly fainting from lightheadedness, a dreadful pounding reverberated in her skull and felt that it was about to crack from the heat. "Help…." she softly cried one last time before gasping several heavy, sorrowful sobs and slumping unconscious around the vent.

"Alive…Barely breathing…" Corly's mind swam in confusion. Murmured voices from far away accompanied blurry images swimming before her eyes. Coughing raggedly, she winced at the pain shooting through her chest. Phlegm and bile rose unbidden in her throat and the disgusting mixture drooled down the side of her face. She gagged at the sensation as the rest of the concoction attempted to slide back down her throat. Corly felt more than saw a gentle hand tilt her head to the side and wipe away the goo threatening to choke her. She mumbled what she hoped was something like an apology, but all she could manage was garbled gibberish before vomiting.

A soft voice from somewhere above murmured for her to rest and she had no will to argue as her eyes rolled back into her head.

Corly woke sometime later in unfamiliar surroundings. Tents were haphazardly scattered about and men with deeply tanned skin and fierce looks spoke in low tones with harsh, brusque voices in a language she didn't understand.

Trying to sit up, her head swam sickeningly in protest. Her stomach agreed with this assessment and lurched to the point where she felt like she might vomit again. It was then that one of the strangely dressed men took notice she was awake.

"Easy there, girl. You've been through a tough spot. It is best for you to take it easy," he said in a cold voice.

She opened her mouth to protest that she was fine, but the man's next words cut through her like a knife. "That wasn't a request girl," he said with such tenacity and such a frightening look that Corly almost cried out in fear; at least she would have if she had had the energy to do so.

The man removed the red cloth covering his face and gave her a small, tight smile. "Do not worry girl. I will cause you no harm as long as you behave yourself."

Corly instinctively shrank back from the fierce man's voice. It had a harshness and hard edge to it she found extremely intimidating. Taking a breath to calm her nerves she attempted to dispel her confusion. It was obvious she had somehow made it out of the bakery alive and it was probably due to these men that she had been able to do so.

The man patiently waited in silence while she took several more calming breaths and shuddered at the sudden realization she was cold. The man handed her a coarse blanket that she gingerly wrapped around herself.

"That's the shock wearing off. Your body is beginning its recovery process. You will be fine eventually as long as you are strong enough to will it so."

"What?" Corly said in confusion as she shivered under the blanket. "I...I don't think I understand."

"Don't worry girl, you will."

Corly had hoped for more of an explanation, but it didn't seem like one was forthcoming.

Despite her condition, being called 'girl' by this strange man several times now grated on her nerves. Even in her confusion she understood she was indebted to these people, but that was something she wasn't going to allow to pass no matter who it was. Thinking about how she would react if Darien ever tried something like that gave her the anger to put her jumbled thoughts into words.

"Corly," she said, finding the strength to look the man in the eyes.

The man made no reaction, not even to blink, so she repeated herself.

"My name is Corly, not girl," she said, trying to put some emphasis behind her words and almost succeeding. She coughed some more and turned so that the man wouldn't see her spit. Taking several small breaths made her light headed again for a moment, but she forced herself to press on. "I'm guessing I have you to thank for rescuing me...um...can you please tell me your name?"

The man sat in silence for a few moments before smiling thinly and extending one large calloused hand. "You may call me Regam."

Chapter 1

It was a bumpy ride on the way to the town of Rowe. Regam had insisted on Corly sharing his mount despite her protests that she could walk once she got some rest.

"You would slow us down considerably should we be forced to match your pace. You will ride with me," Regam had said.

"But…" Corly had protested.

"That was not a request," Regam cut her off.

His tone never changed, but his demeanor took on a dangerous shift and Corly shivered when his hardened gaze settled on her. It was the first time she could remember being completely cowed by someone with just a glance. Not even Oltan at his sternest had been able to manage the feat. She discovered the sensation to be entirely unnerving.

She decided then and there she was going to approach things as they came very cautiously. This wasn't Darien or someone from the village she had known her whole life. Just by looking at Regam she could tell he was the no-nonsense type and his cold and indifferent demeanor made her wonder what kind of life he had lived up until now. He might even have killed someone before. It was a somewhat frightening experience to be in such close proximity to someone like Regam, but she hadn't been given any choice in the matter and she did owe her life to him after all.

Pulling the coarse blanket tightly around her, she tried to ignore the jolts and bumps along the road. Corly grimaced and resisted the urge to rub her backside. She had only ever seen horses before and had certainly never ridden one so these new sensations her body was experiencing were less than welcome. She was sure she would be sore all over once they did eventually stop, but she continued to grit her teeth, determined to show just how much the ride wasn't bothering her.

The ride wasn't even the worst of it; a headache continued to assail her while they rode and the nausea came and went as it pleased. Regam at least had the decency to pause long enough for when she needed to empty the meager contents of her stomach.

It had taken her no time at all to figure out Regam was the leader of whoever these people were. She hadn't had much of a chance to ask many questions since she had woken up, but that much was clear.

All the men traveling with Regam shared the same deeply tanned skin and wore similar clothing in cut and style; leggings of a straight cut and dark color were tucked into serviceable boots while their tunics were of a similarly dark color and loose fitting and worn. There were some minor differences here and there, but with uniformity all wore the same black head covering and red veil leaving only the eyes exposed.

Corly wasn't sure how long it had been since they had left the village, but at some point they must have stopped to rest the horses during one of her bouts of unconsciousness. A small and hastily thrown together camp had been made and the rest of the men were seriously and quietly eating bowls of tepid and quickly made stew. She was surprised when some of the men tossed their bowls aside once finished; leaving them abandoned in the dirt by the roadside. More surprising was her discovery that she no longer had a sense of smell. The stew she had been served wasn't exactly appetizing, but she should have been able to smell *something* from the pseudo-sludge she had been picking at. Her stomach still needed some time to recover and a few small bites were all she could manage.

While they rested and Corly tried to ignore the loss of her olfactory senses, she watched the men for a time while she recovered from her grief and pain with a fair amount of coughing, crying, wheezing and occasionally losing consciousness. There was no humor in them. It made her skin crawl at the lack of normal conversation, laughter or even smiles on the faces of so many people. The oddest part was that despite the lack of levity the men did seem to be quite close to one another. She could hear steady, but low conversations and the sharing of drink and food at meals bespoke a level of camaraderie among people who spent the majority of their time together. It was so different from the lively Village Breathwynd that she was having a difficult time adjusting to her new surroundings. Combined with what Regam had told her about what happened to her village made her heart constrict in her chest and tears fell unbidden from her eyes.

"Does it make you uncomfortable?" Regam suddenly asked.

Startled, Corly tried to understand what he meant.

"What...What do you mean?" she stammered. Her thoughts were still a bit muddled and she was embarrassed at how easily Regam had read her mood. Regam made a small gesture at those around him.

"Our people are not given to much emotion. There are many reasons for this, but I will not go into detail. There are also reasons for what may seem to be wasteful, but again such reasons are not for your concern. Now answer the question you were asked."

Corly shivered under her blanket again, but this time it was due to her being struck by the uncomfortable sensation of how Oltan used to chastise her when he felt she wasn't paying attention. She had *always* paid attention to Oltan's lessons; it was just that Darien was daydreaming half the time so she had to pay attention for both of them.

Pushing her thoughts of Darien aside for the moment Corly sniffed. "I'm sorry if I offended you, but this is all so new. Everyone seems close, but are acting much differently than anyone back at my village and nothing was ever wasted in Breathwynd. It's like you're all on the edge of losing hope."

"I see," was all she got in reply.

Corly tried to wrap herself even tighter in the blanket to hide her discomfort. She wasn't sure why, but she felt like she had just greatly offended the man who had saved her life. Oltan would definitely scold her for that.

After a few moments of uncomfortable silence Regam spoke in a cold, but thoughtful manner.

"It may seem that way to one unfamiliar with both our ways and our purpose, but that will come with time. The assertion that we are all on the edge may not be an entirely inaccurate assessment."

Clutching at her blanket Corly frowned and tried not to sniffle. Regam was staring out at his men as he spoke and the fact he didn't blink even once made Corly incredibly uncomfortable for reasons she couldn't quite place.

Regam remained silent for a time as he stared off at the horizon. Finally, he let out what may have been a sigh, but came out as more of a grunt as he stood.

"We move!" he said in a voice filled with unquestioned authority. He didn't shout, but his voice reached all of his men and they uniformly began packing their meager gear together.

Corly noticed here and there several quiet discussions occurred before certain items were purposely discarded seemingly at random; including kicking down one small tent that hadn't even been used as far as she could tell.

She spluttered as Regam hauled her unceremoniously back onto his mount and kicked it into a trot. Feeling woozy at the sudden movement she decided there must be a reason for their strange actions if Regam said so. Right now, thinking about it was making her head hurt and along with the throbbing in her bottom, legs and back she decided it would be best to decipher the riddle at a later time.

"We will have much better accommodations once we pass through the Grove and reach the city of Rowe," Regam tersely said in response to her reaction. "We will ensure you will receive the care that we currently cannot provide once we do."

"Thank you," Corly managed to say quietly.

She had been so befuddled and sickened by what had happened back at the village that she hadn't thought about what she would do once they reached Rowe.

Questions about what had happened cycled through her memory as she tried to grasp the sequence of events. Regam had filled her in on some things, but she could tell he had left out details. The last thing she remembered before her terrifying ordeal was something about the strange visitor who had appeared that very day. The rest was a hazy nightmare she feverishly tried to forget. Squeezing her eyes tightly shut Corly shuddered as she took a deep breath and slowly exhaled in order to calm her nerves.

After a few minutes of trying to compose herself she tried to think of a way to broach the subject of the missing gaps of

what had really happened to the village with the taciturn
Regam. He had obviously saved her life, and she was very
grateful for him doing so, but what had happened to Darien
and the rest of the villagers? Why go out of his way to save
her when there didn't seem to be anyone else from Village
Breathwynd traveling with them? And why had they come
to Village Breathwynd in the first place? Most importantly
where were her parents?

A hazy conversation with Regam suddenly surfaced and
her heart rent in two. The rest of that conversation came
back to her in a rush and her breath caught in her chest as
she fought down a surge of panic. Maybe she hadn't been in
the right state of mind at the time or maybe she forced
herself to forget, but there was no doubt about the answer to
her questions. "They are all gone. We were too late. You
have my condolences for your loss." Regam's words echoed
in her head relentlessly as they rode.

Despite her efforts she wept quietly for her family, for
Oltan and Mistress Wavely and for Darien. She was at a loss
as to what she was supposed to do now, but Regam had given
her assurance she would be cared for in some capacity so she
clung to that hope. Her head swam a little and she tried to
calm herself only to be eventually lulled into a doze by the
swaying of the mount beneath them.

Regam waited for the girl to fall back asleep. As soon as
he felt her slump against him he began to relay orders to his
subordinates via rapidly moving his hands and fingers in a

complex fashion; what his people called the 'silent language'. It was more than likely the girl would have remained asleep even had a war horn sounded, but he wanted to take no chances, especially with their other precious 'cargo' being transported in tow a good distance behind them and out of the girl's sight.

'Fall back and prepare the old man for a conversation,' he signed to the one closest to him.

'At once.'

'And do not harm him much unless he attempts to defy us or escape. His Majesty wants him alive. At least for now.'

'Understood.'

A cold smile formed underneath his Makavai. He had purposefully kept their other cargo away from the girl for reasons even the densest of his men could understand, but he never took unnecessary risks. Once he finished relaying instructions to the Bloodsetter he made a brief show of obeisance by tapping his pointer and middle fingers to his heart with a quick bow before wheeling away.

Regam watched them go for a moment before he turned his attention back to the road while pondering his good fortune. Not only had this task netted them a major prize, but using this girl should also prove to be a golden opportunity in keeping said prize compliant with their wishes. Normally he would have simply killed the girl like they had the others of the village, but he had decided against it once he recalled the words of one of his compatriots prior to his departure. At first, she had been merely a countermeasure against their other cargo, but he was beginning to think she could possibly become more with the proper motivation and guidance.

Almost in tandem with his thoughts he heard the girl softly mutter a name she had mentioned before as she dozed. "Darien…"

He kicked his horse into a quicker pace now that his subordinate had rode away to carry out his instructions. Regam doubted this Darien was still alive after everything that had happened, but people often believed what they wanted to be true, no matter how unrealistic it may be. *I believe I may have some further use for you girl. Yes, this was a fortuitous day indeed. Our people are that much closer to reclaiming what is ours and you will play a role in that, I guarantee it.*

Tears streamed uncontrollably down Oltan's face. He had long since given up any type of struggle. For the thousandth time he cursed himself for being so ill-prepared for such a horrific and grievous event. He had been whole-heartedly confident he would have advanced warning should King Bamaul ever discover his whereabouts, but that confidence had been shattered in the most violent and terrifying way possible.

He clenched his jaw and squeezed his eyes tightly shut in order to stop the water works, but to no avail. Failing to hold back another anguished sob, Oltan tried to at least take some solace in that Darien had most likely remained undiscovered and that it might take the lad some time, but he was sure the boy would puzzle out the secret of the library in due time.

I should have acted less cautiously and more decisively once the Bloodsetter scout played deaf and dumb to my pleas. Had he had more foresight as to what level of atrocity the scout's presence foretold, he might have been able to do something to prevent the tragedy that had befallen them. Even if it meant getting his own hands soiled. If only he had been more persuasive and persistent with the village folk, they may have given in to his desperation. He had far too many 'what ifs' and 'if onlys' spiraling in his thoughts while he jostled around in the large sack serving as his current prison. The shackles tightly binding his ankles and wrists were cinched in so completely that they were already cutting into his skin and blood was seeping out from raw wounds.

Taking a deep, shuddering breath and trying to push aside these feelings of self-pity Oltan attempted to organize his thoughts. Continuing to bounce haphazardly around, he was struck by a spark of inspiration. His wrists shifted ever so slightly against the wetness coating his skin as the shackles continued to create a macabre lubricant. If he could at least get his arms free he may be able to utilize one of his last resorts in order to escape. It was more likely he'd end up killing himself, and a good number of Bloodsetters as well in the process, but if there was even a minute chance of escape and survival then he needed to take it.

Anything will be better than what I'm sure awaits me at the

Castle of the King, he thought with grim determination. *May the Godling of Providence Pronea protect and guide me*, he prayed as he tried to contort his body in a way that would allow him to work himself free from his manacles. Gritting his teeth against the blinding pain he forced the bindings to cut even deeper into his skin by pressing down on them against the horse underneath him.

It was gruesome and bloody work, but with some time he was realistically sure he would be free from the constraints on his wrists. The mount underneath him whickered and snorted in protest at his movements and Oltan temporarily froze in place.

Being discovered by the Bloodsetters that had bound him and were presumably acting as his escort would be troublesome, but it would be better if Regam was among them when he used his last resort. He took a deep breath and was about to silently send a prayer of thanks to Pronea when the movement underneath him ceased and he was suddenly and unceremoniously tossed to the ground.

Oltan winced at landing on his ailing hip; an old injury sustained in his younger days, and bit back a cry of pain. Letting the Bloodsetters know just how much pain he was in would only make it certain they would use it against him to cause even further anguish. Little did he know he was about to experience despair in a much more terrifying and vile manner.

Callused hands lifted him up and roughly pulled the sack off his head. Oltan blinked in the sudden sunlight and estimated it was late afternoon the day after the attack. As his vision focused and cleared, the last person he wanted to see loomed above him. He had hoped to at least be free of his constraints before confronting this person and utilizing his last resort, but Pronea had ignored his pleas. Cold and murderous eyes stared balefully down at him and it took all Oltan had not to shudder under the scrutiny.

"Good afternoon Oltan," Regam began cordially, his voice slightly muffled by the blood red veil of the Makavai covering his face. "I trust your journey so far has been less than comfortable?" Oltan remained silent, his plans of escape temporarily put on hold as he chose to see where Regam was going to take this conversation. "Feeling less than conversational? No matter. Concerning our sudden stop, I am sure that a man such as you would have some kind of contingency for this type of situation, am I correct?"

Oltan refused to be baited by Regam's taunts. Keeping his face impassive, Oltan lightly brushed his tongue up against the false teeth at the back of his mouth and cursed at his lack of luck in not having enough time to work himself free.

Regam suddenly grabbed Oltan by the face and roughly pulled him to his feet. A wave of dizziness washed over him from both the blood he had lost and the sudden movement. The blow to the head came swiftly as Regam cuffed him across the cheek with a balled fist, knocking Oltan heavily back to the ground. Oltan grunted as he hit the dirt, but refused to show the Bloodsetter just how much it hurt.

"Let me inform you of the reason for this unscheduled stop. I am well aware of just how soft-hearted you really are, especially when it comes to children, so I wanted to make sure you fully understood your situation."

Oltan's heart started to thump heavily in his chest. *Please Godlings above, no.* Outwardly he maintained calm despite all his pain and fatigue, but inwardly he was panicking. If Regam had somehow found the boy and discovered his connection to Aplesi and Elze he didn't know what he could possibly do to ensure they both escaped. Regam's next words were startling, but concerned him just as much.

"You are not the only guest we are bringing back from that abomination of a backwater village. Would you like to know who else has joined us for the journey back to the Castle of the King?"

Oltan's stomach dropped into his boots and he felt sick at the thought Darien had somehow also been captured. Despite his efforts, his concern must have shown on his face as the creases around Regam's eyes indicated a hard smile had formed under his ritual headdress.

"I wonder just how valuable a piece this youngster is? It would have been far less trouble to simply kill the child, but from your look of concern perhaps she has some value to you?"

She?

Oltan was confused, but managed to keep the surprise from his face. His mind whirled furiously as he thought about who Regam could possibly be referring to. There shouldn't have been anyone else in Village Breathwynd who held any relevance or value to Bamaul besides Darien and himself. Everyone else had been a native villager who had always lived under the shadow of the Breathwynd Mountains.

He continued to maintain his outward composure, but his heart pained at the thought that another innocent villager was suffering due to his ineptitude. The others had all had their lives ripped from them simply for living in the same village as him and he knew he would carry that pain, guilt, rage and grief with him for the rest of his life, but now he was sure whoever Regam had taken with them was suffering even worse. Oltan couldn't imagine how much grief and confusion the youngster must be experiencing and it threatened to tear his already worn heart in half.

Despite his fears, Oltan tried to hold onto the meager hope that this was a bluff; a way for Regam to exert total control over him. He wouldn't put it past the man to employ such a tactic. His thoughts must have shown on his face as Regam removed the red cloth and his mouth split in a thin, cold smile. Regam removed a small, thin object from within the folds of his tunic and the blood drained from Oltan's face. Dangling the ribbon inches from Oltan's eyes Regam quietly spoke, his words dripping with venom.

"This was taken from her as she slumbered. I believe her name is Corly. Does that sound familiar old man?"

Oltan's body went limp as all of his will to resist instantly drained from him. Slumping to the ground in defeat, he temporarily forgot his wounds as his mind reeled at this revelation. The lavender ribbon was the same one Darien had bought to celebrate her Name Day years past that Corly always used to tie her braids together. Oltan could never mistake it for anything else.

The lines around Regam's eyes crinkled with malice at Oltan's reaction. "So, the waif is known to you. Rest assured; no harm will come to her so long as you do as you are told."

Oltan mutely nodded. His entire body remained numb at Regam's news. *Why didn't I think of putting the girl together with Darien? Surely I could have convinced both Wavely and her parents that it would have been fine! That woman was always pushing the two of them together every chance she got and was probably more excited at the inevitability of their betrothal more so than even Corly's parents!*

His mind was stumbling over his thoughts as he processed this new information. If the Bloodsetters under Regam's command had Corly in their grasp, then there really was nothing he could do; not even his plan for an emergency escape was feasible any longer. It was a completely hopeless situation.

A satisfied look flickered across Regam's eyes at Oltan's response to the information about Corly. "It seems you have come to a decision. Truly your soft-hearted attachments will finally be the end of you. Fitting."

Hanging his head low, Oltan grimaced at the bitterness he felt deep in his heart. It was unfathomable to him that someone could be so callous and cruel and not be as insane as that madman Bamaul.

"Do you not care for those around you in any way at all?" he said softly.

Regam slowly knelt and grabbed Oltan by the hair so that he was looking the old man eye to eye.

"I have a greater love for my people and our land than you could ever imagine old man," Regam spat with a surprising amount of disdain. "However, I would sacrifice any and all of them without a moment's hesitation to achieve our ends. Each one of us not only understands this, but feels much the same. Our end goal is all that matters and we will do whatever, sacrifice whoever, plunder, pillage, and destroy to take back what is rightfully ours. Only then will we rebuild and offer penance so that future generations can inherit the fruits of our labors."

Releasing Oltan with disgust, Regam sneered. "You are a fool who blindly ignores the past and its blatant transgressions while clinging to the present and with an eye only toward the kind of future you want for yourself. Letting your bleeding heart lead you to take in worthless refugees and giving them a place of supposed honor for whatever petty 'services' that ignoramus Tammaz and his ancestors found laudable. There were others far more in need and far more deserving of aid that were not only wholeheartedly ignored, but exploited and displaced. You disgust me."

Oltan knew he had been utterly defeated. His only hope

now was that Darien had remained undiscovered and would leave Breathwynd far behind while Oltan somehow found a way to keep Corly from harm. However, the first was out of his hands completely while he had little hope of success for the second.

"There is little need for the sack any longer. Place him on the back of your horse. His behavior is guaranteed," Regam told one of his men.

Rough hands grabbed Oltan and he winced in pain. He was hauled up onto the backside of one of the mounts and his appointed escort was no less rough than Regam had been. Blinking back tears, he looked up at the sun beating down overhead and ground his teeth in frustration.

Godlings above, what do I do from here?

Chapter 2

Corly sneezed. Trying to discreetly wipe her nose on her sleeve she was concerned about the small amount of blood left behind, but she put that particular worry aside for the moment and looked around their current camp. It seemed like the one they had set up previously, but the men around her were more nervous and on edge. Several of them were peering down the road into the distance with obvious worry. It was the first sign of emotion she had seen any of them exhibit since her rescue and it unsettled her for reasons she couldn't quite put her finger on.

The man currently assigned to her barely even spared her a glance as she took everything in. He hadn't spoken a word since taking over from her previous escort with only a slight grunt of acknowledgement.

She sniffed. None of them had even given her their name besides Regam and she was pretty sure that wasn't going to change anytime soon. She mulled a few things over in her head before deciding that no harm could come from at least trying to draw the man into conversation, especially considering the constant silence was starting to drive her nuts.

"Excuse me, but why does everyone seem so nervous? Is there something dangerous up ahead?"

"Yes."

"What?" she yelped. She hadn't expected to even be acknowledged, much less answered directly, and the stark simplicity of his answer frightened her.

"What…what is it?" she asked with a slight warble in her voice. Her lower lip quivered and she felt the sudden urge to relieve her bladder, but she wasn't about to embarrass herself in front of one of the people who had rescued her. Instinctively gnawing at her nails she nervously waited for an answer.

Her escort shifted his focus to her for an intense moment before looking away and speaking two simple words.

"The Grove."

Corly's breath caught in her throat. The Grove was legendary to even those who had never left Village Breathwynd. Very few from the village, other than Oltan, ever risked the Travel Road cutting through the mysterious Grove. There were many, many stories about the place circulating amongst the villagers and none of them were good. It was one of the major reasons, along with the Breathwynd Mountains themselves, that Village Breathwynd was so vastly segregated from the rest of Katama.

"Why…why would you want to go through there?

Haven't you heard all of those horrific stories? We could all go missing, or worse! We could all die in there!"

Her heart was hammering in her chest and her panic rose higher by the moment as her adolescent mind conjured all sorts of horrific fates surely waiting in store for them. The thought of being subjected to the mystic uncertainties and horrors of the Grove so soon after being saved from being roasted alive was enough to break her. She began recalling all the stories she had heard over the years and those played out by Hulgar's Traveling Troupe that had recently visited Breathwynd were at the forefront.

A girl had gone off the Travel Road and went missing during the troupe's journey. Supposedly she followed them from just out of sight until they had left the Grove without ever reuniting with them no matter how much they pleaded. Hulgar himself had described the terms of her pursuit as if she had become a fairy of the forest and by the end he doubted the girl was the same as she had been and most likely would not have meant them well should she have chosen to reappear.

Before she knew it she was up and stumbling in a hurry to get away, to be anywhere but near the Grove and those willing to travel through it. In her beleaguered state and still wearing her restrictive baker's smock and dough clothes she was only able to move a short distance before her escort caught up and grabbed her by the collar, hauling her off her feet with minimal effort.

"Let me go! Are you crazy!" She kicked and flailed as

best she could, but none of the blows she landed with her diminutive fists had any effect. She was far too small and weak to break free of the man's vise-like grip. Her cries soon dissolved into incoherent babble as her frustration with her weakness only added to her mounting fear. It was enough to draw the attention of the entire camp and within moments Regam had arrived.

"Put her down." She was immediately dumped to the ground and found herself facing Regam before she had the wits to try to scramble away.

"You will remain calm," he said in an icy tone.

Corly sniffed back the tears forming at the corners of her eyes at Regam's no-nonsense manner. The inner turmoil caused by years of stories and tales of the Grove she had listened to uncountable times during her childhood warred with her fear of angering Regam. Despite still barely knowing the man his presence gave off an overwhelming aura of danger. Her mouth opened and closed a few times, but no words would come forth.

Regam said no more; he just stared at her. After a time Corly was able to get her breathing under control and calmed down. Regam nodded curtly while she composed herself.

"Good. There is nothing to fear for us from a place such as the Grove. However, to ease your troubled heart, know that we have secured additional security to ensure our safe passage."

Corly wanted to know what he meant by 'additional

security', but decided not to trust her voice until she had pulled herself together. Taking a deep breath she regained her feet, wiping away the dust and grime from her smock and rear with as much dignity as she could muster.

She felt a tiny bit foolish. It made sense that Regam and the others would know how to travel safely through the Grove. Otherwise how would they have gotten to Breathwynd in the first place? *Ugh. If Darien had seen that I would have died from embarrassment for sure!*

Regam waited for another few moments to ensure she wouldn't break her composure a second time before briskly stalking away without another word. The man assigned to her had never taken his eyes off the road stretching out before them during the entire exchange, but now he loudly snorted and turned back to Corly. "We eat."

Corly wrinkled her nose and fidgeted with the hem of her garb. Now that the excitement of the past few minutes had passed she realized she had a more pressing matter. The man had turned away and when she didn't immediately follow he turned back with an eyebrow arched in irritation. Blushing furiously, she mustered the courage to convey her dilemma.

"I need to...um...go," she stammered, mortified about having to explain this to a stranger.

The man stared at her for a moment before the light of understanding entered his eyes. He nodded and slightly changed direction. "This way."

Corly breathed a heavy sigh of relief despite the lingering

feeling of embarrassment. She followed nervously behind the man whose name she still didn't know for a few minutes before stopping at a hollow ditch carved into the earth a slight ways away from where they had stopped to rest.

The man casually waved at the ditch, indicating she should take care of what she needed to do.

Corly flushed a deep crimson. "Right here? Anyone can see!"

The man shrugged before waving away a fly that had alighted on his arm and turning to stare back in the direction of where the Grove lay once more.

Corly was beyond flustered, but gritted her teeth. It had been quite some time and her lower half was protesting against being held in for so long. She understood she didn't have much choice in the matter, but that didn't stop her from feeling that her sense of propriety was being torn to shreds. Taking a deep breath, she decided to make it as quick as possible and pray to the Godlings above that no one else showed up while she was there.

"Here goes nothing," she muttered darkly.

Corly could still feel how red her cheeks were some time later as the sun set and Katama's large moon slowly rose above their heads. Not even the cool breeze of eveningfall was helping much and the chirping of crickets in the distance, oblivious to her discomfort, irritated her somewhat. She was at least thankful it was still late summer and that it was getting warmer the further they traveled so the nights hadn't been too cold; certainly not as chilly as evenings under the Breathwynd Mountains usually were. As if to mock her the wind picked up slightly and Corly pulled the coarse blanket Regam had gifted her tightly about her slight frame.

"Every time!"

Each and every time she had had to utilize the makeshift latrine someone else had inevitably shown up to also relieve themselves.

They have no shame! she inwardly screamed. She felt the need to scream out loud, but knew that would be severely frowned upon. If only Darien was there she could pick a fight with him in order to feel better, but that obviously wasn't an option. She clenched the tepid bowl of stew in her tiny hands. The sudden thought about Darien caused a knot to tighten in her stomach and her feeling of embarrassment faded somewhat.

Staring at a bowl of stew that had been a staple of their diet since leaving Breathwynd and frowning at still not being able to smell anything, she tried to stamp out the crushing sadness and loneliness welling up in her chest. She barely had had any time to internally process what happened back at the village, much less grieve for those that died, but she didn't want to face the fact that Darien might be dead along with her parents and Oltan; not to mention Mistress Wavely, Master Beldhar, Marsa and all the others she had known her entire life. That would completely break her spirit. She just had to hold out hope Darien and some of the others had found a way to survive. *If I was able to get rescued that means others were too, right? But why didn't they come along with me?*

Regam hadn't said much more about what had happened other than the village had undergone a crisis that he and his men had been sent by King Bamaul to avert, but they arrived too late and all but her had perished.

Reminiscing about even more memories of Darien, her parents and others dear to her caused her to choke back a sudden sob that she covered up by pretending to choke on an oversized spoonful of the mediocre stew. None of the men around her even spared her a glance. They were all far too preoccupied with the looming monstrosity in the distance. Corly pulled her blanket even tighter as she stole nervous glances at the forbidding sight.

At some point during the failing light of day the Grove had finally come fully into view. It was even more expansive and foreboding than Corly had ever imagined.

More trees than she had ever seen in her life rose menacingly in the distance in either direction, silent sentinels looming over them and causing her to shiver in spite of her blanket. The calm night sky and the ethereal light from the stars and large moon overhead combined to make the silence of the waiting Grove even more intimidating.

It was probably her imagination, but she felt like even at this distance she could hear the leaves and branches of the Grove's massive and dark trees swaying in restless anticipation of their arrival. Her stomach rumbled at the variety of emotions rampaging through her and she had to force herself to eat the remains of her earlier meal. Regam had been insistent about needing nourishment for some reason and she had to force herself to finish what she had left from earlier. Tears started flowing again despite her best efforts and she quickly wiped them away with a free hand.

Argh! Her frustration and grief were about to boil over so she focused all of her energy on attacking the now sludgy stew as if it were responsible for all of her recent trials.

"Are you insane?"

Oltan glared at the man with bleary and bloodshot eyes.

Regam had come to pay him a visit just as he had the previous day.

"Is that the proper tone to take with the one taking responsibility for the waif's safety? Especially since you failed so miserably at doing so yourself?" Regam stared down at him coldly.

Oltan swallowed his heated words and wiped the sweat and grime from his face, a difficult task with his wrists still bound as they were. He wasn't sweating because of the weather, but because of what Regam had just told him.

"Are you truly caring for her safety after saying such a ludicrous thing?"

Regam smiled his familiar thin, cold smile. "The path we take is bartered and negotiated for. There is nothing to fear from the elements of the natural world for ones such as us.

You and your young friend however, will need to…behave yourselves to the utmost. I assure you it will most certainly be a matter of life and death where our broker is concerned."

Oltan worked his jaw several times, but no words were forthcoming, a rarity for him. The absurdity of what Regam was telling him defied all logic and common sense any sane person in this region of Katama would follow as absolute. He did have to take into consideration he was being toyed with as a matter of course in order to increase his stress and worry to keep his mind dull, but Oltan got the distinct impression from Regam's demeanor that what he had been told was the absolute truth.

Swallowing heavily, Oltan's mind tried to grasp the implications of Regam's plans.

"Are you truly confident you can safely travel this 'alternate route' through the Grove? Not even the Travel Road is guaranteed safety! Who or what is this broker? How can you be so sure it will keep its end of the bargain? There's no telling what sorts of wonders of the old world await those who venture into the undergrowth!"

Oltan was never one prone to panic, but when it came to the places of the world such as the Grove, even he was uncertain at best about its numerous wonders, mysteries and dangers.

Regam crossed his arms and glared at him from behind his Makavai.

"I need not give you any more assurances than I already

have. You will conduct yourself in a manner befitting your new station. Who knows what could happen to the waif should our additional baggage cause our broker offense. The creature is quite temperamental."

Oltan swallowed hard again. What madness was he about to bear witness to?

The two men standing nearby roughly knocked him to the dirt as Regam stalked away without another word. Oltan barely had the energy, stamina or mental acumen to right himself, but he forced his body into a seated position so as to not give his Bloodsetter captives the satisfaction of seeing him struggle.

Sighing, he struggled to comprehend any scenario that could present itself within the deep confines of the Grove. Considering Regam's words carefully Oltan surmised that both he and Corly were somehow not an expected piece of whatever pact had been struck. What were the terms of the agreement? What would happen when extra people not known about beforehand showed up without warning or explanation? The thought frightened him. He hung his head limply in order to gain even a few more moments to think.

No, I at least should be expected. They came to Breathwynd specifically because of me so that leaves Corly as an unknown variable in the agreement. Godlings above I need to do something, but what can I possibly do when presented with the plentiful unknowns of this situation?

He felt as if the Godlings themselves were testing him as he raised his dirty and sweat-streaked face to the darkening sky to ponder what was about to occur. A sudden blow to the back of the head sent him reeling, but he had expected it and had braced himself. He knew there was no chance that a Bloodsetter would allow a captive even a moment's peace if they could help it.

At least the boy is safe, he thought as rough hands forcefully hauled him onto his knees and shoved a spoonful of stale stew into his face.

Corly held her fear in spite of herself as they approached the indomitable Grove. Her heart pounded incessantly in her chest and her mouth had long gone dry at the inexorable approach. A sense of unease in the men around her was so palpable that even she could feel it. However, what had her truly worried, no terrified, was that Regam had informed her they wouldn't be taking the normal, more conventional route of the Travel Road they had been using so far. The only reason she had been able to keep her fear in check at the news was that Regam had given her a stern and intensive talking to about the need for her to keep her composure in the coming days. His tone had not only brooked no argument, but implied it would be dangerous to do so otherwise. Oddly, she had somewhat been reminded of how Oltan would scold Darien in the past for one thing or another, but she tried to suppress that familiar feeling and comply with Regam's instructions.

Once the group had finished final preparations they began to advance on the Grove looming large before them.

The Grove seemed to swallow the Travel Road whole as it disappeared into the legendary woodland and Corly had to fight off a sudden chill at the sight. She glanced nervously both left and right, but the Grove unilaterally stretched off forever in either direction. Cold sweat beaded on her forehead and she gritted her teeth as the group prepared to enter.

Dusk had fallen and a light breeze swirled, rustling the green, gray and silver leaves among the thick boles of the Grove. Here and there leaves of an indescribably vibrant auburn, gold and even soft lavender mixed in to add to the ethereal surroundings.

A pleasant earthy scent tickled the inside of her nostrils which was odd considering her recent lack of sense of smell and Corly couldn't resist the urge to breathe it in and let out an explosive breath. The scent coated her tongue as she breathed in and she found it to be not a wholly unpleasant sensation. Looking in awe at the massive boles surrounding her as she hesitantly stepped foot into the Grove for the first time she was almost certain the bark of the nearest tree expanded slightly, as if itself was alive and timing its breaths with her own.

The men around her still had that palpable sense of unease about them, clutching their weapons tightly and eyes never stopping for a moment as they surveyed the eerie surroundings. Regam was the only one who was nonplussed. Corly was certain by this point the man only had two emotions, serious and annoyed. Glancing sidelong at the man who had saved her life she guessed he was both at the moment.

"Hold here," were the only words Regam uttered. The message was quickly relayed among the rest and Corly wondered why they were just standing around. They had just entered and were only several yards into the Grove. She could still see the road leading up to the Grove from where she stood. *He could at least tell us what is happening! I feel like I'm about to burst!* From her perspective there didn't seem to be anything that should be causing them delay or concern, but knew enough that she didn't have any experience with a place like the Grove and kept her mouth shut and eyes and ears open in case of an emergency; a skill she had acquired over years of watching Darien constantly being admonished by Oltan for not thinking ahead.

The light wind stirred up again and Corly became acutely aware of just how overturned her life had become. Each breath she took infused her being with the myriad sensations of a woodland that few had ever dared to trespass and even fewer were worthy of. Reveling in the exotic sensations of the Grove Corly hyper-focused on her immediate area, from the particular tang in the air to the soft and earthy detritus beneath pressing up into her toes. More and more of the trees around her seemed to be mimicking the same expansion and breathing she had noticed earlier and a sense of bemused contentment infused her entire being. She briefly wondered why she had ever been afraid and how anyone could ever want to leave such a wondrous place. The feel of nature on her tongue was the most comforting and natural sensation she had ever known. Corly didn't need to fear a place of such comfort. She never needed to leave. It felt like home. It *was* home.

A rough shaking of her arm woke her from her reverie. Corly yelped in surprise as she found herself almost pressing her nose up to the bark of the tree she had noticed 'breathing' earlier.

"Be wary!" the man shaking her hissed.

"What…What?" she stammered, stumbling backwards and falling onto her rump.

"Be wary of the woods and the allure of leaving the road."

Shivering, Corly took a deep breath and caught herself just as that sweet and mysterious nature of the woods began assailing her senses again. Deciding it would be best to take shallow breaths for the foreseeable future Corly took a look around to see how the others were faring.

Several of the men were being shaken out of a daze by others and Corly couldn't be entirely sure, but she felt like there might have been less of them now than when they had entered. She glanced at Regam and noticed that he had fully immersed himself in his odd headdress that left only his eyes exposed. Corly was curious about the garment since all the men had one, but she hadn't had much of an opportunity to ask about it; especially since Regam was probably the only one who might even answer her. The dark black fabric wrapped tightly around his head and fell down to his shoulders while the deep red veil covering his face except for those unnervingly emotionless eyes served to enhance his intimidating demeanor.

"Isn't that enough?" he growled loudly into the stillness.

Corly blinked in surprise. That was the first time since her rescue she had heard any real emotion in Regam's voice.

Everyone stopped what they were doing and looked at their leader in confusion.

A light suddenly sprang to life off to Corly's left a few feet into the dense undergrowth. The glowing light slowly moved closer and closer until Corly had to squeeze her eyes tightly shut and look away from its intensity. The wind that had sprung up died back down in an instant and when Corly was able to open her eyes again the light had greatly diminished and in its place was a…person?

Corly's confusion stemmed from the fact this was the oddest and most mysterious person she had ever laid eyes on. Even her questions about Regam seemed insignificant in lieu of what was now gliding across the road towards them. She gasped and shook her head in order to clear her mind in case she had been bewitched again, but 'gliding' was the only way she could describe what she was witnessing. The figure looked to be female, but after almost getting eaten by a magical breathing tree she wasn't about to trust her normal senses just yet.

She held her breath as the mind-bending sight before her completely registered on her brain. The woman languidly gliding across the Grove was not only the most exceptionally beautiful person Corly had ever laid eyes on, but she was also exceptionally naked. Not a shred of cloth or clothing could be found, but the woman either didn't notice or didn't care about the world bearing witness to her nudity. Corly felt her face go hot at the brazen display, but couldn't tear her eyes away.

The woman was suffused in a light golden glow softly radiating off of her like the warmth of the sun. Light red hair was swept back from her face with a regal ringlet of gold and her fine porcelain features were sharply accentuated with penetrating green eyes sparkling even in the darkness surrounding them. Smooth alabaster skin without blemish or imperfection completed her appearance and the only word Corly's mind could come up with to describe the figure was 'immaculate'.

The woman continued her slow glide over to Regam while ignoring the rest of them and soundlessly alighted in front of him.

Corly started to feel a little lightheaded and realized she was still holding her breath. She slowly forced herself to again take small, calm breaths and fervently prayed this wasn't about to turn into a confrontation. She had the distinct impression there was little hope for them if it was.

Regam and the elegant woman stared silently at each other for an uncomfortable amount of time before Regam finally broke the terrifying stand-off.

"Turn that down, there's no need for that much," Regam said from behind clenched teeth.

The woman's regal countenance instantly changed. The

small, condescending smile among peaceful features suddenly became a raging tempest of anger and fury.

An invisible force erupted out of her, hurtling all of them to the ground and before Regam could regain his footing the woman had straddled atop him, her hand firmly grasping his neck.

Corly shook her head and spit out soil and detritus as she lay in the dirt and silently checked herself over for injuries. She winced at the soreness in her ribs, but otherwise she seemed to be fine. Regam, on the other hand, looked to be not so fine.

The woman's face was so close to his that they were nose to nose and the soft glow around her had begun pulsating in a steady rhythm. Corly tried her utmost not to make a sound. She had no idea what this woman was or what was happening, but the thought she might be killed so soon after being saved terrified her.

Glancing sidelong at the two she could barely make out the woman's mouth moving so she hoped some sort of dialogue was taking place. Unfortunately, she couldn't read lips and Regam still had that cloth covering his face so she couldn't make out what was being said.

Normally a naked woman straddling a man where she could see would be outright scandalous and embarrassing to say the least, but considering their lives were clearly at stake she squeezed her eyes shut and prayed to every Godling above she could think of for salvation.

"You will know your place trespasser," the woman whispered, each word dripping with honeyed venom.

These creatures had become far too bold and reckless of late for her liking and she wished upon every being of the Early Dawn that she could just take all of them for herself and be done with it, but she had given her word. Even if she *did* plan to take a smidge more from them this time around than what was agreed upon, what did it matter? Especially so now that she had to move two groups instead of one. If the Great Elders were bothered by her actions she would surely have been reprimanded in some form by now.

The one now at her mercy was the most vexing one she had had to deal with yet. She was conversing, *conversing,* with a human! It disgusted her to the very fabric of her creation. Not to mention unlike the other insignificant creatures spread out like flotsam around her this one showed no sign of fear or deferment. It annoyed her to no end, but a bargain was a bargain and she was still owed. She could not take this human; however, there was nothing in that bargain about how much harm could be inflicted. The woman flexed a delicate looking hand and the man's eyes narrowed at the deceptively vice-like grip around his throat. A few tense moments passed with the two of them locked in this tense embrace. Inwardly sighing, she begrudgingly admitted she had pushed as far as she could despite her desires, but these 'things' needed to be taught their place.

"If you have finished your wholly unnecessary display of power and dominance, I believe our debt for this crossing has been paid?" the man beneath her said, ignoring the hand at his throat and keeping a level gaze free of fear or intimidation. Such rare and impossible defiance made her want his aura more than anything, but she forced herself to hold back.

She gently ran a hand along the man's face underneath his ridiculous headdress, removed his veil and placed a single, long and elegant porcelain finger upon his lips.

"Shhhhh… You shall pass when I say you shall pass and not a moment sooner." Her precious home was not for others to use as a plaything whenever they so wished. These humans had lost any and all semblance of respect for that which they should revere and she would not fulfill her end of the bargain without imparting that knowledge upon those still remaining.

She especially wanted to teach these particularly filthy creatures a lesson due to the lecherous desires leaking off them despite their fear as they ogled her glorious entity. Only one other besides the one beneath her was free of that emotion and instead maintained an odd mix of terror, curiosity and…shame? *How curious.*

The woman spared a glance for the small one she had pinpointed, but immediately dismissed it. The only one she truly needed to passingly acknowledge was the infuriatingly defiant one beneath her. She roughly pulled back and bucked her hips as she sat upright, hoping to elicit a reaction she could then use against him, but she had no such luck.

This one has some semblance of self-control. Hmmm.

There were not many humans who could willingly resist her allure, especially within the expanse of her home, but it was not impossible. A fact she hoped to one day rectify. That one small goal had played a part in why she had agreed to a pact with these things in the first place.

She gave a mocking sigh of disappointment as she gently pressed her fingertips into the man's chest and shoved off, lightly landing on her feet a few yards away. She did get a satisfying grunt from the man at her thrust and a small smile played at the corners of her lips. There had been no need for the extra movement, but she wanted to keep playing with her toys a bit.

The man quickly regained his feet, not even bothering to brush away the debris clinging to his tunic and leggings from his time in the dirt.

"Now shall we continue with our agreement?" he asked as if nothing untoward had occurred.

Corly and the others took their time slowly and carefully regaining their feet. It looked to her like whatever impasse had occurred was about to be resolved. At least she hoped that was the case. Despite Regam's earlier assurances they had met with trouble almost immediately after entering the Grove and she felt their chances of coming out the other side unscathed were relatively small.

Barely daring to move Corly continued to take small, measured breaths in case of any lingering effects in the air from earlier. Straining her hearing to its limits she was able to catch some of the conversation, but still couldn't hear much and there were lots of things said she didn't understand. She wasn't even sure what the discussion was about, but she hoped it involved the return of the few who had vanished.

Involuntarily shuddering at the thought of what might have happened to them; Corly kept up her silent vigil of her surroundings, including what might be lurking amongst the interweaving branches eerily creaking above them.

It was an old habit she had acquired after attending many of Darien's lessons with Oltan when they were younger. Darien always had a tendency to face only what was directly in front of him and trying to plow through problems without thinking things through. He had a terrible habit of deciding the first thing that came to his mind was the best solution and was always perplexed when this approach failed to work out the way he expected. Oltan had tried time and time again to impress upon him that paying attention to above, below and the unseen was crucial to finding a solution to many problems. She had come over time to understand the purpose of the childish game of 'hide the object' Oltan sometimes used was to pay attention to everything around you and approach difficulties in multiple ways, but Darien had often been rather frustrated until Oltan patiently explained it to him. He had gotten better over the years, but it had taken far longer than Corly would have liked.

Looking warily above her, she was almost certain there had to be something else out there. From her position it was hard to tell for sure, but she could feel the eyes of unseen watchers from deep within the trees. It was unnerving.

Nervously brushing away the detritus clinging to her, she began to unconsciously bite her nails. Her heart had been beating rapidly for some time now and she forced her agitated nerves back to calm. The men around her remained tense, but their unease seemed to have lessened somewhat.

The 'conversation', if it could really even be called that, between Regam and the unclad woman seemed to have progressed to a less aggressive and life-threatening state. Corly again wondered about the missing men and where they might have gone. She decided it was best not to think too deeply about it and sent up a prayer to the Godlings for their safety.

She glanced at the pair and quickly looked away. She couldn't keep her eyes on the naked glowing woman for more than a few seconds without feeling a wave of embarrassment wash over her.

How can she walk around like that without any shame? It's scandalous!

She *did* briefly wonder if Darien would be interested in that sort of thing, after marriage of course, but she quickly shook her head.

What am I even thinking about right now?

Her thoughts were interrupted by an authoritative shout.

"Gather yourselves and get ready to be moved! There are those nearby we do not have the leisure to deal with right now so we will be moving further than last time. Prepare yourselves!"

"Wha-"

Corly barely had time to register the sudden order before she was roughly grabbed by her escort and hefted unceremoniously over his shoulder and brought into the group forming around the glowing woman.

"Close your eyes and mouth and clench your gut," the man muttered between gritted teeth.

Understanding something unpleasant was about to happen, Corly didn't have time to protest being treated like a sack of grain and instead decided to follow the man's terse instructions.

Squeezing her eyes closed and tightening her stomach Corly acted just in the nick of time as the entire group was enveloped in the golden glow emanating from the strange woman.

The world lurched sickeningly around her and her stomach felt like it was twisting into a knot. When the sensation passed she opened her eyes with a gasp and the man holding her slumped to his knees while she slid off his shoulder onto her rump and tried not to vomit.

"What just happened?" she gasped.

Her question hadn't been aimed at anyone in particular, but her escort answered her quietly with a pained expression that he quickly masked.

"We were moved."

"Moved? Moved *where*? How? What does that even mean?"

Foregoing the small and calm breaths of earlier Corly found herself sucking for air as her eyes rolled wildly at their new surroundings while trying to glean an understanding of what had happened. She was surprised by what she saw.

She blinked away a few tears blurring her vision to ensure what she was seeing wasn't an illusion. Looking behind her and back again a few times she pieced together what must have happened. The Travel Road now stretched out before them instead of behind. It was as if someone had flipped the terrain of the Grove around in a moment. It was disorienting at first, but the more her mind processed it as the only likely possibility the more she was able to accept that they had somehow been transported from one end of the Grove to the other. What was normally a multiple day's journey had taken only moments. The mysterious and foreboding Grove was now mostly behind them and the woman was nowhere to be seen.

Once the remaining men had more or less composed themselves, Regam barked another order.

"Get moving!"

Heaving a sigh, Liana took a deep appreciative breath of the intoxicating night air. Moving such a large amount of fodder, even ones as insignificant as humans, had taken a surprisingly heavy toll on her both physically and in terms of her aura.

She was surprised to find that she was even lightly sweating from the effort, the cool and comforting breeze of her private sanctuary within her home giving the perspiration a not unpleasant sensation. She frowned slightly at the thought that perhaps her most recent migrations might not have been sufficient selections, but what was done was done.

Stretching languidly in the comfortable surroundings she continued to soak in the essence of her home. It would take quite some time for her to recover what she had lost so she might as well get started.

The place humans called 'The Grove' had so much more to it than any of them could ever even imagine. Not only was it a wondrous and beautiful reminder of what once was and should be again, but it gave to its denizens in abundance. Those that inhabited the Grove were mostly naturally occurring wonders of the world that had existed far longer than the other inconsequential creatures polluting the landscape of the world at large and were the true inheritors of what had been left behind.

Liana was not only one of these natural beings, but was one of the oldest, having been birthed not long before the arrival of the Two Fallen Gods. She had never been one to worship them due to her reverence for the true ruling class of the world and her lack of devotion had proven correct when they had ultimately destroyed themselves and created the infestation humans referred to as 'Godlings'.

Liana desperately wanted to acquire the strength and power to eradicate the very existence of these new pretenders, but even she had enough self-awareness to understand she was as of yet far too weak for such an undertaking. Even had she been at the absolute peak of her powers she knew it wouldn't be nearly enough to accomplish such a lofty and noble goal.

"Still, the day will come," she uttered into the night. Lightly shivering at the thought of bringing the pests to their glorious demise Liana slowly sat in place upon an earthy mound and folded her legs beneath her. She took a moment to revel in the sensation of the grass and earth cradling her lower extremities in an intimate embrace. The air lightly swirling around her was tinged with the glorious scents of the woodland and she nearly climaxed in ecstasy.

"Calm," she whispered, her words forming thin white wisps just before her lips. Now was not the time for pleasure; she needed to focus.

Taking a controlled breath and closing her emerald eyes Liana began the process of slowly absorbing the abundance her home so graciously offered her. She lightly sighed as she did have one minor regret at the moment, but she unfortunately had had a bargain to keep. There were other nuisances who had strayed much further than they had any right to, but she currently didn't have enough remaining of her aura to properly dispose of them.

Surprisingly these ones had been respectful towards her home despite moving off the approved path, but had she not had to engage with the others they would still have been dealt with harshly.

"Ah well. Should they remain when I wake I shall deal

with them appropriately," she murmured as her eyelids became heavy and her steady, rhythmic breathing lulled her deep into sleep.

Chapter 3

Liana's eyes snapped open and rolled wildly in her head.
She gasped as the brisk air swirling around her fused with a
sudden and forceful saturation of magic so dense it coated
her skin and sank deeply into every pore. She instinctively
knew it had been more than a few passings of the moon since
she had begun her meditation and process of renewal, but all
of her previous thoughts and plans were erased from her
mind as she shuddered in the darkness. She had just had
her entire being drenched with an infusion of her home's
very essence in overabundance, but was uncertain as to why.

Normally such an occurrence would fill her with glorious
wonder, but something within her beloved woodland had
shifted in a monumental way. Beads of sweat formed on her
brow while she took measured breaths to regain a semblance
of calm while her mind reeled at what such a shift could
possibly foretell. She found herself shivering at both the
sensation and the feeling of foreboding rising inside her.

It took several minutes for both her mind to clear and her

body to cease trembling. Fluidly uncoiling from her seated position, the dew that had formed during her meditation glittered and glimmered over her nude body. Tilting her head and closing her eyes to focus on the feel and fabric of her surroundings she began to ascertain what had transpired while she slept.

Steadying her breathing, the familiar golden glow enveloped her as she extended her senses out to her immediate surroundings. Quickly discerning there wasn't anything amiss in her general area Liana began to glide further into the woodlands while she searched for what could have possibly caused such a massive shift in her homeland's stability and majestic presence. A frightening scowl marred her porcelain features as the fallen leaves littering the earth lightly rustled at her passing.

"Should any of those interlopers have scarred the perfection of this place there will be no escape from the horrors I shall inflict upon them."

Corly sat wide-eyed at the table with her current escort seated stoically next to her. This particular man gave absolutely no indication he was aware of her presence and spoke not a word unless she asked him a question directly. Even then his answers were only grunts, if he answered at all. Quickly giving up on drawing him into conversation, she took in everything around her and couldn't contain her excitement and rampant curiosity. The lively bustle and din of the tavern Regam had brought them to was as lively and chaotic as it was intimidating. People of every variety and walk of life crammed themselves into this intimate space and Corly couldn't help but gawk at the boisterous throng.

Unconsciously bouncing in her seat she tried to soak in everything around her. It was hard to hear anything coherent among the cacophony of the other customers, but that didn't really bother her. She ran her eyes over everything she could, from women dressed in uniform clothing serving ale and food while deftly swatting away curious hands of overzealous customers, to the patrons laughing, arguing and boasting of deeds dubious in nature, to the man sitting cross-legged in the corner on an elevated platform expertly plucking a tune from the strings of an instrument she had never seen before. The place wasn't much bigger than Master Gellam's inn back in Breathwynd, but Regam had mentioned the Flask of Iron was a tavern that only served food and drink and did not offer rooms to patrons. Corly found this odd, but her curiosity about her new surroundings took precedence.

At first she wondered how so many people could gather in one place without getting out of control, but shortly after arriving a man who had gotten too deep into his cups had tried to forcibly drag away one of the serving girls. He had swiftly been beaten senseless with wooden clubs and unceremoniously tossed out by two brutish looking men who appeared like specters from the shadowy corners of the tavern. It left a definite impression that such foolishness would not be tolerated.

Since she couldn't get anything out of the man seated to her left, she wanted to at least ask Regam since he was the only other one to accompany them, but he had disappeared into the back with someone immediately after arriving.

The sights, sounds and smells of her new surroundings were enough to make her head spin, but it also served as a welcome distraction from the stress, fear, uncertainty and grief she had been battling since her rescue from Village Breathwynd.

The last few days had felt like she had been looking through someone else's eyes at some surreal play like the ones her favorite traveling troupe, Hulgar's, used to perform when they would periodically visit her former home.

Tears welled up unbidden at the thought, but she blinked them away when a steaming plate loaded with veggies and a slab of meat slathered in some kind of sauce was plunked down in front of her by one of the serving girls who appeared as if by magic. Corly's mouth instantly began to water as the smell quickly reminded her of just how hungry she was. This was her first proper meal since leaving Village Breathwynd and she was excited to finally have something other than bland stew and dried travel rations.

"Here you are sweetie! You're so tiny and cute that I had the cook add a little bit extra to your portion. You need to fill out a bit more! Consider it a special bonus for you and your man's first visit!"

"Wha…" Corly yelped, turning bright red at the insinuation she and the abrasive man next to her could possibly be a couple, but she was able to keep her manners like her parents had taught her. *Do we* really *look like we're betrothed? Impossible!*

Most would say the girl was unremarkable in appearance with dark curly hair, small eyes, a crooked nose and a slightly overweight bearing, but her demeanor, smile and ease with which she melted into din made her incredibly impressive and exotic to Corly. She suddenly had so many questions, but the serving girl had already vanished back into the throng just as quickly as she had arrived.

Corly's stomach growled as the aroma wafting up from her plate lightly tickled her nostrils and all thoughts of the server quickly faded away. Her mouth was watering at the prospect of some real food, but the manners ingrained in her since childhood kept her from diving face first into her meal like her escort had done with an ample amount of grunting and other unruly sounds. She would have been appalled at such a lack of manners had she still been back in Breathwynd, but her mind was occupied with more pressing worries.

Staring at her plate she gripped her wooden spoon so tightly her knuckles turned white. Was it really okay for her to be sitting here eating such a lavish meal and being cared for when the others from the village had suffered such an abominable fate that she only escaped due to sheer luck? Was it fine if she continued to accept aid from Regam and his men when no one had come to save any of the others? Why was she the only one who got to experience this kindness? Tears formed at the corners of her eyes and she had to do her utmost to not start bawling like a newborn.

Regam's sudden arrival startled her out of her guilt-stricken trance. Thumping down heavily in the empty seat across from her he practically slammed his own plate down.

"Eat," he said with his usual seriousness as he consumed his own meal by shoveling measured mouthfuls into his face. Corly resisted the urge to scrunch her nose at his tone and the way he was eating. This man was the leader! He should have a better grasp of manners and decency! If she had seen Darien acting in such a manner, she would have smacked him good!

However, Regam's brusque admonishment and the gurgling in her belly was enough to convince her that she needed to eat something more substantial than what she had been fed lately. Taking a deep breath to settle her raging emotions she began to tentatively eat her meal now that it had cooled somewhat.

Taking small, careful bites her hunger eventually overtook her criticisms on etiquette and she ended up devouring her meal. Now with a full belly and her inner turmoil having quieted somewhat she soon found herself nodding off despite the din around her. Within moments she felt Regam's strong calloused hands easily lifting her small frame and carrying her to the rear of the tavern. Vaguely recalling this place didn't offer rooms for guests she supposed she should be alarmed, but her head was too muddled from fatigue to dwell on it.

She briefly tensed at the realization that a man had scooped her up and was carrying her in his arms, but her fatigue and feelings of guilt at surviving Breathwynd's destruction combining with her full stomach swayed her into a deep sleep even before Regam was able to lay her down on the stuffed pile of straw serving as her bed.

Looking down at the peacefully sedated child Regam smiled at how quickly the sleep inducing narcotics the girl's food had been laced with went into effect. It was a proactive countermeasure to ensure she would remain oblivious to the old man's presence as part of their party. Thinking about what was next to come, Regam spoke without emotion into the silence of the room.

"Sleep well and worry not. You will soon begin your service to the crown you are now so indebted to."

The rest of the journey to the capital and the Castle of the King went uneventfully. At least as uneventfully as Corly could hope for given her circumstances and what she had already endured. She still couldn't get used to the commonality and lack of shame associated with the makeshift latrines they dug with each rest break, but once they got close to the capital she had much higher hopes in that regard.

Riding along with Regam behind her guiding their mount and ensuring her safety she squinted into the distance. The castle itself was still a good distance away, pennons fluttering in the breeze atop crenelated turrets while they rode in

silence. They had begun passing several farms and small
villages that Regam had curtly mentioned marked the
outskirts of the capital city of Trengylle. Corly had been
hopeful for a level of familiarity with people who lived in
similar circumstances as her, but she had been stunned and
more than a little unnerved at how emotionless and
unfriendly those working in the fields had been.

Everywhere she looked there were the familiar sights of
workers tending the fields and the sounds and scents of an
honest days' labor tugged at her heartstrings a bit. With the
sun beating down overhead and a light breeze whirling
through the land she felt almost as if they had returned to
Breathwynd itself, but there was a very distinct difference
between her village and the outskirts of the capital.

Everyone looked forlorn and less than enthused at their
arrival. The adults paused in their labors long enough to
acknowledge their presence, but none offered a greeting or
attempted to hail them in any way. Not even the few
children visible were excited at the sight of the riders as they
passed. Had this been Breathwynd, the younger ones would
have been chattering nonstop while bombarding them with
questions and just being unruly and excited in general at the
rare event. It was nothing like that here. Anytime a child or
younger person noticed their approach they would quickly
duck into the nearest home or building without fail.

Her concern must have shown on her face as Regam
sternly addressed her like he could read her mind.

"Do not let their reaction trouble you. The transition

from the previous regime to the rightful monarch has been rather stressful for all of us, especially here in the capital."

Corly nodded. Village Breathwynd was so remote from the rest of the country, having the Grove in the way and all, that it wasn't often news of the outside made its way there. Even when it did it was often already outdated information. The ascension of Bamaul, however, had been something even she was aware of; she was also very aware of the rumors and controversies swirling around the sudden change in rulers. Most of the villagers had been slightly concerned at first, but ultimately decided it had nothing to do with them; Breathwynd wouldn't change either way and life would go on as normal. At least that's what all of them had thought. That way of thinking had proven fatal to everyone in the village, save her.

Regam continued in his oppressive monotone. "Those who rightfully live here will come around when they see the results of his majesty's rule. I am sure that you will become well-known to them all in due time so be patient with those who seem uneasy."

Corly didn't really understand what Regam was saying, but she nodded again and kept her eyes glued to the horse's mane in front of her rather than endure the uncomfortable feeling of the residents' morose reactions. *Why in the world would I become known to all of them? That doesn't make any sense!*

Once they had passed through the outlying lands, they finally began to approach the capital proper. There was a long line of travelers, carriages, wagons, mercenaries and the like all waiting to enter the massive gate barring entrance. Corly took a quick look to her left and right, but couldn't discern an end to the large, thick, alabaster walls surrounding the capital city of Trengylle. The din of those waiting in line became noticeably subdued once the people at the end of the queue became aware of their presence. Corly had assumed they would be waiting a while to enter considering how long the line was, but Regam and the others made no move to join the line, instead ignoring it completely and heading straight for the gate.

Corly marveled at the gate itself. There had been nothing like it back home, not even in Rowe. It was a large wooden door comprised of thick planks alternating horizontally and vertically in a layered pattern and reinforced with metal plates engraved with an odd symbol in the center. She wanted to ask if the symbol meant anything important, but the oppressive atmosphere kept her mouth closed.

Trundling past those waiting in line Corly became acutely aware of more and more stares as the quieting murmur soon became an uncomfortable silence. She didn't know why, but she ducked her head in embarrassment and maintained her gaze on the mane of Regam's horse.

The two guards inspecting people at the gate stiffened at their approach and quickly gave a nod and slight bow towards Regam as they passed through unhindered. Peeking out the corner of her eye at the guards Corly wished she had more time to admire the shiny steel armor and embroidered accents they were wearing, but Regam made no attempt to stop or even acknowledge them at all.

Finally entering Trengylle, Corly's senses were immediately assaulted by all manner of sights and sounds that made the tavern back in Rowe seem tame in comparison.

More people were packed into this one space than Corly had ever seen in her entire life. Not even the boisterousness and bustle of the Flask of Iron could compare. People in all manner of dress hurried to and fro about their business while vendors from food stalls shouted the deliciousness and benefits of their goods and shop merchants loudly exhorted the value of their wares. Some were simple, but proper stalls while others displayed their wares on blankets spread out on the ground.

Inhaling deeply, Corly was struck by a tantalizing smell that reminded her of the sweet rolls Mistress Wavely used to bake that Darien had loved so much. She felt a lump in her throat at the sensation, but forced it back down and took a settling breath. It seemed her sense of smell was slowly starting to recover so she counted that as a minor blessing.

Regam and the others made no effort to avoid or maneuver around the throng and instead moved ahead at a deliberate pace forcing people to scramble out of their way. The bustling and boisterous crowd became less enthusiastic at their passing and the shopkeepers and stall vendors seemed less vocal about their wares, but Corly attributed it to what Regam had told her earlier. They *were* an intimidating bunch after all.

Corly was also amazed at just how quickly the dense crowd of people began to adapt and make way for their procession. She hadn't thought it was possible for such a large mass of people to coordinate for such freedom of movement for a party as large as theirs, but it seemed to be so.

She did hear the din of the crowd swell back to its previous level behind them so she shrugged off the odd atmosphere and chalked it up to just something else she didn't understand.

Now with the crowd behind them Corly stared in wonder at everything around her as they rode. There wasn't a cloud in the sky and the sunlight beaming down from above gave everything an immaculate gleam as if straight out of a fairy tale.

Once they had made their way a bit further the stalls and minor merchants began to give way to buildings and structures Corly had never seen before and some whose purpose she couldn't begin to guess at. It was the first time in her young life she had ever seen a building with three floors; some even had four! She was astounded and wondered how they didn't fall over or tumble to the ground. Surely a strong wind would topple them right over!

She also noticed while they trudged along that the ground was steadily rising as they made their way to the castle proper. Soon the buildings that had intrigued and mystified her gave way to even more elegant and lavish homes with gates, gardens, and elaborate decoration all kept in immaculate condition. Here and there, a worker or someone dressed in a servant's livery could be seen tending to the needs of their respective households. Corly was impressed at the level of dedication the people who lived in such extravagant homes must have to work so hard to keep things in such pristine condition and she mentioned such to Regam.

Regam snorted in derision at her observation.

"Those who dwell in such places never lift a finger themselves. Those with affluence cannot be bothered to soil their own hands to labor on what the land has given them. You've seen the servants of some places already. Do not make such baseless assumptions again."

Corly ducked her head in embarrassment, but still grumbled a complaint since Regam wasn't being very fair.

She sniffed and lifted her head to look defiantly back at Regam. "Well, how would I know? I've never seen anything like this in my entire life you know."

Regam remained silent at her protest, but as they passed one particular manor she noticed his face tense for just a moment, but it passed so quickly she might have missed it had she not been looking directly at him.

Following Regam's gaze to the meticulously maintained garden surrounded by a low, almost blindingly white fence, she noted a simple swing gate in the center barring entry. Flowers of indescribable color bloomed in abundance and the greenery of the grass and multitude of vines sparkled in the sunlight. Further back past the garden she could just make out a much larger gate of iron barring entry to the manor beyond.

The object of Regam's scrutiny was the individual diligently digging through the expanse of plants and flowers adorning the main walkway semi-paved with cobblestones. Corly wondered what was so special about this servant compared to the others, but before she could ask Regam must have sensed her curiosity.

"Look closely. You will need to see more clearly in the future if you are to grow in any respect. Look as we pass and tell me what it is that makes him differ from the others."

Frowning, Corly was again reminded of Oltan at his tone, but did as she was bid. Passing by the worker in question he rose to his feet, brushing the dirt and grime from his worn and stained smock as he did so. Light green leggings were tucked into scuffed and stained leather boots that had seen far better days. The darker green tunic he wore underneath the smock was also worn, but serviceable. She noticed nothing out of the ordinary until she scrutinized his face as best she could despite the distance. His face showed no emotion, but his eyes locked onto Regam and Corly was struck by a sudden sense of familiarity. This person looked just like Regam and his men!

She looked over her shoulder at Regam again, who was wholeheartedly ignoring the servant and confirmed her suspicions.

"Is he one of you?"

Regam gave a curt nod. "He is. You will see a few like

him here and there in Trengylle, but thankfully they are few and far between."

Corly got the impression there was more to the story than he was telling her, but she knew by now pressing for more of an answer wouldn't get her anywhere. She wondered just what the situation with Regam and his people really was, but ultimately decided it wasn't any of her business. Maybe in the future she could ask and learn more, but for now she had enough worries of her own.

The man continued to stare at them even after they had passed and Corly wondered what other surprises awaited her as they continued their gradual ascent to the Castle of the King.

The closer they got to the castle the more expansive and elaborate the homes around them became; each one meticulously maintained and crafted to an otherworldly degree. The number of servants and workers who seemed to be of the same people as Regam and his men also increased despite his earlier claims of them being few and far between. Each and every one of them reacted in much the same manner as the one from earlier and Regam ignored them all. However, Corly didn't miss the whitening of his knuckles on the reins.

Giving her head a light shake, her braids lightly swinging about, Corly focused her thoughts on what she was supposed to do once they reached the castle. Regam hadn't exactly been forthcoming about what they were doing or what was expected of her, but no matter how hard he tried she couldn't think of any reason as to why she was being brought all the way to the castle itself. She supposed she would find out when she got there.

Oltan steeled himself for what was sure to come. How long it had been since they had passed through the Grove he couldn't be sure, but he instinctively felt they should be getting close to the Castle of the King by this point. Despite his earlier protests, curiosity had gotten the better of him and he had spent the majority of the trip since the Grove trying to ascertain exactly what had happened when they traversed the wood.

The chains remained in place and the sack was restored over his head, but the tingling along his skin and the unnatural heaviness suddenly permeating his entire body told him they had entered the mystical wood shutting off Village Breathwynd from the rest of the world.

The Grove itself was a precipitous and unpredictable place; traveling through it was no easy task even should one adhere strictly to the Travel Road. Even someone as knowledgeable as Oltan, who had gained quite the amount of experience through his years of service to the crown and countless hours of study and trial and error, wouldn't dare do so without proper preparations made in advance.

He had expected to endure a short break while the others moved further into the wood so that Corly wouldn't become suspicious of the second group trailing along behind, but he had been shocked to hear a sudden commotion just moments after the lead group had entered the confines of the Grove.

There had first been what he recognized as an infusion of the essence of the Grove, something that always made his hair stand on end, or at least it would have had he not had a sack over his head. Shortly after hearing some brief shouting that reached even his part of the entourage there was another intense burst of energy shooting through him as the heaviness in the air became so unbearable he felt his bones were about to be crushed into meal.

Grunting at the sudden and intense pain, it evaporated almost as quickly as it had come and a few minutes later his hood had been removed and some water splashed onto his face. Blinking several times at the sudden change Oltan felt nauseous at how disoriented he was. Despite his confused state he was able to swallow the spoonful of stale stew-like sludge that had been shoved into his mouth. Looking around he tried to gain his bearings and ascertain where in the Grove they currently were.

Oltan's jaw dropped when he realized they had made it clear to the other side of the Grove already. It had only been minutes since they had entered! He didn't have much time to think about it more than that as one of his escorts roughly cuffed him on the side of the head and he had fallen unconscious.

Now at present he sensed from the scents and sounds around him that they must have finally reached Trengylle and would soon come face to face with the self-styled rightful king of Katama, the Silver Tyrant Bamaul. Suppressing the

urge to sigh he again ran through any options he might have
and yet again reached the conclusion that he had none. The
fact they had taken Corly captive was both vexing and
confusing.

Bamaul and his co-conspirators like Regam having
knowledge of his whereabouts were understandable and to a
lesser degree it was possible they knew Darien had a
connection to Aplesi and Elze. However, was taking the girl
part of a larger plot or just coincidental? Besides, how
would they have known about her and her relationship with
Darien in the first place?

He couldn't dismiss the possibility this had all been
planned out from the beginning and lamented at just how
tied his hands were from acting on his own. The power of
Bamaul's artifact was vague at best and he couldn't reliably
rule out any possibility at this juncture. If he had in his
possession that artifact of his own stored away in his secret
study within the castle then perhaps he might be able to
accomplish something, but even he had little grasp of what
that strange object was capable of. If only he had had time
enough to retrieve it before his hurried flight from the castle
perhaps the tragedy at Breathwynd could have been
avoided. Again resigning himself to whatever fate the tyrant
had in store for him Oltan jostled along through the muted
din of what must have been the stall market and common
folk quarters of the capital.

Oltan longed to hear the joyful and enigmatic hustle and
bustle he remembered from years past, but what saddened

him most was the unmistakable pall over the noise that sounded forced to his practiced ear. Even that dimmed to almost total silence as he was escorted along. He was sure he was being made into a spectacle for the crowd. A filthy and ragged reminder to all who saw the sack-clad prisoner of what could befall any one of them at any time should they displease those in power.

Another thing he found curious was the fact he had remained concealed once they had entered the capital. He had been convinced once they reached this point both Bamaul and Regam would want his identity revealed to the public to further bow the populace to his rule and to gloat over the capture of one of his greatest rivals.

He thought through scenario after scenario and just couldn't figure out what exactly the madman sitting on the throne had in store for him. He was reasonably sure he wouldn't be executed right away; Bamaul was certain to want to obtain and abuse the knowledge Oltan had accumulated over the years and felt that Corly must be a guarantee against his cooperation. Beyond that he was at a loss.

Thankfully it didn't seem like his old secret study or the artifact hidden within had been discovered. He was certain Regam would have lorded it over him had that been the case.

Continuing to force his exhausted mind to work out any possible scenario or solution that could work to his benefit Oltan felt the ground begin to gradually rise in elevation, signaling they had left the merchant stalls and common quarter behind and had begun the final approach to the castle grounds through the noble quarter.

Oltan gritted his teeth and steeled himself for whatever Hells the mad tyrant had in store for him.

Chapter 4

Coming up to the castle itself was a stunning sight to see. Corly was in awe at the awesome majesty of the gigantic structure as Regam directed his mount towards a long and winding pathway paved solid and leading towards the main gate of the castle.

Small rolling hills swelled up around the snaking path and Corly wondered why such a roundabout way was used to approach the gate. It must be an awful burden to have to do this every day when they could have just made it straight!

Putting aside her sudden irritation Corly took in what she could see of the castle while they made their laborious approach. From her vantage point they were steadily approaching a long drawbridge covering a wide moat. Several men in elaborate armor polished to a blinding sheen and marked with symbols Corly had never seen before stood at attention in front of a barbican protecting the large gate beyond.

The gate itself was even more impressive than the

entrance to Trengylle had been. It was easily twice the size and sported the same pattern of thick boards, but was reinforced with large metal spikes and had a portcullis looming menacingly above. Corly was struck by an odd memory of how similar it felt to Oltan's library, but that was probably just her imagination.

The same symbol as the one on the guards' armor adorned flags lightly fluttering among several of the crenellations above. The symbol depicted a white hourglass containing falling black sand on a field of crimson and supported by two circles the same black as the sand. Three white crooked lines rose in ascending order of height from the hourglass with the middle one ending in an odd hook.

"Regam, what is that?" she asked, pointing in the general direction of the pennons.

"It is the sigil of our king. You had best commit it to memory."

Corly glanced up at Regam, but no further explanation was coming. Turning away to hide her annoyance at his lack of explaining things properly, Corly supposed she should be used to his reticence by now.

After what felt like an eternity they finally reached the wooden drawbridge connecting them to the castle side; the horses' hooves clattering loudly in the surrounding silence. One thing Corly definitely couldn't get used to was the stillness and silence that followed Regam and his men wherever they went.

The men standing at attention remained stiffly in salute as

Regam trotted past, neither one making a sound or otherwise acknowledging their existence. Corly resisted the urge to bite her nails at the tension. One thing she had noticed was the amount of respect people showed Regam and his men and she didn't want to tarnish that reputation by doing something so unseemly. She was aware that people also seemed somewhat afraid of Regam and those under his command, but she attributed it to what Regam had told her earlier about people adjusting to change. However, that was only the beginning of the things that were starting to bother her.

Up until now her travels from Breathwynd had been a dizzying whirlwind of events that she had just been trying to keep up with, but now that they had actually arrived at their destination all sorts of worries came bubbling to the surface.

Not much news from the rest of the world ever made it all the way to a place as isolated as Breathwynd was, but what little they had heard about King Bamaul was never anything good.

She supposed much of the information they did get often came from Hulgar and his traveling troupe so some exaggeration was to be expected. They were people who made their living through storytelling and showmanship so she was sure there must have been more than a small amount of embellishment on their part. They always *did* tell a good story though.

Corly steeled herself and decided right then that all she could do was wait and see and decide for herself what the

king of Katama was truly like if she really did get the
opportunity to see him. It still didn't seem real that a
normal peasant girl like herself might be introduced to the
king. Regam had mentioned it during their journey, but she
supposed he might have just been saying that in order to
calm her fears while they traveled. She wasn't sure how to
feel if that was the case. On the one hand it would alleviate
her concerns about her future, but on the other how often
does a person like her get to meet actual royalty? She
wanted to ask Regam about the rumors, but figured doing so
would be a waste of breath at best; and at worst an insult she
wouldn't be able to recover from.

She didn't have long to dwell on her worries as they
quickly made their way through an immaculately kept
courtyard located at the center of four separate pathways
leading to and from in the cardinal directions. Looking
closely as they approached Corly could tell an intense
amount of labor was used to keep the courtyard and
pathways free of debris and maintained to an incredible
standard of cleanliness. Mistress Wavely would have
absolutely *swooned* at such cleanliness and order.

Servants in black and silver livery adorned with Bamaul's
sigil scurried about their various duties with a briskness she
instantly felt a familiarity with. It had the same air of how
she and Marsa used to attend to their tasks within the
bakery they had apprenticed to back home.

Corly choked back the emotions rising up in her at the
memory; right now she understood she couldn't afford to be

anything but her very best. She owed that to everyone who hadn't made it out of Breathwynd alive. She needed to conduct herself as the sole representative of Breathwynd and if she was ever going to discover the whole truth behind what happened to her home then these people were the ones she was in the best position to ask for help from.

Regam ordered everyone to a halt once they reached the courtyard itself and they all quickly dismounted. Corly felt it a little odd they were leaving the horses here instead of going with them to wherever the stabling area was, but after giving it a little thought she again supposed she should start to forget what passed for common sense in her previous life and adjust accordingly to what she sees and hears. She had had little interaction with horses in the past and usually only saw how they were handled when Hulgar or the occasional visitor to Breathwynd appeared. Everything and everyone around her were new, different, unknown and far more complicated than anything back in Breathwynd so she needed to adapt if she was going to survive in this new environment.

Corly frowned as Regam easily lifted her off their mount and set her on the ground. She blushed furiously at both the inelegant sound she made and the fact a man had just placed his hands on her in such a familiar fashion. *I'm going to have to learn how to properly ride one of those things aren't I? And I need to get used to how familiar people seem to be outside of Breathwynd, but it's so outrageous!*

Taking her time to compose herself she tucked these

thoughts away in a corner of her mind as even more servants appeared to attend to the horses and lead them away to wherever they were stabled.

"Please don't do that," she said more calmly than she felt. Despite her realization that she needed to get used to the differences between Breathwynd and the outside world there were some things she just could not let pass.

The few servants still within earshot froze at her words and even the men remaining from the group seemed to flinch. The stragglers still wrestling with the mounts hurried in their tasks and an uncomfortable silence followed.

Regam stared a hole in her for what felt like an eternity, but Corly was determined to stand her ground on this particular manner, especially after not being able to speak her mind back in Rowe.

Firmly placing her hands on her hips despite her nervousness Corly tried to put a stern look on her face much like Mistress Wavely used to. She found it easier if she pretended she was scolding Darien. That felt more natural.

"It is entirely inappropriate for a man to lay his hands on a maiden in such a manner! Especially in public and without permission!" She felt proud she had kept any quavering out of her voice. Well, *mostly* kept it from quavering.

Regam eventually uttered a solemn "I see," and turned away to begin barking orders at his men.

His response seemed to shake the tension out of the air and the remaining servants finally all scurried out of sight.

Once everyone was back in motion Regam made some odd gestures with his hands towards one of his men who nodded and turned to sprint off in the direction from which they had just come.

Corly was confused why Regam had sent the man back in that direction and that he had somehow done so just by wiggling his fingers, but she figured she had pushed her luck as far as she could for the moment.

Regam again turned his focus back to her. "You will follow me. You will remain silent unless directly spoken to by myself or one I designate in my stead. Do you understand?"

Corly was taken aback by the sudden command. She took it to mean she should keep her mouth shut and remain obedient, which were two things she wasn't very good at. She did her utmost to swallow the retort forming on her tongue and was thankfully successful. Reminding herself again of her decision to watch and learn, she only nodded. Hoping the obvious sign of irritation on her face was enough to get her real thoughts across to Regam, she grimaced since he was already walking away from her.

She gritted her teeth. *This is going to be harder than I thought.*

The overwhelming stench of mold, mildew and unwashed flesh assaulted Oltan's olfactory senses. Still wearing his blindfold and shackled at the ankles and wrists, he had been blindly led through a twisting and turning path that he was sure was meant to confuse him.

He had been stripped of his tunic and his shackles had been transferred to a mounted device on the wall as he hung limply from the cold and mossy stone pressing into his backside. Ignoring the increased pain coursing through his body he wracked his brain to try and discern where exactly in the castle could give off such an abhorrent stench, but nothing came to mind. It was only after the sound of metal grating on metal ending with a loud clanging was his blindfold removed and he became fully aware of his plight and just how hopeless things had become.

Blinking several times, his vision blurred despite the minimal light emanating from the lone candle Regam held. His vision had been obscured for so long that even this miniscule amount of light was as if he had been exposed to the blazing midday sun.

Regam stood before him silently for a time simply observing Oltan's condition, no doubt salivating at the sight of his master's enemy brought so low. Oltan assumed a detailed report would need to be made on Regam's part so he was being scrutinized for any signs of deceit or dissent; not that he could do as much with Corly being held hostage as she was.

Hanging limply from his bindings Oltan stared at Regam, making sure to keep his face expressionless. There was no telling what Regam would report to Bamaul based on this interaction and it was entirely unknowable just how the madman himself would respond to Oltan's capture. He had been rather surprised he hadn't immediately been hauled in chains before the tyrant himself, but Regam was both a cautious and practical man so there was certainly a reason the chain of events hadn't gone as Oltan thought so far.

"You will wait here for a time until his majesty deigns to grant you an audience."

Oltan maintained his blank expression. No doubt Regam stating the obvious was a way to bait him into some response he was sure to later regret, but he had lived too long and endured too much to fall for such a common tactic.

Regam waited a few minutes in silence before finally snuffing out his candle and plunging Oltan's cell into complete darkness. Straining his hearing to its limits, Oltan focused on the fading sound of Regam' boots as he tried to get a feel for anything that could prove helpful. He heard another, much louder metallic slamming of what was probably a door followed by the familiar hum of magic being invoked.

Oltan was stunned for a variety of reasons. For one, there had never been anything in the castle as far as he knew requiring the amount of magic being utilized. Additionally, he was not aware that Regam was adept with the use of magic and had never heard of the man even attempting to use any type of tool requiring magic infusion. Frustration overwhelmed him both at his lack of knowledge and the inability to at least see what it was that was making his skin crawl and arm hairs stand on end.

His curiosity warred with his reason and he rolled his

tongue over his back molars as he pondered what his next move would be should an opportunity present itself, limited as his options were. He actively began to loosen his rear teeth just in case they became necessary.

The magical hum and heaviness in the air slowly faded and he was soon left in absolute darkness, silence and solitude to await his fate. He sighed.

"Nothing to do now, but hurry up and wait."

Corly's stomach growled. She had been led by one of Regam's men to a small building near where the stables were located. It had been a while since she had last eaten and she couldn't stop thinking about having something other than the dried jerky and stew they had been eating the entire trip, save for that one inn Regam had briefly stopped at. Not even the smell of the horses in such proximity could discourage her hunger and she wondered when she would be able to eat something more substantial.

As usual the man stationed as her escort remained silent and any attempt to engage him in conversation was met with single word responses or unintelligible grunts. He wouldn't even give her his name! She had gotten used to this sort of thing over the course of their travels, but it didn't infuriate her any less.

Making up her mind then and there Corly decided she would do whatever she could to get these men to open up to her, starting with this one. She did owe them her life, so she could tolerate the dismissive and standoffish behavior, but her patience with their lack of manners had run its course.

Corly began to pepper the man with more and more questions and began to ramble about anything she could think of just to keep the words flowing in the hopes of eliciting a response more than an annoyed grunt.

Continuing her torrent of one-sided conversation her eyes took in her surroundings. There wasn't much to the room they were in, but Oltan had mentioned multiple times in his lectures about the importance of always paying attention to your environment.

It was a very small room, just big enough for a few people to sit rather uncomfortably on the wooden bench currently rubbing her already sore backside the wrong way. A worn desk with no ornamentation sat opposite her with a rickety chair that looked as if it would fall to pieces if someone so much as coughed. Cobwebs could be seen in the corners of the ceiling and she kept fighting back the urge to sneeze from the motes of dust lazily floating in the air. She couldn't begin to guess what such an unkempt place could be used for so she included it among her endless stream of questions and comments.

"Just what is this place exactly? It seems really run down to be part of a castle that's so gorgeous. All the stories I've read have castles filled with magnificent things, but that isn't always the case I guess? Can't you at least tell me your name? I feel like I'm talking to myself here! It's kind of rude, isn't it?"

The man had barely been able to keep up with Corly's

verbal assault even with single word answers and she noticed a slight sigh escape from his lips. She knew the signs of someone about to crack after years of convincing Darien to see things the right way so she pressed her advantage until she got what she was after.

He eventually held up his hand and finally gave her a response that was more than a grunt or single word. "Cease! If I tell you my name will you end this tantrum and wait for Lord Regam? *Quietly?*"

Corly smiled at her victory. He had a deep, baritone voice with just enough of an accent that one could tell he wasn't speaking his native language. Corly thought it was a nice voice. "Of course! I promise!"

The man looked down at her with suspicion evident in his eyes. Tugging at the blood red cloth hanging loosely from what Corly had come to understand was called a Makavai the man finally gave her what she had been after.

"Aditsan."

Corly waited in hopes that more was forthcoming, but that was all she got.

"Aditsan? That's a nice name! I'm Corly, but you already know that. So, what is this place then?"

She tried asking again in hopes of getting something more out of Aditsan, but he folded his arms and stared at her. "Quietly, yes?"

Corly pouted a bit at the reprimand, but figured this was the best she was going to get out of him for the moment and she was happy she got that much.

Corly swung her legs and hummed a little in satisfaction as they waited in silence for a time, but she felt far less awkward now that she had finally gotten a name out of one of Regam's men. She smiled in the middle of humming her nameless tune when Aditsan glanced at her, but he didn't say anything. She counted not being reprimanded another win for her.

Regam eventually returned, his impressive frame silhouetted in the doorway for a moment as his eyes narrowed and swept the tiny room as if trying to find fault with it. Entering, he dismissed Aditsan with a wordless gesture and turned his attention to Corly.

"You will come with me."

Corly turned her mouth down in annoyance, but felt pushing for more courtesy from Regam would be a bit of a stretch so she quickly masked her frown by putting on her most pleasant expression.

"Of course!" She hopped up off the bench and brushed off her clothing as best she could despite not having bathed or changed clothes since her rescue.

She wrinkled her nose as she caught a whiff of both her and Regam and the thought of appearing out of sorts here at the castle that was home to so many powerful and affluent people greatly worried her.

"Is it possible to bathe somewhere in private and find a change of clothes? I'm certain that I should be doing that much before I'm brought to wherever it is you plan on taking me?" Corly was making an educated guess based on everything she had seen and heard since entering Trengylle so she was sure this one small room was the outlier and the rest of the castle proper would be as stunning as everything else she had seen. Plus, she was determined to win over Regam more so than any of the others so she needed to try extra hard when he was around.

Regam didn't respond and only stared at her, crossing his arms much like Aditsan had. Corly briefly wondered if that was the universal gesture of annoyance of Regam's people, but she didn't have long to dwell on the thought.

"No worries there, dearie! I'll help you get right cleaned up without a care in the world!" Regam glanced behind him, but made no effort to move out of the way as the newcomer squeezed herself past him.

The woman the voice belonged to was the skinniest person Corly had ever seen. There wasn't an ounce of fat on her and she had little to offer in terms of bust and waist. She looked like a strong breeze might send her flying away at any moment! The woman wasn't as tan as Regam, but her worn and leathery skin gave a comparable appearance to him and his men. A straight nose hooked slightly at the end and small, beady eyes gave her a furtive appearance and her hair was streaked with enough gray to prove that she had been around for a while.

Comparing the sight of this woman with the boisterous and voluptuous Mistress Wavely made Corly a little more assured of her own diminutive frame. She did at least have some more time to grow unlike whoever this person was.

Regam moved to sit behind the desk and almost as if by magic another one of his men entered the room to stand by his side, neither of them saying a word.

The woman continued, unaware of Corly's scrutiny and seeming to have already forgotten that Regam was even there.

"Godlin-, ahem, goodness me you're a tiny one aintcha? What have they been feeding you until now? It certainly isn't enough! You need to be bathed and fed immediately! Don't you worry though, I've been told everything and old Doris here will have you squared away right quick! No need for any worries lass, now come, come!"

Before Corly could process the whirlwind of this woman's words she grabbed Corly by the wrist and whisked her out of the building without so much as a glance in Regam's direction.

As Doris began to practically drag Corly around she tried to get a look at her surroundings and get a better feel for things, but Doris wasn't having any of that.

"Come along dearie! No time to be gawking and dawdling now. We have so much, so much to do!"

Corly had many questions for Doris, the first and foremost being who in the Godlings Doris even was, what was going to happen to her, where they were going and would she be sent back to Regam afterwards? He and his men were rather an off-putting and strange bunch, but they were the only familiar people in an unfamiliar place and she would rather not lose the only tether to a sense of belonging she had at the moment.

The people, buildings and scenery were all a blur as Doris pressed on and continued to chatter away without a care in the world.

"Right dearie, we're almost there. A nice little bathhouse where you can rid that rustic stink right off ya. And don't worry, we'll have some nice clean and proper clothes for you so you toss those rags right out afterwards."

Corly was mildly annoyed at being called rustic and her 'dough clothes' as she called them referred to as 'rags', but she decided to let it pass; not that she could get a word in edgewise.

She was thankful she was going to have a chance to bathe, but normally she just jumped into the nearby river running through her parents homestead where no one could see her so she wasn't sure what this 'bathhouse' would entail.

Thankfully she was able to finally ask once Doris paused long enough between sentences to catch her breath.

"I've never used a bathhouse before. What's it like?"

Doris paused and actually stopped in her tracks to stare at Corly in confusion. For a full five seconds Doris only blinked and Corly was almost sure she could hear the whirring of the woman's mind.

"My, my! How in the world did you even take care of yourself before now? Where out there is a place where a young lady of courtable age can't even take a proper bath? That's unheard of! Outrageous even!"

"Well, I usually just used the river…" Corly began before

Doris cut her off and began pulling her along again. Corly was stunned just how tight a grip such a frail looking person could have.

"A river! Of all the...I've never heard of such a thing! Dearie, you needn't worry your pretty young self any, not one bit. From now on you'll be taken care of properly I can promise ya that!"

Corly didn't like the insinuation she hadn't been taken care of properly. Her parents certainly hadn't been perfect and sometimes insufferable when it came to the proprieties of her relationship with Darien, but they had been good people who had loved her and had always worked hard for the benefit of the village.

Corly forced herself to talk over Doris when the woman took another second to breathe. "I was taken care of, but Breathwynd didn't have anything like a bathhouse so we made do however we could."

Doris glanced at her and hurriedly adjusted her wording.

"Of course, dearie. Meant no offense, but once you experience bathing at its finest you'll never want to go back to jumping into rivers I can promise ya that!"

Corly was exasperated. She didn't know quite what to make of this woman, but if allowing herself to be pulled along meant finally getting cleaned up then she was all for it. She ignored most of what Doris had to say on the rest of the way to their destination as she turned her attention inward. Getting a chance to wash up would be a blessing, the Godlings above knew that, but what was still worrying her was what would come afterwards.

Regam hadn't mentioned much during the course of their travels no matter how many times she had asked and even now she wasn't entirely sure if she would even see him again. It was possible his role in her rescue was complete now that they had reached the castle and the prospect of being distanced from the only people she had any familiarity with frightened her.

She kept her worries from showing on her face, not that she thought Doris would notice, but her fears were allayed once they reached the bathhouse Doris wouldn't stop yammering about.

"Here we are dearie!"

The site of the bathhouse nearly stole Corly's breath away. The building itself wasn't overly large, but was so ornate and intricately designed Corly had trouble making sense of how so much care and meticulous detail could have gone into constructing just one structure.

The entire building had been constructed out of an unknown shiny black stone that glistened wherever the sunlight struck. Intricate designs and ornamentation depicting both people and animals Corly had never seen the likes of were carved into two pure white columns guarding the entrance and provided a stark contrast to the black stone of the building proper. She found herself staring in awe as the silver accents tastefully embedded in parts of the décor glittered and shone under the sun.

All of this just for taking a bath?

Stumbling along behind Doris, one thing she *didn't* notice was the flag atop the building flying high in the light breeze; one that bore the sigil of King Bamaul.

The sight of the majesty of the bathhouse had lulled her into a temporary stupor, but she snapped back to reality as she finally started to pay attention to what Doris was saying. She was swiftly ushered past a confused looking female clerk in black and silver livery standing next to a counter of dark stained wood. Corly got a brief glimpse of numerous containers smelling of soap and oil laid out, but Doris's next words made Corly quickly forget her curiosity.

"By the by dearie, I'll be the one getting your change of clothing so I needs to be getting your measurements and knowing if you're on your moonflow or not, it makes a difference in smallclothes."

Corly's ears burned furiously at such a brazen question spoken so loudly she was sure the clerk had heard. She had been getting her moonflow for a little over a year so she had gotten used to the pain and discomfort, but having her privacy intruded upon in such a public setting was more than a little shameless.

Doris wouldn't let the topic go as she led Corly through a thick curtain into a changing area adjacent to the bath itself.

"Come, come, arms up!" Doris clapped her hands and Corly was so dazed from her questioning that she began to comply as Doris made to help her remove her clothing.

"Wait, wait!" Corly gasped as she tried to regain control of both herself and the situation. "I can undress myself!

And as far as that other thing it is rather improper to discuss with someone I've just met, but I am not experiencing anything at the moment."

Doris paused and a look of concern flashed across her face before being replaced by her usual vapid one.

"I see then! Well, no worries dearie! Just needed to know for your clothing is all! You should be needing to know here in the capital such…rustic ways of thinking will be challenged and overruled so best be getting used to it! Well then, strip naked and dunk yourself to your heart's content. But first, measurements! I'm sure you'll be called for before long so best be getting clean as a whistle as soon as I'm done. Now then, I'll leave you some clothes here that seem like they'll fit though it might be difficult since you're so small! Once we obtain clothing perfectly suitable for you we'll be sure to turn you into a dazzling young lady!"

Corly ignored Doris' last comment, but wasn't sure what the woman meant by 'getting called for' or why she would need to be dazzling. She supposed she'd settle for the woman leaving her be as soon as possible. Biting her lip, she undressed down to her smallclothes as Doris quickly and rather invasively took her measurements with a thick string she marked with the charred end of a small piece of wood shaved to a point. It went more quickly than Corly had anticipated, but far more slowly than she would have liked.

Once Doris had finally left in search of permanent clothing, Corly fully undressed and stood for a moment looking at herself in the large mirror adorning one wall.

Normally the sight of something as expensive and luxurious as a mirror, especially one of this size and made of actual glass, would have stunned her, but she still hadn't caught her breath from the whirlwind known as Doris.

Inspecting herself in the mirror and turning in a full circle, she frowned and suppressed a sigh. Corly had never been exactly thrilled with her tiny frame and less than spectacular features, but she supposed there wasn't much to do about it since this was the way she was born. She had to remind herself again there was still time for her to grow a bit more. Hearing Doris harp on it so many times was a bit aggravating though. She *did* wish some things were more defined like Mistress Wavely had been. Maybe Darien would have been less oblivious and she wouldn't have had to work so hard to get his attention that way. *Well, maybe I don't need as much as Mistress Wavely had, but something a little bit more would have been nice!* This time a sigh did escape her lips at the memory of two of the people who had been closest to her and she bit her lip as she held back sudden tears.

She hadn't had much time alone since her rescue and never was truly able to fully process her grief so she found herself overwhelmed with emotion now that she had a moment of respite. Feelings of guilt and depression threatened to overtake her as she stared at herself in the mirror. Why was she still here? Why did something like that even happen? How come she was alive and no one else was? What should she do? Hiccupping, tears started to fall before she knew it. For several minutes all she could do was shiver and cry, all thoughts of taking a bath having vanished. Thankfully the clerk stationed outside must have sensed something was amiss and called out to her from beyond the curtain in a gentle voice.

"Miss? Do you require any assistance? The water will cool down if you don't hurry. I can attest to the benefits and quality of this establishment so please don't be shy and enjoy the opportunity."

Corly started at the sudden interruption. Sniffling back her tears she took a breath and slapped her cheeks with both hands. *Pull yourself together Corly Mathias! Bawling like a newborn won't help anyone or change anything! Take it one step at a time and figure out what's going on around you first, and then come up with a plan! That's the way!*

After psyching herself up some, Corly finally stepped through a long red hanging curtain and into the bath itself. It was a relatively small room, but just as ornate as the rest of the place. She couldn't see very far in front of her due to all the steam, but she was able to find her way to the sunken recess in the floor that served as the washing basin. Stepping into the water, an involuntary sigh escaped her lips. The bath was the perfect temperature even despite her delay and a comforting warmth seeped into her as she slowly sank into the water. As she soaked her eyes closed halfway and she could feel the stress and tension in her body begin to melt away. She might have even fallen asleep if it wasn't for the clerk who again called out to her, this time from within the changing area.

"Your temporary clothing is here. Please use the provided soaps, green for hair and blue for skin, to bathe, lather and rinse thoroughly. Once you have finished please dry off with the provided towels and change then wait with me in the lobby."

"Yes ma'am," Corly responded as she inspected the aforementioned items arrayed along the outer rim of the bath. Sniffing each one, she was amazed to find them both to be scented! A luxury like this would never be found in Breathwynd and she again wondered if it was really okay for her to be enjoying herself like this and being treated so kindly when everyone else had suffered so horribly? She shook out her braids in frustration and meticulously untied them before vigorously indulging in the care of her body to quell such morbid thoughts.

It took some time, but Corly eventually got herself to a point where she was satisfied with the results and prepared to exit the bath.

However, she emitted an embarrassed yelp and felt her face go crimson at the sudden appearance of a fully nude Regam striding through the curtain. The steam in the room had evaporated enough to where she got a *very* good view as he entered the bath opposite her without a care in the world.

Corly hurriedly sank back into the bath as far as she could without drowning herself. Regam didn't speak a word, but just leaned his head back as he soaked. His long, dark hair floated atop the water and Corly wondered how he kept so much hair hidden beneath his Makavai. She also noticed that he pointedly ignored the scented soaps, which irritated her.

She desperately wanted to be anywhere but here, but leaving now meant that Regam would see her and *that* was something she wasn't willing to compromise on.

Fine, I can wait this out if this is how it's going to be. She decided even if this was something that was common here at the castle there were just some things she would *not* accept. *Why does he insist on being so outrageous?!*

"You are going to learn to get used to it."

The look on the visible portion of her face must have given her thoughts away as Regam finally spoke. Corly frowned and inadvertently blew a few bubbles at his sudden admonishment.

Regam looked at her through hooded eyes.

"Among my people, bathing between men and women is something that occurs often and from an early age. There is no reason to show concern or embarrassment. We are as we were made by the Mother and there is both joy and pride in that."

Corly didn't quite believe that, but Regam continued undeterred.

"You will be in my care from now on. I have already received tentative approval for this. You will become accustomed to the ways of our people if you are to both survive and be useful enough to repay your debt."

Corly's underwater frown deepened. *What is he talking*

about?

She had assumed she would be handed off to someone better suited for helping someone like her and far more personable than Regam and his crew. Did this mean she was going to be permanently assigned to Regam's group?

Corly had mixed feelings about this sudden revelation. On the one hand her fears of being separated from the only people she was familiar with had been put to rest and she somewhat knew what to expect from them. On the other hand, getting even one of them to crack enough to tell her his name had been a major pain in the butt.

However, she *had* just a little while ago decided to force the issue with the taciturn group of men so she supposed this was what the Godlings had in store for her based on that decision. Not that she wholly agreed with this outcome, but she doubted Regam had any reason to lie.

Regam wasn't forthcoming with any more information so she worked up the courage to tilt her head above water just enough so she could speak.

"What exactly does that mean?"

She waited for several minutes for a response while Regam soaked in silence. Before leaving Breathwynd she would have been aggravated and more than a little annoyed at being kept waiting so long, but she had grown somewhat accustomed to this type of thing from Regam.

"What is it that you do not comprehend? You are to be placed in my care. You will live and learn as my people do and will swear service to his majesty Bamaul as an agent of the crown. Those remaining from our journey will all take a turn in overseeing your care and the training you will receive. And before you voice any frivolous objections this is not a request, offer or negotiation. This is what has been decided."

Submerging the lower half of her face again Corly grumbled at Regam's words and tone.

Regam finished his soak and emerged from the water just as shamelessly as he had entered. Corly squeezed her eyes shut, but her adolescent curiosity was just enough to catch another glimpse of adulthood before shutting them even tighter. The sound of Regam casually toweling off while she waited for him to leave caused her to blush furiously at the mental images coming to her unwanted and unbidden.

These people are so scandalous!

She swore to herself once more that there were just some things she would *not* compromise on no matter how much she owed him!

After a tortuous amount of time had passed Corly heard the padding of Regam's feet as he finally exited the changing room. She blew out a breath in frustration and embarrassment and took out her anger on the frothing and bubbling water with a small fist.

"What in the name of all the Godlings above! He could have just waited to tell me that!"

She grumbled to herself for a time, but eventually got around to finishing her bath so that she didn't get that weird wrinkling of the skin that came with submerging too long.

Finally getting to wash away the dirt, dust and grime felt wondrous, but she wished she could have enjoyed it a bit more, especially without the unexpected company.

She frowned again at the all too recent memory as she dried off and made her way to change into the clothing that had been left for her.

Despite how flighty Doris seemed Corly had to admit she had a good eye for clothing. She experienced some slight difficulty with the strings and buttons but was able to manage with some effort as she carefully inspected each garment before donning it. The only thing to not get a thorough inspection was the smallclothes; those went on immediately before Regam or the Godlings knew who else decided to intrude upon her privacy.

Gently rubbing her fingers on the soft fabric she closely inspected the stitching on the seams. She was stunned at the quality, fit and feel and instinctively knew these were clothes far beyond her means. *Is...is this silk!?*

This outfit was something no one in Breathwynd could ever hope to acquire or create in their lifetime. Finely stitched deep emerald embroidery ran along the neck and hemlines of the light green dress and even the soft, white chemise she had been provided with sported the same! The dress fit her nearly perfectly and Corly was stunned at just how different it felt to wear clothes so vastly superior to her 'dough clothes'. Was it really ok for her to be given them on a whim? She was shocked that such a fine thing had been given to her. *These are the* temporary *ones?*

Once she finished some final adjustments she gave herself a once over in the mirror to ensure nothing looked amiss or out of place. Satisfied that she probably looked fine she sat on a nearby padded bench and began to meticulously brush her long hair before braiding it back into her customary braids and tying them together at the ends with the lavender ribbon Darien had gifted her on her thirteenth naming day. Not a day went by since then she hadn't incorporated it into her wardrobe in some fashion. She smiled at the memory of how awkward he had been when he had given it to her and her breath caught in her chest as a wave of emotion swept over her. She took a deep breath to keep from breaking down and carefully wiped away the tears forming at the corners of her eyes.

She had thought it lost after what happened back at the village, but Regam had surprisingly had it in his possession and returned it to her, saying that it seemed precious to her since she had been desperately clutching at it when they found her.

"You alright in there dearie?"

Corly nearly jumped out of her skin at the sudden presence of Doris as she whipped back the curtain to the changing area without a care in the world.

She couldn't help but scowl. *It's a good thing I decided to get dressed first!*

"Ah, I see you're almost done. It's a shame you decided to re-braid your hair, there was so much we could have done with it had you just asked! But don't mind me dear, take your time, take your time! Do be quick though, there's so much more to do!

Corly wanted to know how she was supposed to be quick about taking her time, but decided to just do things like she normally did so she tuned out most of what Doris was saying from that point on. After a bit she made another final appraisal in the provided mirror and nodded in satisfaction.

Doris blinked and stopped mid-sentence about whatever it was she had been saying and gave Corly a visual once over.

"Not bad dearie! Aren't you just the most adorable thing! I guarantee all sorts of suitors will be flocking to you once you reach your majority in a few years!"

Corly felt her face go flush, not in embarrassment, but in annoyance. She had forgotten how those outside of Breathwynd viewed her during the brief interactions she had had with outsiders over the years.

She made sure to look Doris directly in the eyes and put on her most serious expression.

"I will be at my majority when next summer's naming day celebrations begin. Please do not make the assumption I am a child."

She felt like she had used the proper tone and demeanor to effectively get her point across, but Doris only blinked blankly before launching into another verbal torrent.

"Is that so dearie? Well then, let's proceed with the rest of what we have to do shall we? Off we go then!"

Corly resisted the urge to scream in frustration as she was ushered out of the bathhouse before she could object or get

Doris to acknowledge what she had said. It was important for them to know she was practically an adult!

She did appreciate the sympathetic nod thrown her way by the attendant as Doris hurried her along and barely managed to yelp a "Thank you!" before they had left the bathhouse behind.

Now where are we going? she wondered as Doris pulled her along.

"Right, now dearie I'm supposed to get you fed before anything else now that you're all cleaned up and adorable! Or was I supposed to do that first? No matter! Perfectly presentable as you are, aren't ya!"

Corly was stunned at how vapid this woman was. Of course she should have eaten first if that was part of the plan. Now she had to be extra careful not to ruin any of the ridiculously expensive clothes she was wearing and avoid undoing the results of the bath. She also didn't know what Doris meant by being 'perfectly presentable', but she didn't bother asking. She had somewhat of a handle on what type of person Doris was at this point and decided not to ask too many questions until she could ask someone more reliable.

"We're almost there dear! So exciting for you!"

Corly still didn't know where 'there' was or why she should be excited, but based on everyone else around them she assumed it was another fancy place far beyond anything she had ever experienced.

As Doris forcibly guided her along the number of people dressed in the livery of the king increased drastically and so did the quality of the architecture and landscape around them.

When she had first arrived she had been amazed at how incredibly well constructed and maintained everything was. The bathhouse had exceeded even her initial wonder, but now she had no words to describe the splendor of the people and things around her. Even the servants were all women and men of uncommon beauty and handsome good looks and they all moved with a practiced fluidity more reminiscent of dance than of those performing daily menial tasks. She also took note of the increase in the number of flags, pennons and decoration bearing the oddly designed sigil of Bamaul.

However, she didn't have long to gape at the opulent surroundings as she bumped into Doris when the woman came to an abrupt halt.

"Here we are! Now do be on your best behavior from here on dearie!"

Corly was fairly certain she had already been behaving herself properly based on all the commentary in her head about Doris she had been keeping to herself, but she put on her best smile and nodded anyway.

"Good, good! In you go then!"

Doris ushered her inside as if shooing a troublesome house pet and vanished from her side before Corly could even wonder what was happening.

Before she could get her bearings, a small group of men and women dressed in silver and black livery suddenly swarmed her and bustled her along amongst a torrent of chatter.

"Wait…" was all she could manage in slight resistance as pushing back against the surge only seemed to embolden the servants to speak faster, louder and with more urgency.

"Come now! We must make the final preparatory steps before turning you back over to Lord Regam. Your tone and demeanor must be addressed immediately!"

"At least her dress isn't that same shabby mess from earlier." Corly heard someone say.

The others surrounding her all made some similar comments and Corly was struck by an odd sense of being surrounded by a gaggle of geese. *What happened to getting something to eat?* She sighed. She guessed Doris must have already forgotten about that part by the time they reached wherever she was now. Her stomach certainly hadn't forgotten, but it was a bit late for that.

The chatter persisted until she was brought into a small room without decoration in contrast to everything else she had seen so far and housing a small wooden chair in the center and a thick, sturdy podium heavy with wear near one wall. The people surrounding her, who had been so talkative before, went instantly silent upon entering the room.

Corly was in a daze, but was thankful for the respite. At least she was until the presence of the person standing rigidly at the podium registered on her.

The almost comedic bustle and chatter of the servants had vanished and Corly felt a pall fall over the room as the woman glared at them so sternly she felt like a hole was being bored into her skull. The woman's gaze was so intense Corly couldn't help but feel guilty and ashamed even though she hadn't done anything wrong.

The woman stood behind the podium with back straight as an iron rod and hands clasped behind her waist while appraising the intruders with hawkish eyes enhanced by thin rimmed spectacles threatening to fall off her angular nose. Her mouth pursed in a disapproving frown as her gaze swept over them and Corly noticed more than a few of the servants actually flinched. Stone gray hair tightly pulled back into an immaculately kept ponytail only added to her severe and unforgiving appearance.

The woman looked to be later on in years, but her piercing eyes still held a healthy amount of vigor and her clothing was just as severe and impeccable as her appearance. Her own dress of livery looked to be tailored to fit her specifically and unlike the other servants had silver and black accents offsetting the pristine white blouse and black vest that had the top button out of three buttoned closed. She wore men's trousers the same blinding white as her blouse with a thick silver line running down the sides. The contrast of her shoes, black as midnight and with sheen so glossy Corly thought she might be able to see herself in them, made the only audible sound as the woman tapped one foot impatiently.

Before anyone dared to speak, the woman who was very obviously in charge snapped in a calm yet authoritative voice. "You all may go. None of your services shall be required."

No further explanation was given, but the servants who had been so eagerly escorting her suddenly couldn't wait to be anywhere but in that room.

Corly assumed the instructions were for her as well, but she was pulled back by the woman's voice as she turned to follow in the wake of the others.

"Not you lass! Why would you assume such a thing when I went to all this trouble bringing you here! Did that insufferable woman tell you nothing?"

Corly froze in place as the words were spoken so sharply it was like being cut with a knife. She had a very good idea of who the 'insufferable woman' was, but decided to play it safe and bobbed her head in apology. She chose to remain silent in fear of her voice cracking under this woman's intensity and that she would bring trouble to Regam should she cause offense.

The woman's frown impossibly deepened, accentuating the wrinkles at the corners of her mouth.

"I see you have at least a basic concept of both manners and following instructions. I suppose that does bode somewhat well for both your usefulness and potential."

Corly didn't understand what she was talking about, but she remembered what Regam had told her earlier and remained silent. She assumed she would be told more as long as she followed Regam's instructions so she relied on the patience she had spent years honing and perfecting while spending the majority of her free time with Darien.

"Well and good then. I see you are at least intelligent enough to adhere to Lord Regam's instructions. Very well. You may sit. I am Elnora. I will be your instructor and guide for the time being. You will find none of Doris's flighty nonsense nor the chatty noise of the others from me. I will speak. You will listen. You may ask questions when I allow you to do so. When I tell you to answer a question, complete a task or anything of that sort you will do so in a manner befitting a young maiden worthy of being brought forth before his majesty."

The blood drained from her face as she properly sat down at the rickety desk at the casual confirmation she would indeed be meeting King Bamaul. Her stomach tightened in a knot and all thoughts of hunger fled entirely. A cold sweat broke out on her forehead as Elnora smiled thinly at her obvious discomfort.

"Let us begin."

Chapter 5

Gliding through the dense interior of the Grove Liana seethed with unchecked fury. Thick and lush branches, leaves, hanging vines and other parts of the densely packed underbrush left nary a mark on her flawless alabaster skin as she phased through everything in her path.

She had *felt* it. An Elder's epic song of the glory of creating new life and powerful magic infusing itself into the very fabric of her existence. She had reveled in it. Praised it with every ounce of her being and gave it proper reverence. Only then had it suddenly and forcibly been siphoned from her in a heart shattering moment that threatened to tear her aura apart. There was only one denizen of her home that could introduce such a powerful and world-altering magic into existence; the Great Elder who resided in the deepest and least accessible recesses of the Grove and kept herself hidden within the Birthing Circle. And *something* had just violated this glorious process that should have been inviolate.

She could feel the immaculate essence of her home

growing denser all around her, becoming purer with each passing second as she made her way towards that hidden area deep, deep within the Grove.

Only those such as herself with an excessive amount of magic and aura, or blessed enough in extremely rare cases to be invited, could even get close to where the Birthing Circle lay. It was the only portion of her home that was both its heart, but somewhat separate; occupying a space in the world all its own and was generally inaccessible even to her. Liana found it both fascinating and glorious and her heart swelled with pride and adoration at just the thought of the Great Elder residing inside.

Despite her rage at the notion that the sanctity of the Circle had been violated, a look of awe and wonder etched onto her delicate features as she felt a sudden, yet subtle, shift in the very essence of the Grove. A gentle tug compelling her onwards to a portion of her home that had previously been shrouded from her.

I have been invited! Gliding along, she could feel the full brunt of the Great Elder's aura enveloping her to the point where she briefly fell to her knees and wept crystalline tears of joy. She could have spent the rest of her existence in that state and been ecstatic to do so, but the powerful call of the Great Elder was too much to bear and it continued to draw her to it as if she was enchanted.

A slight vibration in the air caused goosebumps to form on her skin and she shivered in a continued state of ecstasy.

Before her very eyes the holiest of places slowly

shimmered into view. Massive, thick boles packed tightly together stretched so far into the canopy above that the interior could never possibly be viewed by any other than the worthy. Bark, branches and leaves sparkled and shimmered in shades of green, emerald, silver and gold even in the dark. The air was heavy and lush with power humming gloriously in her ears and she basked in its glory as she glided along.

Her eyes grew heavier the closer she approached, but her limbs felt lighter than ever. With her heart thumping loudly in her chest Liana gasped at the sensation as she floated around the magnificent boles continuing to thrum and vibrate with the essence of her home. Instinctively tracing her fingertips across them and reveling in the sensation she smiled while following this wonder, this privilege, bestowed upon her. Just coming into contact with the mighty boles caused small sparks to fly and she shuddered in joy. She fervently wished for this moment to never end.

Soon she came to a small opening among the boles. She was vaguely aware that such a thing wasn't naturally occurring, but despite her heart swelling further at what she saw as an invitation she declined to crawl through and instead respectfully peered inside to bear witness to the majesty contained within.

Despite her desire to remain respectful, a slight cry of wonder escaped her lips at the sight of the Great Elder now stretching her mighty black wings to the heavens as she sang her dragon's song.

Liana threw her arms out in front of her and tightly

gripped the sides of the opening. Her whole body shuddered as the indescribable notes of the Elder's song washed over her in a blessing she was not worthy of. The enchanting words and melody echoed endlessly in her mind as it spoke of new life, new glory, and new magic born into the world.

There was one thing Liana found odd despite her raptured state as she continued to listen to the song. She took note of a much smaller dragon she had never sensed before lying sleepily at the Great Elder's feet. Gray scales glistened from what must have been the mother cleaning her young and Liana ached to cradle the infant Elder in her arms and revel in the feel of the newborn's claylike scales before they blossomed into whatever jewel-like color they would become. The membrane of the newborn Elder's wings lightly trembled with each breath and Liana's chest swelled with joy at the sight. She could barely hear the infant Great Elder's mewling as it tried to mimic its mother's glory, but the magic of its essence strangely felt both near and far away when it should be nearly as overpowering as the mother despite being newly born.

That's when Liana came to the realization of what must have occurred and what exactly had been stolen from her home. It must have been why she had been summoned by the Elder's song!

Rage erupted internally as she warred within herself against the elation she was feeling. Someone had *stolen* from this moment that the very fabric of the world and everyone in it should be rejoicing in! This new life, this new Great

Elder, had come into the world perfect and new and had thus been violated by the most heinous of acts.

Shuddering again in both ecstasy and anger Liana inhaled the scents of the woods and magic enveloping her, all the more heavily saturated by her proximity to the Circle, and felt an infusion of essence like she had never before experienced. So much was being gifted to her that she could even feel those recently chosen for her latest migration recoil in uncertainty and fear within her.

Despite her current state of worship Liana felt irked at the sensation they provided. Both because their presence shouldn't have still been noticeable and that they both should have accepted their fate already; her deal with one notwithstanding. Perhaps it was due to the sheer power of the Birthing Circle itself? It was entirely possible. Not even she, who was among the oldest of the Grove's denizens, fully understood the almighty power of the Birthing Circle and the Great Elder who called it home.

Taking another deep breath and trying not to lose consciousness at the sensations coursing through her, Liana calmed herself while she bore witness to a new member of this world's true ruling class begin her first throes of existence.

She stared in awe as the miniscule Great Elder took its tentative first steps around her mother's immense frame. A tiny roar, nowhere near as massive or immaculate as the ones her mother was capable of, reached Liana's ears as the young one cautiously flexed her wings; still wet from her recent birth and her mother's ministrations. Liana's heart filled to bursting with joy at the sight as the young one continued to waddle around unsteadily, intermittently emulating her mother as she did so. Despite her elation at what she was witnessing Liana had the distinct impression the young Elder was looking for something and was rather distressed about it.

Seeing this precious and majestic Elder in such a state of disarray so soon after gracing the Grove and this world with her presence sent Liana into a homicidal rage overwriting all of the extreme euphoria she had been experiencing. The migrations within her wailed at the sudden burst of emotion and Liana forced herself to tear her eyes away from the heart-wrenching scene.

Reluctantly turning her back on the Birthing Circle, she shuddered as the black Great Elder slowly finished the last glorious, haunting traces of her song. Before she could move another step Liana felt a powerful inrushing of air surging by her. She was almost hurled to the ground by the intensity of this unseen force, but she was able to phase out enough where she could retain her dignity before those who were the rightful rulers to the treasures of this world.

Long ago she had borne witness to this phenomenon so she was prepared for the blast-back of air that followed. Holding her breath as the reverse pressure of the Elder's relocation hit, she was again struck by the warring emotions of rage and ecstasy within her.

Just the sensation of being engulfed by a portion of the

essence of not one, but two of the Great Elders was enough to quell her rage to a simmer and quiet her inner struggle as she fully phased back in near the tail end of the reverberation.

The Birthing Circle began to fade from view as Liana felt a gentle separation from the space within the Grove housing such a precious relic. She was saddened her allowed stay was so short, but elated that she had been gifted such a boon. As she stood lightly trembling in the darkness she vowed to herself an oath.

"I *will* find what was taken from the young Elder and will make whosoever stole from her suffer such that they will wish to have never existed."

Liana's visage was an indescribable mix of fury and joy as she glided her way back to her favorite place where she could absorb as much of the essence of her home as she could.

She had much to do.

Corly couldn't keep her knees from trembling as she knelt on the cold and filthy stone floor of the throne room. The black and white patterning beneath her was grimy and unwashed so she was terrified of the scolding she would get later for sullying the clothes she had been gifted. Trying her best to stay calm by focusing on the floor she could feel the intense gaze of the king boring into her and judging her worth. She was also aware of Regam's presence since he arrived shortly before King Bamaul had been announced.

Corly wished she could have asked him for advice, but Elnora had been thorough in her instructions to already be kneeling, immobile and silent before Regam and the king even entered the throne room lest she desire a fatal punishment.

A slight breeze fluttered in through the large un-shuttered windows lining the far wall and she utilized every ounce of willpower she possessed to repress a shudder at the realization these must be the 'jump-holes' she had been recently instructed about.

It had already been several minutes since Regam and King Bamaul had entered, but so far neither had uttered a word.

Even the herald, both knees bent and back bowed to the point of almost being prostrate, seemed more terrified than nervous and Corly wondered if all the rumors trickling through Breathwynd over the last few years were actually true.

She resisted the urge to shake her head to clear it of horrid and rambling thoughts since Elnora had been *very* clear about staying both silent and still; two of the 'keys to survival' as she had called them.

She steadied her breath with some effort, but having been in this position for so long was beginning to make her legs and back ache. Her knees were already smarting from kneeling on such an unforgiving surface for so long and she again lamented the fact that her new, expensive clothing had been marred by the unkempt floor.

Corly had been informed during her instruction that his Majesty had his reasons for the state of the throne room, but her instructor had been unclear and evasive as to what those reasons could possibly be.

After what felt like an eternity King Bamaul finally uttered his first words.

"So this is the one who survived."

Corly's whole body tensed, but was able to remain still despite the biting impact of his assessment. His words felt laden with accusation and contempt despite how calmly the king spoke. His voice didn't have the harsh and biting tone she had expected, but was rather calm and precise; each word carefully enunciated with precision as if each held meaning, although he did speak with a slightly odd accent. Despite the calmness of his voice, she had the distinct impression of what it was like for livestock being appraised and was rather unsettled by the implications of being assessed in such a way.

She idly wondered if the sheep her family had raised had felt much the same, but her train of thought was interrupted by Regam.

"Yes, my liege. This young one goes by the name of Corly. As we have previously discussed she is the survivor of the tragedy that befell Village Breathwynd and will be placed under my care from now on. She has shown some flashes of potential and *will* be useful with the proper training and knowledge."

The emphasis on the phrase 'will be useful' was not lost

on Corly. She was intelligent enough to understand there were still some major events related to Bamaul assuming the crown still occurring within Katama even now and that she would more than likely become involved in some fashion now that she had been officially given over to Regam as his ward.

"I see. What happened there was truly a...tragedy indeed. So much was lost that day. It must have been quite the ordeal."

Corly kept her expression neutral, but something was starting to feel slightly off about the king's words. They began to sound somewhat strained, like he was having difficulty speaking. She resolved herself to ask Regam later if the king needed to speak in a certain way in public since this was something Elnora had failed to mention, but she doubted the tight-lipped man would be willing to tell her much.

She heard the king sigh heavily and waited anxiously for several moments before he began speaking again.

"I see you Corly Mathias and acknowledge your apprenticeship under Lord Regam. From this moment forward he is not only your protector and guardian, but your lord and master and myself your God above him. You will obey his every command and devote your very being to the betterment of my country of Katama. Our enemies are your enemies and our allies your allies. Strive for strength and greatness at any cost and contribute to building a nation that is always better tomorrow than it is today. You may lift your head and meet my eyes."

She heard a sharp intake of breath from the herald at the king's words and Corly thought his majesty growled slightly, but the herald quickly croaked out a repetition of the king's instructions.

"Corly Mathias of Village Breathwynd, newly appointed to Lord Regam of the Bloodsetters may now lift her head to meet his majesty King Bamaul's eyes."

Corly wasn't sure what was so shocking that everyone in the room needed to hold their breath, but she quickly did as she was instructed; another one of Elnora's instructions had been 'do exactly as you are told and do so immediately without flaw.'

Lifting her head and locking eyes with his majesty, indescribable emotions instantly took hold of her. The king's dark eyes held an overflowing amount of passion, strength and intensity that she afterwards would never be able to accurately describe. The intensity of his gaze was so overwhelming she could only hold it for a few moments before dropping her head back into a bow in a cold sweat.

The king shifted forward intently on his throne and emitted a quiet laugh. "You held my gaze for longer than most twice your age have been able to girl. That shall be your first accomplishment of note. Many have openly wept before me in fear, awe or worse, but you…"

Corly didn't understand the rest of what the king was saying as it was too soft to discern, but it sounded like he was speaking to Regam so she assumed whatever it was wasn't for her ears. She did let a small sigh of relief slip out at having made it this far without incident and froze in place as the king immediately went silent. The very air went still and she felt the weight of her mistake hanging heavily on her shoulders as an enormous pressure emanated from the throne. Corly's stomach dropped and her heart began to hammer in her chest.

I messed up!

Several more tense moments passed before the king heavily rose from his throne and strode to stand before her.

Corly had never been more terrified in her life. All she could think about was being thrown out the window to fall to the courtyard below and how much it would hurt before dying. Tears welled up and her lip began to quiver, but before she lost herself to her terror the king spoke in clear, even tones that brooked no argument.

"Do not ever be content enough to relax for even a moment young Corly Mathias, even in the presence of your greatest allies. Such behavior is enough to warrant you free passage to the courtyard below."

Corly's breathing became ragged, but she tried her utmost to keep her composure despite having broken one of Elnora's teachings after almost having made it through this insane situation without issue. All the rumors and warnings about the king that she had forced herself to push aside in order to remain calm came tumbling back quicker than she thought possible, but she gritted her teeth and willed her body and mind to remain still despite being under the king's terrifying scrutiny.

"I see. Regam, now I understand more of what you have told me about this child," the king spoke calmly as he turned sharply on his heel and resumed his place on the throne with an ominous creaking.

What do you understand?! Corly's nerves were so frayed she wanted to scream.

"Yes, your majesty. I do believe she will be both an asset and a boon for our country should she apply herself as desperately as she seems capable of."

Corly was thankful for the reprieve and almost found herself relaxing again, but the terror from a few moments ago was enough to stop herself in time. Instead, she decided to focus only on what was said and concentrate intently on not making another mistake.

Despite her fear she found herself a little irked at how talkative Regam had been while in the presence of King Bamaul. Her best efforts at drawing him into conversation had always gone nowhere and to hear him so open with communication frustrated her for some reason.

Corly resolved to make it so Lord Regam would eventually be the same way with her, but she was smart enough to know she would probably have better luck first with pressing forward her earlier decision to break the ice with the other Bloodsetters. Then maybe Regam would find it easier to open up to her.

She didn't have time to dwell on it as the king suddenly dismissed her from his presence and she pressed her forehead firmly to the floor. The king stood from his throne and strode with purpose from the room with Regam closely in tow.

"You will receive further instruction shortly. An escort will fetch you momentarily and bring you to your lodgings. Do *not* disgrace us," Regam said loudly over his shoulder, his words reverberating throughout the cavernous throne room.

She kept her head pressed to the floor like Elnora had instructed as the clacking of the two men's boots faded into the distance.

Silence reigned for a time before the herald raised his voice and loudly proclaimed "Bamaul, the ruler and King of Katama has exited the throne room! All may rise to a knee!"

Corly and the guards rose to a knee as one and the herald continued.

"All may rise to a bow!"

All parties in question rose to their feet while keeping backs deeply bowed in the direction of the throne.

And then finally "All may stand at ease!"

Corly was finally free to relax, but had to fight to keep from fainting on the spot from all the stress, tension, fear and lightheadedness threatening to overwhelm her. Her head hurt almost as bad as when she had woken up after being rescued and her mouth felt like it was stuffed with cotton.

Brushing away loose strands of hair plastering themselves to her forehead from her profuse sweating she was somewhat surprised none of them had gone gray.

Corly took a quick glance around the room and noticed all the guards and the herald seemed just as relieved. After a few seconds passed everyone caught their collective breath and the herald made another loud announcement.

"Corly Mathias may exit the throne room to where her escort is waiting!"

Keeping her head up she proceeded on unsteady legs to where the herald directed her. Another one of Regam's men stood silently just beyond the entrance of a small alcove and immediately turned his back and began to briskly walk away as she approached. Corly had somewhat gotten used to this type of thing and understood she was expected to follow, falling in step with the man after hurrying to catch up to him with the pattering of her dainty feet.

The man glanced down at her briefly and she allowed herself a small smile of satisfaction. Always before she had walked behind her escorts, but she had spontaneously decided to switch things up in order to keep in line with her earlier determination to integrate herself with her rescuers. Despite what she had just endured she had never been one to let things she couldn't control affect her too deeply and now that she was back in a familiar, and far less stressful, situation she began to assert control over her fate with this one small step.

She decided to keep that particular thought to herself at the moment however, and she lightly hummed under her breath as she waited to see where this new escort would bring her.

Corly stood in the middle of a dusty and empty area fenced in with some less than serviceable lengths of rope and rickety pieces of wood. She felt like if she stared at the "fence" too long it might collapse under the weight of her gaze. She frowned as she took in her surroundings and took a look at her newest change of garb.

After leaving the throne room she had been promptly brought to a tiny, empty room where her escort only told her 'Change,' and pointed to a pile of rough and worn looking clothing heaped into a pile in the corner of the room.

"Uhh…Are you going to leave so I can change?" she had asked, but was only given a hard stare in response.

Crossing her arms Corly put on her most stern expression. There were just some things she would *not* compromise on no matter what! "I'm not changing anything with you here. It's both improper and outright scandalous! Didn't your mother ever teach you proper manners while dealing with a young maiden?"

The man had only continued to stare at her, but Corly held her ground and defiantly stared right back. She refused to repeat the embarrassment like with Regam in the bathhouse again!

Eventually the man must have grown tired of her stubbornness and turned his back to her.

"I cannot leave you unattended," was all he said.

Corly glared at his back as hard as she could in the hopes she could somehow bore proper manners into him through sheer power of will alone, but the man refused to acquiesce any further. If she had been able to learn his name on the way here she might have pushed further, but he had been the most reticent of all her recent escorts and she hadn't found any openings to work with.

She did her best not to scowl, but eventually resigned herself to the situation and ended up changing faster than she had ever thought possible.

Corly had been appalled when she had asked what to do with the expensive dress she had just been wearing and was told to leave it to be burned! It was so wasteful, but apparently no one save Lord Regam or the servants assigned directly to the king ever wore the same thing in his presence twice.

Now standing in this empty yard with nothing but the dust swirling in the air and the dirt under her feet to keep her company she took another appraising look at what she had changed into. Brown leggings that were a little too snug for propriety tightly clung to her in uncomfortable ways and she was certain the gray tunic she was wearing had originally been tailored to fit a man as it hung rather loose from her slender shoulders.

The boots, however, did fit rather well and seemed to be relatively well made so she sent up a small prayer of gratitude to the Godlings above for tiny favors. After finishing her short break of devotion she suddenly sneezed when the dust swirling around her tickled her nose.

The lack of any other people, minus her escort, even

servants, was unnerving her a little since she hadn't had a moment to herself since arriving and being exposed to the whirlwind of activity and bustle constantly ongoing within and around the castle.

Clouds had moved in overhead, throwing everything around her under an ominous shadow and she resisted the urge to start biting her thumbnail. Her escort hadn't been very forthcoming with answers to her questions and continued to be incredibly hard to break. Corly found herself wishing it was Aditsan who had been the one to bring her here. At least she could get *something* out of that one.

Thankfully she wasn't left wondering for much longer before she finally got her answer. Regam suddenly appeared from wherever he had gone off with King Bamaul and was dressed in similar fashion as herself, confirming her suspicions she was indeed wearing men's clothing. Corly was sure her mother would be rolling in her grave if she saw her daughter right now.

He carried with him two wooden sticks both carved in a similar manner that started thicker at the bottom and thinned out somewhat to a rounded end at the top. He unceremoniously dropped one of them at her feet and loomed menacingly over her. Assuming she was supposed to pick it up she bent down to retrieve it and suddenly a sharp pain rang through her skull with a loud thwack as Regam forcefully struck her over the head so hard that for a few moments sparks floated before her eyes and she almost bit her tongue in twain.

Her knees buckled at the force of the blow and she stumbled backwards with tears blurring her vision. "What..."

"Never remove your eyes from your enemy! Remember this pain for it is the best instructor for learning to avoid it."

Corly rubbed at the small lump forming on her skull and couldn't avoid scowling. Apparently she was in store for some sort of training. "Who just hits a lady out of nowhere like that?" she snapped before she could stop herself.

Regam responded by quickly stepping forward and clubbing her in the ribs before spinning around to sweep her feet out from under her with his heel.

Corly made a very unladylike noise as all her breath left her body and she landed heavily on her rump.

"Emotions and needless chatter serve only to get you killed quickly. Always be ready and expecting a lethal attack while preparing your own attack, counter, and intent to kill."

Corly was still in the dirt wheezing at both the lack of air in her lungs and being in a *lot* of pain. Regam seemed even more irritated than usual and she briefly wondered what had happened after she had left the throne room.

"What…" she started again and winced in anticipation as Regam once more quickly closed in and towered over her with anger smoldering in his eyes. Instead of striking her again as she had expected he again dropped her training weapon in front of her with a thud. She hadn't even noticed him picking it up.

Through her blurry vision Corly tentatively picked up the weapon she now realized was molded vaguely in the shape of a sword. Still unsure of what was happening or why Regam was putting her through such violent paces she unsteadily rose to her feet and held her 'weapon' awkwardly in her small hands.

She was smart enough to know that right now keeping her thoughts to herself was her best option and to follow along with whatever Regam was planning. She doubted this was being done without reason. It reminded her again of lessons and lectures with Oltan when he would adopt a no-nonsense attitude, although forgoing the physical pain. She would apply herself to this lesson and ask her questions afterwards.

Regam gave a barely perceptible nod.

"Good. Now that you have experienced pain I will begin to teach you both how to avoid it and how to inflict it."

But why? She couldn't get the question out of her head, but she kept quiet while she intently listened to Regam's instructions. He began not by striking her again as she expected, but with the positioning of her feet, legs, and hips. Corly flushed with embarrassment as Regam used his rough hands to physically adjust her positioning without so much as even asking permission. She gritted her teeth and endured it while keeping ready to fight back with every ounce of strength she possessed should he decide to attempt anything more improper.

The feeling of a grown man putting his hands on her in

such a familiar way was uncomfortable to say the least so she found herself asking why this was necessary despite her earlier resolve.

"Is it necessary to be so intimate? It is rather improper. Wouldn't it be easier to watch you and copy what you do?"

Her breathing had become ragged from the constant and merciless exercise and she had taken this chance during a brief and much welcomed break where Regam had once more admonished her and adjusted her positioning.

Her question was answered with a resounding thwack and a ringing in her ears as Regam again thumped her on the head and she was again knocked heavily into the dirt. Looking up, her complaint died on her lips and she immediately shrank back in fear from the menacing glare staring back at her.

"You seem to have forgotten. You were told recently to not speak unless spoken to. Let me remind you of that now. As for your query I will only say this once. The body of a female warrior is designed differently than a male and moves in a much more complex way. The placement of muscles, joints, bones and the like all require different techniques and placement to achieve the desired results. Simply copying myself or another of my men will only serve to be detrimental to your development. As such it is vitally important that intricate adjustments are made to ensure you are learning the correct techniques for your size and physical constitution. We are also using this time to determine just what sort of blade will be forged for you in the future so that you can perform to your optimum at all times. You should be grateful I even possess this knowledge or else your fate might have been much, much different. Now that your curiosity has been satisfied, free yourself of your previous notions of propriety from a backwater village and dedicate yourself to what you are being taught!"

Regaining her feet on wobbly legs Corly bit back a heated reply about her home village and took a deep breath. All sorts of things came to mind as she absorbed Regam's reprimand, but she took to heart what she had been instructed and readied herself as she glared back at Regam with determination.

Regam held her gaze for a few moments before quickly launching into a series of strikes that Corly did her best to block, parry and avoid as she had been instructed, but most still found their mark. With each strike that landed she vowed with tears in her eyes to return the pain tenfold to whoever was behind the recent events that had turned her entire world upside down and stole everything she had ever loved from her.

I swear to whatever Godling listening that I will avenge my family, my friends and the people of Village Breathwynd. I swear it with all my might!

Chapter 6

Following Corly's meeting with the king and just before
he left to meet her in the makeshift training yard, Regam
walked silently behind Bamaul as the monarch strode
proudly forward with hands clasped firmly behind his back.

Regam understood the next few minutes would be
precarious for him, but felt the balance of what use he had
and what he brought to Bamaul's cause would outweigh any
outbursts that may come his way. He knew Bamaul needed
the cooperation of the Bloodsetters as well and should
anything happen to him their continued service to the crown
would be in doubt. However, one could never tell what
emotions Bamaul's bracelet would elicit from Katama's
ruler. Having the girl in tow upon arrival as well as the old
man should also play strongly in his favor, but nothing was
ever a certainty when it came to the turbulent mind of the
king.

Regam had already been concocting plans on both how to
leverage the girl against the good behavior and cooperation

of the old man as well as manipulating her into dedicating herself wholly to himself and Bamaul, not to mention the rest of the Bloodsetters under his command.

Now all he had to do was see how the king reacted now that he had met the girl in person. She had done rather well surviving the encounter for a village bumpkin, save for that one near-fatal mistake, but everything would ultimately hinge on how Bamaul perceived that meeting.

Of course, it was entirely possible Bamaul had already forgotten about the girl, but Regam doubted that was the case. He could tell the king, whether unconsciously or not, was heading in the direction of the old man's cell. This sometimes happened while Bamaul was struggling with what he referred to as 'the bells' in his mind the bracelet elicited, but Regam hoped the king was in enough control that he could still see the possibilities and benefits of fully investing the girl in their cause.

Soon they arrived at the hallway where the door leading down to where the old man resided and stopped upon entering. The guards stationed in the hallway were already kneeling with heads bowed as their monarch entered. After taking a few steps Bamaul paused and looked around with a frown and Regam quickly stepped ahead of him to stride to the end of the hall to open the next door. He had enough experience serving beside Bamaul to know the man was likely looking for an excuse to strike out in rage and bloodlust. However, he judged there was little time for it despite how little he cared for these 'soldiers' that were no more than cowardly decorations of flesh holding no actual value.

The door creaked ominously on its hinges as Regam pulled it open, but Bamaul suddenly spoke as he stepped through to the landing of the stairwell leading down into the darkness below. Regam made sure to close the door behind him so the guards would not hear the king's words.

"That girl you have in your possession. Will she be as useful a piece as you claim? Had you not previously vouched for her I would have thrown her to the courtyard below by those ridiculous braids myself."

Outwardly Regam remained calm and stoic, but his mind was feverishly working. Had the king already forgotten the words he spoke back in the throne room? It was entirely possible depending on his mental state, but Regam hadn't noticed the king stroking that onyx bracelet fused to his wrist which caused his madness.

However, Regam had become accustomed to repeating and re-explaining things after having spent so much time by Bamaul's side over the years and he had become rather adept at often turning it to an advantage.

"Yes my lord. She is connected very closely to our guest resting comfortably below, which has already proven to be of great effectiveness in guaranteeing his cooperation. Additionally, having a survivor unaware of what actually occurred allows us to control the narrative we provide her, which will serve to induce her to feel even more indebted to us for saving her life. There is also the added benefit of having such a survivor becoming so publicly dedicated to our cause that others will become more sympathetic to us even if they may not agree with the application of our principles."

The king didn't respond, but his frown deepened, marring his face and adding to his already dark and brooding complexion. Bamaul took a deep breath and ran a hand through his dark, wavy hair in a gesture Regam knew meant he was dealing with some of the bracelet's effects on his mind.

Regam still wasn't entirely sure what the bracelet really was, but knew how powerful the artifact could be despite its side effects. He was aware it was linked to the origins of his people and that had been one of the more persuasive aspects of Bamaul's recruitment efforts all those years ago. He was also vividly cognizant of what 'the bells' and 'the ocean' meant and what the effects of these things were on both Bamaul's body and mind.

The physical effects were much more noticeable, but frightening enough on their own. Just looking into the king's eyes for more than a moment was a task too monumental for most, even for those under Regam's command. Often bloodshot and unsteady, the eyes of the king nonetheless exuded strength, power and no little amount of madness. Perhaps this is why Bamaul had commented on the girl holding his gaze more than most twice her age and with more worldly experience were able to.

Then there was the bracelet permanently adorning the king's wrist. Calling it 'permanent' wasn't an expression nor an exaggeration. The deep onyx of the bracelet, made of some unknown metal, had a small sliver of silver embedded in it that glinted under the light in such a way and with such a sheen that Regam often wondered if there was something ephemeral about its origins. Not much about it other than its connection to his people was known even to him, but what was immediately noticeable were the blackened, web-like lines spreading outward from where the bracelet grafted to Bamaul's skin. The king employed the best physicians and shamans in the nation to alleviate the malady, but none could completely cure or rid him of it, only temporarily lessen or slow its spread, and occasionally temper its effects. However, no matter what course of treatment was taken the infection would soon inexorably begin to spread again.

Regam valued his life more than his curiosity so he never asked for further information past what Bamaul was willing to confide. The amount he did divulge involved visions and effects capable of making even Regam's blood run cold.

Patiently waiting for the king to regain control of himself, there were a few tense moments where Bamaul placed his hands behind his back in a gesture Regam understood meant he was restraining himself from stroking the bracelet and inadvertently increasing its effects. Knowing the compulsion the bracelet had was incredibly strong and that Bamaul had actively been battling his urges since acquiring the artifact, Regam forced these dangerous thoughts from his mind as the king finally addressed his appeal.

"Hmm, I see your point. I have assigned her to you as my most trusted subordinate, but should she prove a liability in any way or we lose the advantage she allows us then this discussion shall be...revisited."

Regam nodded. He understood very clearly what the king was inferring.

Before they could continue their discussion or progress further down the darkened stairs a rather loud commotion coming from back in the hall caught their attention and Regam inwardly winced at the sudden interruption. There was no telling how the volatile king would react to being interrupted when he was about to visit the old man, but Regam re-opened the door all the same.

Thankfully the guards and the source of the commotion were smart enough to already be kneeling before the door opened; otherwise one or more would certainly have lost their lives during the maddened rampage Bamaul would have gone on.

What foolishness is this?

Stepping back into the hallway, Regam solemnly closed the door as Bamaul slowly turned to face the panicked messenger that had arrived in a state of disarray. Regam had expected Bamaul to immediately relieve this fool of his life, but was surprised to find him reacting calmly as he motioned for Regam to stand by.

The man's obvious fear and the king's strangely calm reaction piqued Regam's curiosity and interest. Either

Bamaul inherently inferred this page bore a missive of true importance or he had the blessings of the Mother herself to avoid execution upon the spot.

Regam stood patiently a step behind Bamaul and off to the side, his hand resting on the pommel of his sword should his liege require it.

The king looked down upon the page through hooded eyes, his calm expression both cold and calculating.

"Speak."

"Yes sire. A messenger agent has returned from the field to deliver an urgent report concerning the status of Philip Lockhart. He is working under Bloodsetter Daras and insists the information he possesses needs to be presented before your majesty directly as previously ordered."

Bamaul's eyebrow twitched at the mention of Lockhart, but he remained passive much to Regam's surprise. Normally the mere mention of Philip Lockhart's name would cause the king to fly into a murderous rage and lash out, but he stood calmly considering the words of the man kneeling before him.

Regam assumed it was the man's demeanor and phrasing combined with Bamaul's preoccupation with the girl and the old man that allowed for a moment of clarity with the king; he had no doubt had the man chosen a different method of delivering this information the outcome would have been much more gruesome. Regam grudgingly gave a small amount of respect for the page since he must have practiced his delivery as much as possible en route to sound both humble and informative, while also giving the indication he was not at fault for either the timing or the information contained within his report. Naming Daras also showed the Bloodsetters under the king's command were involved and Bamaul would have to give some consideration to that information since Regam was their head.

Had there been even a sliver of blame on the messenger for the sudden and unwanted intrusion upon the king's time his life would no doubt have ended up forfeit. Regam disliked having to admit it, but this man was capable in his role. Many others would have stumbled over themselves due to both nerves and fear or spoken in a way that would have either brought blame upon themselves or in a tone Bamaul would have found offense with in some way.

"Dismissed. Regam."

"Yes sire?"

"We will return to the throne room to receive this important missive."

"Of course."

Regam had been unable to get a clear view of Bamaul's face due to his positioning, but he quickly realized he had been mistaken as to how calm he was.

Moving forward to kick the kneeling man out of the way, Regam got a full view of the king's visage. His face had become a twisted mask of anger and resentment hardly concealing the murderous intent rolling off him in waves. Regam was stunned the man hadn't succumbed to whatever was happening inside his mind as an ominous clicking filled the tense silence in the hall while Bamaul stroked the onyx bracelet.

The small piece of silver shining with an otherworldly gleam glittered under the sparse light filtering in through the paneled windows of stained glass adorning one side of the hall. Even Regam suppressed a shudder at the thought of whatever it was currently invoking itself within the king's mind.

As Bamaul began to move, Regam quickly and quietly again moved to open the door for him. He glanced one final time at the form of the man who had brought this urgent matter to the king's attention, but he remained as still as stone even after getting kicked. Regam pulled the door closed after they had exited, but had he waited a moment more he would have seen the page collapse unconscious from the stress and pain.

"Please don't! I'm sorry! I'll do more! I'll be better and of more use I swear!"

Regam barely heard the pathetic wails of the man he was forcibly dragging along by the collar. Now that he had finished the girl's initial instruction he had another important matter to attend to per the king's instructions.

This particular messenger had previously reported some rather interesting news to the monarch, information that had kept the blubbering fool alive, albeit upon one condition.

The king had instructed the man to learn to fly; No small task, but even Regam was at a loss as to what that meant.

He had been ordered to take the wailing mass of human skin to the shamans working exclusively under Bamaul's employ so Regam could at least make an educated guess that whatever was in store for this fool wouldn't be pleasant.

Regam smiled under his Makavai; the ritual headdress of his people covering his head with a dark cloth the color of midnight while a blood red veil masked his face save for the eyes. The possibilities of what this sobbing mess would undergo were nearly limitless where these shamans were concerned. He normally wouldn't have his full Makavai in place, but the effect it had on his charge was pleasing. It also had the added benefit of muting the scents and smells of their destination somewhat.

The few servants encountered along the way were experienced and wary enough to notice the tell-tale wrinkles creasing the corners of his eyes and nimbly avoided even potentially obstructing his path; they knew better than to bring attention to themselves.

The man's incoherent ramblings meant he still didn't understand his life had been spared, at least temporarily, but that suited Regam just fine. He was sure once they reached their destination he would get a more than satisfying demonstration from the head of the shamans, known by their people as The Haatal; the man was almost as twisted as Bamaul, although he rarely showed it and would never admit it. Regam suspected this was due to all the narcotics and other means of inducing shamanic revelations prevalent in that line of work, but he should be more or less coherent at the moment.

Glancing back briefly, Regam sneered as the man devolved into a pathetic state of sniveling and muttering forlornly. Tears and mucus were plastered to the fool's face and the lines of age marking his countenance seemed to have increased in the last few minutes. Gray hair, sticky with perspiration, matted to his head and the stench of urine was still rather strong from when the man had soiled himself.

The stained clothing wouldn't be a problem since Haatal Peyeiza would probably need to strip him anyways either into some ritualistic robe or simply nude. Hopefully they would burn his current clothing on the spot. The smell was starting to get to even Regam, but at least the man's wailing no longer grated on his ears.

Regam took note of the closest servant who had quickly stepped out of his way and bowed. "See to it that this hall is cleansed immediately and thoroughly," he hissed at the woman who bobbed in a modified curtsy in an indication of understanding. Never breaking stride, he dismissed the servant from his mind as shouts about cleaning supplies faded into the background.

Regam knew he was getting close to his destination when the cloying scent of incense and the Mother above knew what else began assaulting his nostrils even through his Makavai. His earlier smile quickly turned to a frown. He had hoped Peyeiza would be in a coherent state, but his current task may prove to be a bit problematic should he be otherwise indisposed.

Taking shallow breaths, Regam pushed on while the sniveling whimpers behind him trailed off into muted sobs. Regam resisted the urge to silence the man on the spot for good, but he had been given specific instructions to relay to Peyeiza although he himself was unsure what the meaning behind most of those instructions actually entailed. He was sure the king had a purpose behind every word, there was no wasted thought or action when Bamaul was coherent, so Regam brushed off his annoyance and trundled on with his hapless charge in tow.

Soon he found himself entering an area exclusively inhabited by Peyeiza and his disciples. Regam wrinkled his nose in disapproval of the heavy scents that had been steadily increasing to the point where they became a miasma thickening the air.

The door marking the entrance to what was known as the 'Shaman's Den' was currently unguarded. It never was because who would be foolish enough to unlawfully enter a shaman's residence unannounced and unwelcomed? Someone with poor decision-making skills and without much use of their own life, that's who, but Regam was different. There was no part of this castle that was off-limits to him and Peyeiza knew that. Should it come down to it he would have to remind the man of that fact by disposing of a lesser disciple, one not of their own people of course, but he doubted he would have to make that point.

Gritting his teeth, Regam pushed open the heavy wooden door engraved with runic markings representing the teachings and ideologies of the shamans. He assumed there was more to it than that, but that was all the information even he could get from The Haatal. The shamans always claimed graven markings and images were essential to uncovering and understanding the power and wisdom of what they called 'the unseen world', but Regam was never one to buy into spiritual teachings outside of the Mother herself. Although he did have to admit Peyeiza and his acolytes were usually rather potent with their results, no matter what the source of that potency was.

Striding into the antechamber, a discernable cloud of an indescribable hue enveloped them as he left the door open in hopes of airing the den out a bit lest he lose some of his senses. Peyeiza wouldn't like it, but he would have to accept it for the time being.

It wasn't long before a beautiful and scantily clad woman in sheer dress appeared from behind a thick violet curtain on the far side of the room. Sheer, loose fitting sarouel pants covered her lower extremities and she sported a light rose-colored scarf with small bells at the ends over a band covering an ample bosom. Her midriff was bare save for sporting a jewel in her navel and she held a half-niqab decorated with beads in one hand. Most men would find her appeal more than a little alluring, but Regam didn't have time for that. She languidly bowed with a placid expression, her nearly transparent clothing slipping in places and leaving little to the imagination as to what lay beneath.

"Welcome, Lord Regam."

Her speech was drawn out and slurred, each syllable stretched to the limit as far as it could go.

Regam felt a spike in irritation. This was *not* how a woman of his people should behave or dress, but he was aware that certain allowances were made in terms of the nature of shamanic work; no matter how much he may disagree with it.

"Get Peyeiza. Now."

Regam was in no mood to entertain the abhorrent display before him and was irked that Peyeiza himself had not been there to greet him.

"Haatal Peyeiza is...currently occupied with vision questing. May I be...of assistance?"

Regam stepped forward and roughly grabbed the woman by the hair and yanked her upright. He removed his veil and brought her face so close to his he almost received a contact high from the opioids and narcotics lingering on her breath.

"Get Peyeiza. Now. This is an order. From the king."

Regam shoved the woman away and quickly drew his sword, placing the blade at her neck and pressing just light enough to draw blood. The woman collapsed to her knees and he glared menacingly down at her as a sudden realization of horror spread across her face.

The drugs and visions induced may dull one's senses, but even that wasn't enough to eliminate all understanding of what it meant to cross Regam or King Bamaul. She must have realized her error and assumed it was too late. Tears fell from the corners of her eyes and she prostrated herself at his feet in complete apology.

"My apologies…I will retrieve Haatal Peyeiza at once. Please…forgive me."

She quickly inched away from Regam; her face still firmly planted into the floor. Regam waited for her to vanish back behind the curtain before sheathing his blade.

He looked down at the object in his other hand that he had almost forgotten about during his tedious interaction with the woman. The sniveling mess of tears and snot that named itself Gelas stared mournfully back at him with a distant look in his eyes. The thick fog in the air must have begun to have an effect on the man. Regam found himself being thankful for the intense and often life-threatening training he had undergone in his youth that allowed a greater tolerance than most to these types of substances.

He did wish more than anything to take his blade and pierce straight through this fleshpile's skull so that he could revel in the satisfying crunch and squelch as he shattered bone and eviscerated what little brain matter this Gelas might have. He knew his irritation was starting to get the better of him, but there was only so much one man could be expected to tolerate.

As he was contemplating the pros and cons of his murderous ire the one he sought finally deigned to make an appearance. The Haatal's face was lined with age and his long hair, white as snow with multiple beads and feathers delicately intertwined, was finely groomed and hung down his back to the waist. A necklace of small claws and talons rested upon his chest that left him scratched and lightly bleeding at times. He wore the light blue robes of one at the height of his profession and the bleached antlers of the desert-horned embok embedded with various stones and crystals adorning his head gave little doubt as to the power he possessed. Despite his age, the eyes of The Haatal still held obvious strength and vigor and he walked unbowed with purpose.

"Ahh, Lord Regam, welcome to our centrum of knowledge and seeking of the lost within the arcane. Sainai was in quite the state when she came calling for me. I understand the stresses placed upon you under the command of his majesty, but please try to refrain from terrorizing those under my care and tutelage."

Regam was surprised to find Peyeiza in a coherent state since he had supposedly been questing, but it should make things go more smoothly. Peyeiza was an eloquent man when not inundated with the tools of his trade and even then the shaman had a unique and some claimed awe-inspiring way with words. Regam was in no mood for any type of debate or push back so being sound of mind should indicate Peyeiza would understand the severity of the situation and of the words he spoke.

Regam's eyes narrowed at Peyeiza's request and when he didn't answer the shaman seemed to realize the implications of his complaint as he took a small step back and slightly bowed in an apology. Regam ground his teeth and suppressed both his irritation and his urge to kill the piddling mess of a human that he roughly dumped at Peyeiza's feet.

"This one is for convergence. Per the king's order. I highly suggest you succeed. And quickly."

As Peyeiza straightened from his apology the only sign of worry crossing his face was a slight dilation of his pupils and a tiny increase to the wrinkles at the corners of his eyes.

To the man's credit he quickly masked whatever concerns he had and silently looked over the clothed heap of a man hugging his knees and rocking back and forth at Peyeiza's feet.

It wasn't long before Peyeiza's eyes went distant and Regam felt the room go chill as the head of the shamans began muttering in an unfamiliar tongue.

He would have preferred to leave at this juncture, but being on an errand as a result of a direct order from the king meant he had to see this all the way through to where he could be certain Bamaul's wishes and intent were met. Not to mention that meant he would be able to escape culpability in the event of things going awry as well.

After several minutes Peyeiza loudly clapped his hands and two acolytes appeared from behind the curtain. They were dressed in a similar fashion to the head of their order, but had white leggings and with far less adornments on their vests and braids. These two belonged to the very bottom of the shamanic hierarchy and Regam paid them barely a glance as they hefted the quivering Gelas up by the armpits and began gently escorting him towards the curtain.

Something must have finally clicked in Gelas' mind at this point as he suddenly lifted his head and looked around with a wild look in his eyes. "I can't do this!" he screamed. He quickly broke free from the acolytes who both gave a slight "Ah!" in unison at the sudden change in their charge. Frantically looking around the room Gelas saw the exit and stumbled towards his perceived freedom.

Regam moved quickly to intervene, determined to inflict as much pain as possible on someone who had proven to be an incredible nuisance in such a short amount of time, but Peyeiza was surprisingly faster.

With a stunning amount of fluidity and grace the shaman flowed across the room almost as if dancing and struck a forceful, although non-lethal, blow to the back of Gelas' head with the heel of his palm. The resounding crack reverberated throughout the room and the only sound following was the immensely satisfying thud of Gelas' unconscious carcass falling to the floor. Narrowing his gaze Regam forced himself to look at Peyeiza in a new light.

Peyeiza was not exactly your typical elderly as he was not close to the end of his days nor was he slow or decrepit, but he was by no means a spry young man at the peak of virility. Regam admitted the shaman's movements were worthy of praise.

"One could say there might be some Bloodsetter background in your history Haatal. Perhaps you would like to reassess your calling?"

The fact Regam used the official title was not lost on Peyeiza as it indicated at least a modicum of respect on Regam's part and he was not a man exactly well-known for his respect of others, especially outside of the Bloodsetters under his command. The shaman also knew he could be treading on dangerous ground where the Bloodsetters were concerned if he wasn't careful.

"Please, it was nothing at all, Lord Regam. I assure you I am pursuing my proper calling and have thrown away any and all vestiges from before my questing began, but I graciously and humbly thank you for your offer."

The shaman's answer confirmed Regam's suspicions that Peyeiza had indeed once been a Bloodsetter, or at least been in training to become one, at some point in his life and had somehow made the transition to the shamanic order. It was rare that something piqued Regam's curiosity, but he supposed it was irrelevant in the scope of what they currently were tasked with accomplishing.

"I'll leave it at that. For now."

Regam smiled coldly and Peyeiza momentarily froze, but quickly recovered. Regam couldn't leave the conversation as it was without some kind of implied threat considering what leaving the Bloodsetters normally entailed, which is to say one did not leave the Bloodsetters once joined, not by choice, circumstance or desire. Only one's death, severe injury, or in very rare cases where old age made one no longer useful and could retire with honor, held the appropriate avenue for end of service. There were those few who were allowed exit due to a rather extreme circumstance, but Regam had done what he could for those noble souls who had sacrificed so much even if it ultimately left him feeling unsatisfied.

Peyeiza seemed to receive the intention behind Regam's words, but remained nonplussed. Regam was satisfied to leave it at that for now as they had far more pressing matters at hand since the pile of flesh had started to twitch and it seemed he might wake.

"Let us get this over with. I will be accompanying you for the initial stages. That is not a request. Unless you would like to directly file a complaint with his majesty like some of your contemporaries. Forgive me, *former* contemporaries."

Peyeiza had opened his mouth to argue, but quickly snapped it shut at mention of Bamaul and the reference to what had befallen those who had made the ill-fated decision to voice complaints directly to the king concerning the construction of the door leading to the special dungeon.

Several talented people had lost their lives as a result and even some elders were cast down when they decided to ask the king to relent a bit on his excessive demands. It had not ended well for any of them and Peyeiza had still not been able to raise any of the senior acolytes to fill those vacant spots. Apparently finding new acolytes was not going very well either.

"Very well Lord Regam. Please accompany me as you wish. Nala and Yazi, pick that thing up and follow us. Do not drop it again."

"Yes Haatal," they spoke quietly in unison and hefted

Gelas' limp body off the floor with deceptive ease.

Sainai reappeared to hold the curtain back for them and Regam reattached the veil of his Makavai to curtail the swirling cocktail of odors wafting out to greet them. Sainai's eyes widened in terror at the gesture, but Peyeiza gently chided her before Regam had the chance to snap at her in irritation.

"Relax child. He will not harm you without due cause. Please return to your studies and remain there until called for. Understood?"

Peyeiza's voice was gentle, but had an iron tone that brooked no argument, not that Sainai would have anyway; she was much too terrified of Regam now that the effects of her questing had dissipated some. She didn't have the courage or the desire to argue being sent away from her master's side.

"Now then," Peyeiza said while he looked over Gelas as the acolytes trundled by. "This may prove to be rather interesting."

Chapter 7

Inhaling deeply, Regam reveled in the screams coming from the test subject as Peyeiza deftly administered his shamanic skills.

Peyeiza had led him deep within the bowels of the shaman's den to where the convergence was to be performed. They had passed a myriad of rooms en route to where the ceremony was being conducted and most contained scenes beyond even Regam's comprehension, but he assumed there was a proper reason behind all of them. There had been a slight delay with the removal of a corpse from one particularly foul-smelling room in particular, but it hadn't been one of their own people so Regam had dismissed it as nothing more than an annoyance once Peyeiza apologized for the inconvenience.

Now he stood along the fringe of a large and dimly-lit room with a floor comprised of a shiny metallic substance. A large circle carved into the ground and full of the many runic symbols of Peyeiza's trade dominated the room. Each precisely engraved symbol faintly glowed and pulsed with every intonation of Peyeiza's voice as The Haatal slowly and painstakingly labored through the ritual.

The old shaman carefully un-stoppered a vial of dark, viscous liquid and poured it over the naked and violently shaking Gelas while one of the acolytes reverently wiped the sweat from Peyeiza's brow.

Gelas had been stripped nude and dumped in the center of the circle and shackled by the ankle to a small iron ring in the floor. Upon waking the man had blubbered and pleaded in such an incoherent rambling Regam assumed his mind had completely broken.

However, Peyeiza had spent several minutes speaking patiently and quietly into Gelas' ear while Regam waited impatiently for things to progress. Several long minutes were spent before Gelas had calmed down enough to where he only produced an occasional whimper and Regam had wondered aloud why they didn't just render him unconscious again and get started.

Peyeiza's response was surprising. "The subject must remain conscious throughout the majority of the process, especially at this stage. This is imperative to the forced bond we will be implementing." The Haatal shook the oversized vial of light red liquid in his hand for emphasis.

"Do those vials contain…?"

Peyeiza bobbed his head in apology to the unfinished question.

"No, not entirely. We only have a faint trace amount to

work with so what we do have is a dilution of sorts. Not perfect by any means, but it should provide enough for a catalyst to work from as long as he survives. Of course, the survival rate is rather low."

Regam gave Peyeiza a hard stare at the second half of his explanation. Peyeiza's eyes widened as he realized that he may have said a little too much, but before he could cover his mistake Regam strode into the circle, effortlessly avoiding the glowing symbols as he did so, and leaned down so close to Gelas they were almost touching nose to nose.

"Cease your pathetic sniveling and heed my words. You *will* survive this procedure and fulfill the requirements the king has decided upon for you. Should you not meet our expectations I can assure you that precious wife and child of yours will not live past eveningfall. Their deaths will be neither quick nor pleasant. Is that understood?"

Gelas whimpered as the mix of tears, fluid, and mucus flowed unabated down the wretch's face, but he was barely able to muster a nod.

"Lord Regam, please. I must ask that you refrain from entering the circle again, especially during the ceremony itself. There could be unexpected consequences even we are not aware of."

Regam glanced at the shaman. The man's words held some weight, not to mention he could end up taking some of the blame in the case of failure should he cause things to go awry and he needed to avoid that at all costs. Disgusted and annoyed, but satisfied his message had been received, Regam retreated back to the edge of the room to await the next steps the shaman and his acolytes had in store for Gelas.

Some time had passed since then and once Peyeiza had doused Gelas with the strange liquid he had begun leading his acolytes through a complex pattern among the runes on the floor while always keeping Gelas to their left. The acolytes usually would follow in Peyeiza's path, but occasionally would step to a different rune than the one The Haatal had chosen before quickly falling back in line. Each step was made precisely from rune to rune and when one of the acolytes almost missed stepping on one in the pattern the murderous look Peyeiza threw in his direction was enough to wither stone. Cold sweat formed on the acolyte's forehead as he swallowed hard and took a breath before Peyeiza continued on.

Each time Peyeiza or his acolytes stepped on one of the runic markings it would pulse with a much brighter glow and would briefly change color to match the deep red liquid in the new vial in Peyeiza's hand. Gelas would react each time with a scream or sob in time with the runes flaring, but Regam's mind was elsewhere. He couldn't help but notice the process was similar to opening the door to where the old man was being held and resolved to ask about it later. Once the procession had completed their pattern Peyeiza stopped in front of Gelas where a thin red mist also matching the color of the vial began to form around him.

Peyeiza leaned down and began softly whispering into Gelas' ear as the man shuddered and convulsed spasmodically at irregular intervals.

Regam turned his attention back to the ceremony and was annoyed at being kept out of the loop about what was being said, but kept his irritation in check. He understood enough to know, even without Peyeiza's earlier remonstration, that he could not interfere or interrupt less he cause a catastrophic failure. Still, he would rather beat some sense of subservience into Gelas to cease his pathetic display and get this done; Regam still had much more to do before this day was out.

Peyeiza finally finished speaking with Gelas and the two acolytes held him firmly by the arms and lifted him up with his body hanging limply between them. Peyeiza took yet another vial out from his robes and this one was decidedly different from the first two. Instead of a glowing mystical liquid this was a deeply blackened sludge oozing and writhing within the vial as if it had a life of its own.

Peyeiza un-stopped both vials and his chanting increased in intensity and volume until he was shouting and Regam gave an involuntary shudder at the intense cold and deep sense of fear and foreboding filling the room.

Gelas' face was etched in obvious terror and even the acolytes were unmasked in their fear, but Peyeiza remained calm despite screaming at the top of his lungs.

Pouring the first vial of glowing liquid quickly down Gelas' throat, Peyeiza forced him to swallow it all before thick tendrils of an oily black slowly flowed out of the last vial as if alive. Initially they slowly stretched out towards one of the acolytes and his eyes widened as his fear turned into pure, unadulterated terror. Regam took note that it was the acolyte who had nearly made a misstep earlier and had no sympathy for the man.

Peyeiza remained unfazed at this development and continued his chanting, his words taking on a more demanding and authoritative tone. Sweat poured down the shaman's face as each symbol they had previously stepped on intensely flared all at once. Regam noticed that instead of the vibrant colors from earlier the symbols now glowed in muted blacks and grays getting denser and denser with the rise in Peyeiza's pitch. The thick tendrils of ooze stopped and quivered for a moment before slowly turning towards Gelas and hovering just inches from his face.

Once Peyeiza regained control of the strange ooze and gave his acolyte another reproachful glare he began to sway away from Gelas while continuing his chanting. To Regam's eyes the pattern was the same, just in reverse while the runic carvings reduced in intensity with each step. The tendrils of ooze hovering in front of Gelas remained where they were, but new lines thinly stretched out from within the vial, weaving a web of terror that looked like it had been woven from a giant spider out of nightmare. Regam was sure this must have some profound meaning behind it, but was not as knowledgeable of the shamanic arts as he was in other disciplines.

Peyeiza's voice became hoarse and strained as he continued to maintain control over the web of tendrils seeping from the container, but his efforts were not in vain. Once the shaman reached the outer edge of the circle he turned and approached Gelas again, deftly finding a path around, under and even over the web. Regam crossed his arms in appreciation to how dedicated Peyeiza was to his craft; the old man never even touched a sliver of the ooze as he winded his way back to the center.

As the shaman approached the subject, the ends of the tendrils still hovering near Gelas inexorably stretched out as if yearning for him.

Gelas' eyes held pure terror, and not a little bit of madness, but he remained conscious, which surprised Regam.

I suppose his mind may be so far gone by now that he's in a state of shock, he mused.

Regam supposed it was a stroke of luck the man had remained conscious this long, but the concoctions Peyeiza had fed him plus the terror he must have been feeling may have made Gelas push past any physical limits since the entire ceremony would be for naught should he lose consciousness for even a moment; Regam had made very clear what would happen to Gelas' family should that occur.

Standing directly in front of Gelas, Peyeiza's chanting grew to a final crescendo as the tendrils began to caress and fondle the man almost lovingly before violently infusing themselves into every available crevice and orifice. His mouth, nose, eyes and more were filled with the black liquid forcing its way into his body.

Gelas gagged and shuddered violently as the tendrils showed no mercy in their intrusion and Peyeiza slowly lowered his chanting to a mere whisper once the liquid had begun to take hold of its host. The thin web of fluid filling the circle rapidly raced passed Peyeiza on all sides to follow suit and Regam was surprised that not a drop so much as grazed the Haatal.

Gelas continued to shake and shudder more and more violently until Peyeiza had to physically grab a hold of the man to keep him somewhat still while the strange liquid did its work. The acolytes, their part having been completed, retreated to the relative safety of the edge of the room where there were no engravings.

Regam sneered at their cowardice. Had they been under his command such an inexcusable act would never have been tolerated. The fact Peyeiza had ones such as these as acolytes was concerning to say the least. It was a telling sign of their struggle; such an act was a discredit to those who practiced the craft and an insult to Peyeiza as one of his people.

Peyeiza had finally ceased chanting and now cradled the spasming Gelas tightly. The tendrils of liquid finished intruding into the man's insides and the shaman took a deep breath before gently laying Gelas down in the center of the pattern. Sighing heavily, he stood and spoke to his acolytes in a hoarse voice.

"He may sleep now while the remaining effects take hold. Lord Regam, please consider these two are still relative greenhorns and the fact they were able to participate without failure or true folly is commendable."

Peyeiza must have sensed his discontent and Regam assumed this intuition was part of the reason Peyeiza had achieved the position of Haatal. He didn't like the fact the shaman was obviously ignoring the reproach he had had to give during the ceremony, but he had to take the expert in his craft at his word.

The two acolytes flinched at the annoyed grunt Regam gave in response, but Peyeiza had already moved on to the matter of Gelas' recovery and future steps.

Ignoring the sweat and fumes visibly enveloping his body Peyeiza slowly walked over to Regam, avoiding the symbols on the floor as he did so. The runes had almost died out, but a very faint glow still remained and Regam assumed making contact with any of them would have dire consequences. He held his breath as the shaman came up to him, lest he inhale anything that may prove harmful or lethal. Peyeiza noticed and had the decency to step back a bit so Regam could safely breathe.

"It will be about a week before Gelas is properly adjusted to the first stage should all go well and we can then proceed with the remaining rituals, at least as far as we can currently conduct them."

Regam frowned. "There is more than this? The king is expecting results, and quickly." Regam didn't like the insinuation they didn't currently have the ability to complete the cycle, but Peyeiza answered the unspoken question before he could ask.

Peyeiza bobbed his head in acknowledgement of Regam's worries. "As I am sure you are already aware, we are missing a key element for the final procedure. I understand the need for results, but the king will surely be pleased with today's success. This Gelas' body is more tuned and receptive than any other I've ever seen. It's truly remarkable and a very good indicator of things to come."

A slight groan caught their notice and they turned their attention back to Gelas.

"Ah, this is expected," Peyeiza said quickly before Regam could ask what was happening.

Ripples were forming along the outer layers of Gelas' body as something writhed and wriggled just under the skin. It was a surreal sight to behold; ripples bulging, thinning and flowing throughout his entirety for several minutes before the involuntary twitching ceased.

"Do not worry Lord Regam. The final vial takes some time to fully replace the blood in his system. What we just saw was part of that assimilation and is no cause for concern. To be honest, I am surprised he has yet to start vomiting blood and have it spilling out of more unmentionable places. I do not recommend sticking around for that unpleasantness."

Regam glanced at the shaman to see if he was stalling, but had no choice but to accept the explanation. Peyeiza may be a little off-center mentally, but he was a perceptive and intelligent man; he would never willingly put his own life or the lives of his acolytes at risk either in the course of their work or by the king's whims. Regam would have to carefully frame his report to the king, but as long as Bamaul was in a state of clarity he supposed there might not be an issue with what Peyeiza was telling him.

"Very well. I will inform his majesty of the positive results; however, I must remind you that I cannot guarantee the nature of further demands."

Peyeiza ran a weary hand over his face. The man looked exhausted beyond his advanced years; no doubt the ritual had taken a great toll on him as it took a considerable amount of physical and mental fortitude to endure. However, despite Regam holding a certain respect for Peyeiza's ability and dedication to his craft, there were things that needed to be accomplished soon and Bamaul was not one known for his patience.

Regam waited a few more minutes as the runes in the floor finally stopped glowing. The recovered acolytes began attending to the comatose body of Gelas while Sainai quietly entered and handed several vials of thick viscous liquid of varying colors to Peyeiza before beginning to cleanse the room from the ceremony with traditional cleaning supplies.

Regam remarked on this since he had assumed the head shaman would have used some other arcane method to clean the room and prepare it for the next steps.

"You are correct in that assumption, Lord Regam, but that will come later after Sainai finishes her tasks as an upper acolyte. She and the lesser acolytes will then be attending me for the remainder of today's tasks so I can assure you I will be the one administering each and every step of this process."

Regam was starting to get annoyed at how Peyeiza was able to perceive the meaning behind his words so easily. He had sensed Regam's concern that parts of the process may be left in the hands of an acolyte and had expertly assuaged his doubts.

"Very well. When this process is complete I will return with further instructions should the king have any for you. There is someone the king wishes to pair with Gelas once he is capable of deploying into an active role."

Peyeiza nodded again in understanding and bowed fluidly to Regam. "Of course. Please be assured he will be ready. The most difficult part of the process has been completed with today's ritual and we will proceed forward as soon as possible."

Regam grunted and turned on his heel before stalking his way out of the room and back through the shaman's den. Once he exited through the large door that had thankfully remained open he took a deep breath through the veil of his Makavai.

Now let's see what the defector has to say about what the king has in store for him.

Regam's cold smile formed under his Makavai once more as he relished the thought of the next conversation on his agenda.

Corly groaned in pain. Even closing her eyelids felt like an abysmal chore. Regam had been relentless in his training and she had never been so sore in her entire life, not even after the rough ride from Breathwynd to Rowe. She had given up on counting all the bumps and bruises and now all she wished for was the sweet release sleep would bring.

Unfortunately, her brain refused to let her battered body rest as questions and concerns about her future cycled relentlessly around her head. She sighed and let out an explosive breath.

"Ugh. I need to sleeeeeep…" she mumbled as she tried to convince her brain to shut itself down. It was some time before she succeeded and her eyelids eventually closed with some finality. It felt like only moments later when she was suddenly and violently awoken by a swift strike to her midsection. Breath exploded out of her lungs in a short burst and she had no time to comprehend what was happening as she was pulled roughly from her pallet.

Survival instincts quickly kicked in and she began blindly kicking, punching and even biting whatever and wherever she could on her unknown assailant. She sank her teeth into what felt like an arm as hard as she could until she tasted the tang of hot iron indicating she had drawn blood. Her unseen opponent grunted in pain and tried to throw her to the floor, but she held on for dear life as they continued to flail about. It felt like an eternity to her, but in reality the entire exchange only lasted several seconds.

Another, more forceful attempt to dislodge her succeeded in sending her crashing to the floor in a heap. Several sharp blows rained down on her from above. She tried to crawl away to safety, but her tired body betrayed her and she collapsed in a heap heaving for breath with the taste of blood still in her mouth. Having reached her limit, she resigned herself to whatever happened next when the blows suddenly stopped.

A lantern blinded her as it suddenly brightened up the room. One of Regam's Bloodsetters, this one unfamiliar to her, stared harshly from behind the folds of his Makavai.

Still heaving for breath Corly again tried to will her body to move, but the wear, fatigue and soreness from the last few days had taken their toll and her muscles simply refused to listen.

The man looking down at her swung his weapon, what she now recognized as nothing more than a thick wooden rod, and she winced in anticipation. After a moment of silence with nothing crashing painfully into her skull Corly risked a peek and found the Bloodsetter had stopped his weapon just before her eyes.

She stared up at her assailant in both fear and confusion. Her body couldn't take any more abuse and her mind was at its breaking point after everything she had been forced to endure up until now. She was too exhausted to try to understand what was happening or even to lick the blood drying on her lips.

"Be prepared at any time. No matter the time or place. No matter how tired or injured. No matter how safe you feel in your bed. *Always* be at the ready. Lord Regam wishes you to take this lesson to heart. You will not disappoint him."

The man brought his makeshift weapon up to his shoulder, extinguished the light, and stalked silently out of the room. Corly followed him with her eyes the best she could in the darkness, no small feat now that her night vision had been ruined, and waited several heartbeats to ensure he actually left before groaning in pain and frustration. She was so exhausted that not even tears could form to let out the emotions she was feeling. All she could do was lie on the floor in the darkness and pray for sleep to claim her.

This treatment followed suit for several nights after. Then just as she was getting used to the nightly intrusions they abruptly stopped. It had been even more of a sleepless night than the one when she had first been assaulted. Every creak and moan of the building, gust of wind against the window and unknown noise of the night caused her to awake in anticipation, but no one ever came. Then another night passed. And another. And just when she thought she was free and clear and could start sleeping soundly they began again and with more intensity than before.

Despite constantly worn down by getting herded around by Doris, lessons with Elnora and her training with Lord Regam or another of the Bloodsetters, she was still as ready as one could be when the nightly attacks began again.

A slight creak in the floor alerted her subconscious mind of an impending threat and her body reacted out of habit as her eyes snapped open and she rolled off her pallet to the far side. This placed the pallet between herself and whatever threat may be present.

She kept her eyes closed in case of sudden light like the first night she had been attacked and moved into a crouch. Extending her sense of hearing into the now silent room Corly patiently waited. Sensing nothing else amiss she crouched even lower and slowly and carefully opened her eyes while retrieving the wooden practice sword she had gotten into the habit of bringing back with her after her training sessions from under her pallet.

Feeling rather than hearing the attack coming she rolled backwards over the pallet next over from hers. This was a premeditated tactic on her part since she knew it would be unoccupied. Since she was the only female in her peculiar position of being caught between both lessons of ladyship and propriety as well as training like a Bloodsetter she was neither much at home in the Bloodsetter barracks or among the "proper" ladies within the castle so she always slept in a small reserve barracks alone. It hadn't taken her long to incorporate this fact into her defense.

After the first few attacks Corly had spent several hours memorizing the layout of where she slept and had received many painful bruises from attempting to navigate the room with her eyes closed, but now she had the entire room committed to memory.

She flipped the pallet over as hard as she could in the direction of where she suspected the attacker was located based on the creaking of the floor and rustling of clothes and was rewarded with a grunt as it struck her opponent. This hadn't been intended to cause much damage, but to try to pinpoint her attacker's location in the dark room. Satisfied that she had a general idea of where he was she launched herself in that direction with decisiveness, strength and confidence.

This was something Regam had been adamant about during their training sessions.

"Whenever you pick up a weapon you must be both confident and decisive in everything you do. Part of what I am teaching you is the ability to make the correct decisions in those moments. Any amount of doubt or hesitation will cost you or another their life so when you make that decision follow through to the utmost of your ability."

Corly stomped an appel in hopes of distracting her opponent and thrust hard. Her first blow met with flesh, but her second was parried as her knee bent at an odd angle when she landed on a corner of the overturned pallet. Trying not to make noise at the pain she realized a fatal flaw in her plan. Now that the location of some items had changed, the mental map of the room she had was ruined.

Cursing herself for failing to realize something so obvious Corly quickly delivered a few more strikes, which were more to keep her opponent from riposting than anything, before she tumbled to the ground. She immediately tried to roll

away from the threat and regain her footing without turning
her back to the enemy as she had been taught, but her
opponent was quicker. His wooden rod slammed into
Corly's stomach so hard it knocked the breath clean out of
her with an "Oomph!"

The attack ended with that strike as whatever Bloodsetter
had the night training duties quietly exited the room without
so much as a word. Corly sat on her haunches panting in
short breaths for a few minutes before pulling herself to her
feet. She didn't utter a word of complaint and limped about
righting the overturned pallet back to its original
configuration and putting everything else back in its proper
place with grim determination.

I will *meet their expectations! All of them. Then I can
finally get the truth out of Lord Regam.*

She had been told there was much more behind what
happened to Village Breathwynd than an accident and that
there were people responsible for the devastation of her
home. However, he would only tell her the details in full
once she had not only met, but exceeded the expectations he
had for her. She knew he had given her just enough snippets
of information to pull her along the way he wanted to in the
beginning, but when she heard that Oltan and Darien were
somehow involved she knew she had to find out the truth no
matter what.

Grumbling a bit, she continued to put things back in an
orderly fashion. The last thing she wanted was to get scolded
in the morning for her barracks being out of sorts. Doris

was difficult enough to deal with as it was.

Corly had hoped her time with the flighty woman would have come to an end after the day of their initial meeting, but it seemed the woman was permanently assigned to her. Corly caught herself mid-grumble and stopped her complaining. Doris wasn't a bad person, but her personality and constant babble about inane things drove Corly up the wall.

Elnora on the other hand, was the complete opposite. Corly was actually grateful to her despite how strict, rigid and uncompromising she was. She found her time with Elnora a welcome respite from Doris dragging her around and gave her a sense of familiarity since it was somewhat similar to lessons with Oltan, although Elnora lacked his warmth.

Thinking of the lessons looming ahead of her upcoming day Corly began to run through her numbers in her head. She had been somewhat surprised to find she excelled at learning more advanced number lessons than what she had been taught back at Village Breathwynd. After just a few lessons with some parchment and quill she could recall and recite what she had learned with high accuracy the majority of the time. It was the one and only thing she had been praised for.

Finally finished with righting the overturned pallet and cleaning up as best she could in the darkness Corly climbed her weary and sore body back into bed. Thankfully sleep came quickly for once.

"Wake up dearie! This is no time to be lazing the day away…"

Hurricane Doris had barged into Corly's barrack like usual, but after several days of being startled awake bleary eyed and exhausted by the infuriating woman Corly had gotten her body used to the grueling schedule her training was forcing her to adapt to.

As such she was already awake, alert, dressed and had her bedding and belongings in order by the time the Hurricane arrived, including a change of clothes laid out for her training later on.

The look of confusion on Doris' face was worth the extra effort it took to force herself to wake up earlier than usual. Having grown up in Village Breathwynd as one of Mistress Wavely's apprentices she was used to waking before the sun crested the horizon, but her trauma and exhaustion had initially gotten the better of her which led to Doris constantly barging in and chastising her for 'lazing about'. Now that she had settled in somewhat Corly was determined to fight back against Doris with as much innocence and kindness as possible. Corly put on her sweetest village girl smile and gave a fluid and practiced curtsy. It was a little over the top, especially as Doris was not someone anyone would typically curtsy for in terms of social etiquette, but Corly felt like being a little flippant this morning.

"Good morning, Doris. I'm quite ready! Are you alright? You do seem to be a little pale!"

Corly couldn't help herself. It was just a little payback for being constantly pulled by the hand and babbled at like she was some type of doll. Doris opened and closed her mouth without sound a few times, giving Corly the sensation the woman was doing her best impression of a fish.

Corly did her best to suppress a mischievous giggle and Doris blinked a few times before moving past her surprise as if it had never happened.

"Let's go dearie! The day is a'wasting!"

Resisting the urge to roll her eyes, Corly kept her fake smile firmly plastered on her face.

Doris held the door for her and as soon as they had cleared the threshold the woman was back in full Doris mode. Corly tuned most of her babble out and she studied her surroundings while Doris whisked her about all over the place.

Regam had instructed her to always be paying attention to the people around her as well as her surroundings. She was expected to memorize the layout of every building she entered and every pathway she was led down. It was a daunting task, especially since Doris seemed to be blissfully unaware of these instructions. The more time Corly spent with the woman the more she became convinced Regam had paired her with Doris on purpose just to make these tasks more difficult for her.

After their first few usual stops, which included a nice breakfast that was far more exquisite than the simple bacon and eggs that had been a staple of her diet back home, Corly was led to the common bathhouse. This was far less fanciful than the one she had first bathed in and had that mortifying encounter with Regam. This one was used by common workers, servants and other members of the lower classes. It wasn't every day she was expected to bathe, but Doris would seemingly choose on a whim which days she would bring her. Corly didn't see much point in bathing so early in the day, especially since she had Regam's training later where she would get sweaty and dirty all over again, but she had learned early on that arguing or questioning Doris on anything was pointless. Corly sometimes thought there really was nothing in the woman's head since every time she questioned some of the things they were doing the woman looked like her head was going to explode from having to think too hard. It was much easier to just go with the flow where Doris was concerned.

After an uneventful bath was another change of clothes and more seemingly pointless errands run with Doris until it was finally time for her daily lectures with Elnora. Despite how grueling on the mind the lectures could be Corly always welcomed the respite from her time with Doris. Additionally, she likened it to learning from a stricter female version of Oltan. She supposed she had been relying on that analogy a little too much lately, but it was one of the few sources of comfort she had these days.

"Sit down and we shall begin," Elnora barked as soon as Corly entered the small room where she took her lessons.

"Yes Ma'am!" Corly said with more enthusiasm than she felt as she took her seat, the lone chair in the room. She picked up the parchment from her desk and kept her head up, back straight and eyes forward as she had been instructed.

The lesson went as it usually did and Corly was somewhat disappointed that nothing new had been presented. Apparently, Elnora felt like refreshing Corly on certain topics and she was the type of teacher who wouldn't move past a point or subject until she was certain her student could both understand and fully retain the knowledge being imparted.

After her lesson with Elnora, and another change of clothing into her training outfit, Doris reappeared and Corly was quickly led to the training grounds where her escort promptly abandoned her to the mercy of Regam for her daily training.

A few hours and more than a few bumps and bruises later, Corly lay tired and worn out on her pallet. It had been another hectic and intense day, but she had begun to take pride in a sense of fulfillment now that she had gotten somewhat used to the bustling flow of her life here.

She had even developed a routine for herself that she religiously stuck to each night before she allowed herself to crawl into bed. She would first practice whatever movements and techniques she had learned that day in training while visualizing where she had made mistakes. This helped her understand how to avoid those same mistakes in the future. After quickly using the ewer to fill up the wooden washbasin and washing up with a wet cloth lathered in coarse soap she changed into her nightclothes and would then mentally review the different places she had seen and routes of travel she had taken during the day with Doris before reviewing what she had learned during her lesson with Elnora. Only then would she allow herself the reward of falling asleep. Of course, many of her nights were interrupted by an attack of one Bloodsetter or another, but that had practically become a mundane task by this point.

Corly had also been making some inroads on getting to know many of the Bloodsetters under Regam's command, especially those that were often involved in the training sessions when Lord Regam himself was unavailable. She had even learned that a few of them were married and had families! Aditsan was actually one of them!

Thinking of Aditsan made her frown slightly as she rolled over onto her side.

Now that I think about it, I haven't seen Aditsan for a couple of days now.

Normally he would have been the main substitute for Lord Regam once or twice a week for her combat training, but he had been conspicuously absent this past week. When she had asked about it, Lord Regam had glared at her and barked at her about paying attention and focusing on the task at hand. The one day that week she did have a substitute the man wouldn't give his name or even speak to her and every time she tried to engage him in conversation or ask about Aditsan he would only respond by increasing the speed and ferocity of his strikes.

It wasn't until a little while later that she would learn the ugly and heartbreaking truth about Aditsan's fate.

Chapter 8

A few days before her latest night attack Corly had been heading for her usual training when she was greeted by a familiar sight. A grin spread wide across her face when she saw who was waiting for her in the training yard. Aditsan was casually tapping his sword against his shoulder and gave a small wave as their eyes met. Aditsan was usually the one to stand in for Lord Regam when the latter was indisposed for one reason or another and Corly always enjoyed her time with him.

Aditsan was the first Bloodsetter besides Lord Regam who had freely given her his name and had formed anything resembling a friendly relationship with her. She was always appreciative of his soft tone and easy-going manner, which was in direct contrast to how every other Bloodsetter behaved.

He never shirked his duties and never took it easy on her despite their friendship, but Corly felt a level of comfort with him that wasn't present with the others. After getting him to open up somewhat she had been surprised to find that he had served as her escort far more than the others and that he had been responsible for much of her care while they were on the road. She had been embarrassed for not noticing, but Aditsan had waved off her apology and only asked her to continue training her utmost to serve Lord Regam and the crown.

"Hi Aditsan!" Corly beamed with a genuine smile. Having already forgotten about Doris, who had skedaddled as soon as she had laid eyes on the Bloodsetter, Corly excitedly hurried over to where Aditsan waited.

"Lord Regam is unable to attend today so I will be instructing you. I expect improvement so show me how much you have grown since last we sparred."

"Yes sir!"

Corly could barely contain her excitement. She was sure Aditsan would be impressed with how much she had grown since the last time he had subbed in for Lord Regam, but no sooner had the words left her mouth then Aditsan swung his sheathed weapon full force into her side. She barely had enough time to twist her body so the strike would miss her ribs. Thankfully the blow instead impacted the soft area between the ribs and hip as she flexed her stomach muscles to absorb some of the impact.

Instead of complaining like she would have done when she first arrived at the castle she quickly drew her blade and attempted to counter attack while gritting her teeth and bearing the pain. Corly was just glad Aditsan had kept his sword within the scabbard otherwise she would have been sliced in twain.

She had been granted permission to graduate from her wooden training device to a real sword specifically forged to compliment her diminutive frame and was determined to prove to her instructor she was worthy of such a gift.

Swinging at Aditsan's knees, he easily avoided her strike, but she had done so just to create space and gain precious seconds to catch some of the breath she had lost from his blow. Aditsan still hadn't drawn his blade and probably wouldn't for the duration of their training. Lord Regam was the same way; they knew she still wasn't proficient enough to cause either of them serious harm with a naked blade so they kept their own sheathed. They both were hardened veterans of the blade so they had utmost confidence in their own ability to keep Corly from causing them any real harm. Conversely, Corly was allowed to attack with the intent to kill and she was determined to make either one of them draw their sword whenever she crossed blades with them. Her efforts *would* be recognized by the people she owed her life to!

When Regam had first given her the sword she had been hesitant to train as seriously as she had been when using a wooden sword. She had been worried about accidentally hurting someone and wasn't confident in her ability to stop short before making contact.

Corly had been chastised thoroughly by Regam for thinking in this way and she endured a rather harsh lesson in brutality as Lord Regam had beaten into her the fact her blade could never reach him, not even to cause a scratch. The day had ended with her sitting on her haunches and panting heavily covered in dirt, blood and sweat as Regam glared down at her exhausted form.

"You must attack to kill in training or you will die when you are confronted by your enemies. Right now your skills are woefully incompetent compared to even the least disciplined of my men. You will never show me such a shameful display ever again. Is that understood?"

Corly had taken that painful lesson to heart and ever since had trained like her life was always at stake. This had pleased Lord Regam and he had told her something that felt cold to her, but made sense in a way.

"Should the blade of a novice such as yourself reach Aditsan or any other Bloodsetter in charge of your training then he will have deserved any injury or death that results."

She wasn't really a fan of that way of thinking, but she understood the severity of what he was trying to teach her so she was determined to put her best effort forward each and every time she swung her blade.

Aditsan nodded in appreciation as she warily eyed him, looking for any opportunity to strike or to see if she could tell where his next attack would come from. She had been learning to glean information from her opponents' stance, style, facial expression and even manner of dress, but she was still a novice when it came to applying those tactics in real time.

"Let's make today simple. Attack me with the intent to kill as always. I will at first only defend and then we will work our way up to simple exchanges and counters. Now begin!"

Corly immediately launched into an attack as if her life depended on it. It had been reiterated to her multiple times honing such skills as these would inevitably save her life while under the care of the Bloodsetters due to the nature of their occupation so she didn't want to disrespect anyone who took the time to train her by hesitating.

Regam had once told her when she took up her weapon, whether it be blade, fist or dress, that she should always be definitive and committed. 'Make a decision and make it quickly, then follow through on it to its completion', he had said.

"Good," Aditsan complimented her as she executed a series of high and low strikes that Aditsan himself had taught her. He didn't have any difficulty avoiding or blocking and she was panting with exertion before she knew it. She could feel her training garb clinging to her skin with perspiration and the sweat on her palms was causing her to lose a proper grip, but she pressed on.

Aditsan kept his word and slowly began to incorporate counter strikes which almost always found their mark. Corly was sure she would be covered in purple and black marks from bruising later on, but still found herself smiling whenever Aditsan praised her or explained how to properly execute certain techniques he showed her. It was a very intense session, but Corly found herself enjoying it immensely.

Afterwards, Aditsan handed her a clean rag to wipe off the sweat and grime from her face while he did the same.

"You have improved."

It wasn't much of a compliment, but Corly felt elation well up inside of her. Getting even such a small bit of praise from one of the Bloodsetters felt like a complete victory to her. She beamed at the praise and gave a simple "Thank you!"

Aditsan nodded and said something unexpected. "Join me for a meal."

A silly grin spread across her face and Corly almost jumped for joy. Aditsan was the only one amongst the Bloodsetters who took the initiative in getting to know her and this was now the second time he had asked her to accompany him after training. She hoped to learn more about him and the Bloodsetters as a whole; maybe she'd even learn a little bit more about Lord Regam!

She happily followed in Aditsan's wake as he made his way out of the training yard and towards the regular Bloodsetter barracks located nearby.

Corly's stomach rumbled as soon as the savory aromas wafting out from the mess hall adjacent to the barracks tickled her nose and her mouth began to water in anticipation.

As usual she didn't realize just how hungry she was until after training had ended, but now her stomach was rumbling every few moments. The fare served to the Bloodsetters at mealtimes was rather simple compared to some of the feasts Corly had found herself a part of from time to time for reasons still unbeknownst to her, but it was filling and wholesome. Plus, she got a nostalgic feeling whenever she got to experience a gathering of everyone together in one place sharing a meal like the people of Village Breathwynd had done many times in the past. It reminded her of village gatherings on the commons and how much fun those events always were.

Shaking her head to clear it of the sad memories of her former home less she ruin her mood, she decided to enjoy the moment and appreciate the hospitality Aditsan was graciously showing her.

Upon entering the mess hall the few Bloodsetters already taking their meals barely paid her any attention, but she had come to learn through her conversations with Aditsan that this was a good thing. It meant she was slowly earning their acceptance and was getting closer to even gaining a modicum of respect from the rough and grizzled warriors. Should they start speaking out about her presence then it meant there were problems with her performance she would be hard pressed to address.

Grabbing a wooden bowl, she received a heaping portion of thick stew from the serving lady that gave off the same tantalizing aroma she had smelled outside and began eating as soon as she sat down. Although Corly was at first annoyed the Bloodsetters weren't too big on table manners she had begun eating in earnest based on something Regam had told her about never knowing when or where your next meal was coming from or when the one you're eating might be interrupted so eat fast and eat to your fill. She idly wondered what Darien might think if he had seen her eating in such a way, but she pushed that bleak thought aside as Aditsan sat down across from her.

They were seated at one of several long wooden tables with a bench on either side taking up most of the room in the mess hall. They were pretty well separated from the others and none of those who entered afterwards made to sit anywhere near them, but that didn't much bother Corly; she'd get them all on her side sooner or later for sure! She nodded to herself at the thought while they ate together in silence only broken by the clacking and banging of utensils and muted murmurs of conversation from the others.

When they had both eaten their fill Corly asked what Regam had been doing in hopes to learn a little bit about the enigmatic leader.

"The king's will. Was I not sufficient as an instructor? Perhaps we should adjourn back to the yard and continue for a while yet?"

"Ah, no! I was just curious! Aditsan, thank you for teaching me today. I'm sure you would rather be spending your free time with your wife than with me."

Corly began enacting the plan she had been working on with Aditsan in hopes of changing the subject. Ever since he had opened up to her a little she had been progressing their relationship further and further along until they had reached a point where she felt confident she could call him a friend. She felt like by now she could ask things that were a bit more personal in nature without causing him any offense so she plunged ahead with questions about him she had stored up for this particular moment.

Putting on her most innocent expression she began to pepper the unsuspecting Aditsan with questions.

"Are you really married? What about children or siblings? I was an only child so I dunno what it's like to have a brother or sister. There was one person who was a little bit older than me who was basically family, but that was it."

Aditsan looked baffled by the sudden splurge of questioning and gave her a stern look until her questions petered out and she thought she might have pushed her luck too far. Even some of the nearby Bloodsetters had gone quiet as she had been a bit louder than intended so she felt maybe she had touched upon something taboo among them, but Aditsan assuaged her fears.

Holding up both his hands palms out in surrender he gave a surprising answer.

"Easy girl," he said in his soft voice. "You are full of vigor today. Very well. As a reward for how dedicated you have been, I will answer some, but not all of your questions."

Yes! Corly tried very hard to keep a look of self-satisfaction off her face, but she paid rapt attention to Aditsan's answers.

"It is rare for one of us to form a relationship with

anything or anyone but our mission, but there are those among us where marriage and family are present in our lives. As you are aware, I am one of those who does indeed have a spouse."

Despite her joy at getting him to open up Corly's mouth almost hung agape at how easily he was acquiescing to her questioning. She instinctively looked over her shoulder since if Elnora caught wind of her sitting slack jawed at dinner with a man while swinging her legs in excitement under the table she would get scolded and switched across the knuckles for sure.

Despite her concerns about her educational instructor Corly sensed she had a rare opportunity so she tried to keep Aditsan talking about his spouse.

"Really? What's she like? How did you meet? How rare is it for a Bloodsetter to actually get married? It must be tough for both of you!"

Aditsan gave a small, gentle smile at all the questions about his wife.

"Slow down girl. Believe it or not I was married before I joined the ranks of the Bloodsetters so I was betrothed quite young. As far as I know I am the only one in such a unique situation, but there have been a few others among us blessed with matrimony while in service to our people."

"Why is it so rare?"

Aditsan's pleasant smile turned to a frown. "The life expectancy of those such as us is not generally considered to be very long due to the nature of our profession. Most of us

choose not to burden others with the worry, stress and loss
that marriage to a Bloodsetter often brings them.
Additionally, Lord Regam's approval is required and he is
less than willing at the best of times to put one of our people
in that position."

"Then how did you join if you were already married
to...?"

"Ajodit is her name. One of the gentlest and most
beautiful souls you will ever come across in this often harsh
and unforgiving world we occupy by the Mother's grace."

Corly was ecstatic Aditsan was opening up so much to
her. It gave her hope that she could eventually crack the
hard exterior of the other Bloodsetters one day as well.

"As for why and how I became one of Lord Regam's men
I am afraid that is more personal, but suffice it to say that I
lost someone very close to me and that I felt the need to do
whatever I could to avenge that loss. I do not regret that
decision or the sacrifices that have come with it even though
my beloved is never afraid of giving me an earful about it
from time to time."

Corly was hoping he would say more about his wife or
how he became a Bloodsetter, but it seemed he had
concluded with what he was willing to share as he fell silent.

Aditsan had a contemplative look on his face as he stared
into the cup of ale he held clasped in both hands. Corly was
struck by a note of discord as she internally compared how a
man who was so kind and gentle, a man who obviously loved
his wife with all his being, could possibly belong to a group

so taciturn, bloody and violent as the Bloodsetters.

She understood it was the nature of their job even if the reasons for that had not yet been made entirely clear to her, but it seemed strange to her all the same.

Staying her swinging legs Corly dropped her overly curious act.

"Is what you and the others doing really worth so much danger and constantly skirting the line between life and death? It seems very frightening to me."

Corly meant what she said. From what she had been allowed to learn the Bloodsetters were the first and usually the only among Lord Regam's people who were involved in any type of violence and bloodshed. Then there was that incident with the naked woman back at the Grove that claimed the lives of multiple people. The memory of that incident alone was enough to make her shudder and it had taken her some time to cease having nightmares.

Aditsan glanced up from his cup and held Corly's gaze with as serious a look as she had ever seen on him.

"Yes. Even I will do whatever it takes to achieve our goals for we are in the right. And before you ask, if Lord Regam has not deemed fit to fill you in on the more intimate details of our operations I will say no more. No matter how much you pout."

Corly felt like she might have been able to get an inkling as to what the Bloodsetter's true purpose was despite the somber turn the conversation had taken and bit her thumb in frustration at being preemptively stonewalled.

Aditsan smiled at her obvious displeasure and tried to placate her a little.

"I am sure Lord Regam will explain to you what you need to know when it is the proper time, but it is not now. Especially since my next mission would prove to be far more difficult for you even if your abilities were recognized as on par with the rest of us. In the meantime, continue to be patient, diligent and studious. There is much potential in you and your particular situation will one day bear fruit on many levels I am sure."

Corly looked down at her own small hands as she continued to bite down on her thumb and wondered if that was really true. She had been trying her best to perform to the expectations placed upon her while still processing her grief over losing her entire family and home, but she was just one small village girl from the remote mountains. What could someone like her do to actually help those she owed her life to?

Aditsan must have sensed her discomfort.

"Do not worry yourself so much. You are progressing well and we all acknowledge your dedication to the tasks you have been assigned. It is a testament to your character that few others possess."

Corly perked up a bit at Aditsan's words. "Do you really think so?"

Aditsan smiled. "Yes. I hope someday soon to introduce you to Ajodit as an important comrade who has overcome many trials. Hopefully after this mission I will be able to do so."

Corly felt both embarrassment and pride at the praise and encouragement he was giving her. It was one thing to perform well enough to avoid a scolding or switching, but to have her efforts validated by one of the people she valued and respected the most in her new life made her heart swell with pride.

"I will become that person. I swear!"

Aditsan nodded at her determination, but something he had said finally registered with her. "Did you say you had to go on a mission? Can you tell me what it is? And can I go with you? I want to help in any way that I can!"

Aditsan shook his head. "No. I cannot speak to more than that and as I said you are by no means qualified to accompany me or any other at the moment."

"But-"

"For one you will get yourself or someone else killed with your current abilities. It is a risk that cannot be taken. Not to mention leaking details of a mission warrants swift and immediate execution by Lord Regam's hand. As I already said there are other factors that will make it even tougher for you to commit to our mission's goal as well, but I will not speak more to that less I incur Lord Regam's wrath. Continue to do what you have been and in time I am sure Lord Regam will begin to recognize your strength. Be patient until that time."

Corly felt like Aditsan had thrown cold water on her with such a cold and brutal response, but she knew he was right.

She hung her head and mumbled an apology for overstepping. The Bloodsetter reached across the table and gave her a tap on the head.

"Do not hang your head. I appreciate your fervor, but now is not the time. Let us forget your worries and speak of other things more pleasant."

Corly nodded and despite the somber tone of their exchange found a small grin forming at *finally* getting some serious praise for her efforts. She promised herself again that she would undoubtedly surpass the expectations placed upon her and would become the type of companion Lord Regam, Aditsan and the others could take pride in.

A few days later Corly was surprised to find Lord Regam dressed in his normal dark black attire when she arrived for her daily activities with the leader of the Bloodsetters. Before she could even ask why he wasn't in his training gear he uttered a curt "Let us speak for a few moments."

She knew better than to ask further questions or argue when Lord Regam spoke in that tone so she remained silent while waiting for him to speak. A hollow pit formed in her stomach at his demeanor since it reminded her of the way her parents had acted when she was younger and her favorite lamb had to have been put down early due to developing a disease. Her heart dropped into her stomach as his next words confirmed her fears.

"Aditsan has been killed."

Corly didn't realize she was sitting in the dirt until

Regam helped her back up and allowed her to lean on him while she tried to steady wobbly legs.

Tears began to fall as she recalled the soft-spoken voice of the first Bloodsetter she had formed a bond with. Thinking of his wife waiting at home for a husband who would never return threatened to tear her heart in half. She tried to speak, but her mouth wouldn't form words as her brain tried to process all the complex emotions she was feeling. Her chin waggled and she stuttered and began to sob as all the memories of the fire at Breathwynd she had tried so hard to suppress piled on top of those of her time with Aditsan. She held her head in her hands while she cried and as the tears disappeared into the dirt at her feet the only coherent thought that came to mind was *why?*

Despite being one of the rough and battle-ready Bloodsetters under Regam's command Aditsan had had a gentle side that Corly found endearing, not to mention he was the only one besides Regam to give her any type of constructive advice in terms of her training; the others usually just beat the Hells out of her and left.

He would also become somewhat of a gabber whenever the topic of his wife Ajodit came up. It was a rarity to ever see a Bloodsetter show even the smallest signs of a smile, but the one he held while speaking about his wife always made Corly's heart melt at how much he loved the person he had committed his life to.

Regam said nothing more and simply stood there watching her cry. When she glanced up and saw his expressionless face through her blurry vision an intense fury momentarily overwhelmed her grief.

"Why are you so calm!? Don't you care that he was killed? What about the others that went with him? Do none of them matter to you at all? If they are your subordinates, your people, shouldn't you feel *something*? How can you just stand there like nothing happened!?"

Grabbing ahold of Regam's tunic in a tight grip Corly's voice rose until she was shouting. Deep inside she knew yelling at Regam was both wrong and probably dangerous, but she didn't care. The only person she considered an actual friend here at the castle had been taken from her just like all the others back home. It wasn't fair!

She continued to rant and bawl until her eyes ran dry and her throat grew too sore to speak and even then she hiccupped and sniffed for a time while mumbling incoherently until Regam did something surprising.

The head of the Bloodestters silently loomed over her and when he raised his hand she thought for sure he was going to strike her. She winced, but instead of the blow she expected she felt a gentle hand placed upon her head in reassurance.

"I grieve for every one of our people, including Aditsan. Just as I grieve for those lost at the Grove as I have mentioned before. I told you this news not to torment you or for lack of care, but quite the opposite. He spoke quite highly of you despite your being an outsider; a rarity for any of those under my command. You deserved to know his fate."

Blinking away the few stubborn tears still clinging to her lashes Corly sniffled again. Regam offered her his hand and she somewhat reluctantly let go of his tunic and took it as he easily hefted her small frame upright. A bout of lightheadedness struck and it took a few moments for her to get unsteady legs back under control, but she forced herself to get both her body and emotions in check.

Taking several deep breaths Corly regained control of herself. Regam released his grip once he was sure she could stand unassisted.

"Walk with me, I have more to tell you. It also will not be pleasant."

Corly wiped her eyes and nose on her sleeve, incredibly unladylike she knew, but she didn't much care at the moment.

Regam began to briskly walk off and Corly had to hurry her little feet to keep pace with him. Regam stared straight forward and remained silent for a time as they walked seemingly without a destination in mind. The normal bustle and activity of the castle grounds was more muted and gray to Corly and she barely felt the dirt beneath her feet. She would often gawk at how incredible and meticulously detailed the buildings were whenever she passed this way, but now she paid them no heed as her grief threatened to consume her.

Eventually Regam spoke and what he said stunned Corly to her very core.

"What do you know about a boy from Village

Breathwynd named Darien?"

Corly's world stopped. Her head emptied of all thought and she felt she might fall over again. Her jaw worked, but she again couldn't get any words out as she tried to understand why Regam was asking such a thing and how he would know who Darien even was?

Stopping in his tracks Regam looked at her sternly.

"I have asked you a question girl, now answer me!"

Regam's sudden shift back to his usual tone and demeanor shook Corly out of her daze and she took a deep breath to organize her thoughts.

"Darien was someone from Village Breathwynd who was a little older than me. I've known him my whole life."

"And?"

Corly pushed on despite the pain memories of Breathwynd caused until her words erupted in an emotional torrent.

"By now if nothing had changed we would have soon began courting. I made it clear to him just before the fire happened. He was the person I loved more than anyone."

Her face flushed a deep crimson at saying how she had felt about Darien out loud. Her heart felt heavy with speaking about the person she had always thought she would end up betrothed to. Hanging her head, memories of Darien threatened to cause another wave of grief and tears to overtake her.

"Corly, look at me as this is one of the most important things I must tell you. Earlier I told you I would explain more to you in detail once you had not only met, but exceeded the expectations I had for you. I feel now is an appropriate time to tell you more."

Corly felt like her heart weighed ten times more than normal, but mustered the courage to look Lord Regam in the eyes.

"Darien is alive. He is the one who killed Aditsan."

"What!" Corly's brain almost shut down again. Elation at hearing the first part of what Regam said conflicted with the impact of the second half.

"What?" she said again while her mind refused to work properly.

"Darien is the one who killed Aditsan. Not only that, but he is heavily related to the razing of your village and the deaths of the people you loved."

"You're lying! There is no way that could possibly be true! Darien would never hurt anybody! He's stubborn and oblivious and kind and clumsy and handsome and adorable, but he isn't capable of killing someone! You told me I was the only one who survived! There isn't any way he is still alive! Why would you say that? Stop it!"

Balling her small hands into fists and staring defiantly up at Regam, Corly's face twisted as her grief and frustration were driven by anger. She didn't know whether she should cry, laugh or scream. Darien was all the things she had said he was, but he was ultimately a gentle and kind soul who cared deeply for the people around him and hated doing chores, loved sweet rolls, had the best smile and never missed an opportunity to grumble about Oltan making him study too much. He wasn't someone capable of killing another person. He just *wasn't*.

Regam looked at her in silence with that chilling gaze of his and let her rant and rave anew without interruption. Eventually she started repeating herself until Regam gave her a light shake.

"Your confusion, grief and anger are warranted. I assure you what I have told you of is the absolute truth. I have had those most trusted under my command verify this information so I held off for a few days from informing you, but we have confirmed that Darien is the same from Village Breathwynd, but it seems you are unaware of what he truly is."

Corly's throat was so raw from shouting and sobbing that she couldn't speak and she blinked through swollen eyelids as Regam continued to patiently explain how the person she loved had murdered the first friend she had made within the Bloodsetters.

Her mind simply couldn't grasp the enormity of what Lord Regam was saying. *This just isn't possible. It doesn't make any sense!*

Darien had never been anything but the clumsy boy he had always been. She would know better than anyone since she had been watching him for years, even when she was still small. They had spent almost all of their free time together over the years and she could never have imagined a life where they didn't eventually court, wed and start a family before growing old together. She had always assumed that was what their relationship would become and now she was supposed to believe that not only was he alive, but capable of murder?

Her stomach felt hollow and the world around her was distant and dreamlike as she hung her head and processed this horrific new information. Instinctively she reached back and grabbed a hold of her braids, bringing them in front of her and staring mutely at the lavender ribbon tying them together.

Darien had been so awkward and embarrassed when he gave it to her and it had always been one of her favorite memories. The way he had blushed a deep crimson all the way to his ears and couldn't look her in the eyes or speak properly had always made her smile. She had worn that same ribbon every day since, no matter how worn it had become.

So many similar memories came to her unbidden that she almost started sobbing again, but she took several deep, calming breaths to stabilize her emotions. Slowly inhaling and exhaling with practiced breaths she tried to slow down the pounding of her heart.

She couldn't get the myriad images of Darien from over the years out of her head. What confused her the most was that there was not one single memory she had indicating Darien had that sort of temperament, aside from his normal obstinacy about chore-work and studying. They would of course have the occasional argument as two people who are so close often do, but there was nothing extreme or outside the norm of their relationship over the years. So *why*? Why was this happening? What could have caused this drastic change in his personality?

Regam made it sound like there was a hidden side to Darien she didn't know about, but that was impossible. There wasn't anyone save Oltan who knew more about him than she did, but she recalled something Aditsan had mentioned the other day. When she had been pestering him about the next mission he had been selected to participate in he had been reluctant to speak much about it and mentioned something about a difficulty relating to her specifically.

She had been concerned for his safety overall of course, but there had been something off about the way he had phrased that particular part of the conversation and his concern for how she would react once he returned. Now she understood. Aditsan had somehow known her childhood friend as well as probable lover was alive and part of the mission. Now he was dead at Darien's hands if Lord Regam was to be believed, but what purpose would he have to lie?

Regam must have sensed that she came to some sort of a realization and pushed her a little further.

"Take the time you need to think things through carefully and without emotion until you have reached the most logical conclusion. I will answer any questions then."

She didn't know how he knew what she was thinking, but now that her brain had latched onto something to work with, her mind wouldn't stop spinning.

What if Darien really had survived? Was it possible someone else had rescued him or maybe even had been holding him hostage? No, him as a hostage wouldn't make any sense. He would have been trying to get rescued if that was the case, not fighting back against Aditsan and the others to the point of killing. Even if he was being forced, Darien is the type of person who most likely would have thrown down his weapon and asked the other side for help.

More thoughts and possibilities came and went and she dismissed them all as unlikely. In the end she felt the most likely scenario to be that Darien had somehow survived, but was being used by people who had found him or was being tricked into fighting against people he really shouldn't be. Based on the little Aditsan had told her the ones he was being sent after seemed like some dangerous and terrible people.

She couldn't think of any other possibility no matter how much she thought about it and her head was starting to hurt so she relayed her final consensus to Lord Regam. He gave her a small frown as she explained her reasoning.

"Not quite. You still have too much of a tendency to assume the best of people. More so if they are a known entity to you. You are somewhat correct in that he has become a part of those whom we have as enemies, but know this for certain; he has joined their cause knowingly and willingly."

Still staring at her ribbon Corly scrunched up her face and began instinctively biting the nail on her thumb.

Lord Regam continued. "I suppose I should also tell you the one you know from your childhood is far more than what he has always seemed. He is no normal human being like you or I and we highly suspect the one responsible for his upbringing was not only aware of this, but purposefully hid this fact from those around them while cultivating the boy's growth."

Corly was even more confused. "What do you mean? Darien and Oltan were both pretty normal for as long as I've known them," she said while trying to think about anything about the two of them that might have seemed abnormal.

Lord Regam stared daggers at her for a moment as if she were incredibly dense.

"Do normal mountain villagers own an extensive amount of knowledge that dwarfs the common village collective? If your information is indeed accurate it would be a match for any noble library even here in the capital! The old man is much more than you could ever possibly understand, but it is the boy who is the most relevant to this issue and by far the most dangerous."

Corly bit back another protest at calling someone as awkward and kind as Darien as dangerous. There was no less dangerous a person in the whole world. Her mind still refused to comprehend what Lord Regam was saying, but nearly all her energy had run out and had left her feeling tired and worn.

Feeling defeated and more than overwhelmed, Corly finally gave in.

"Can you please explain to me what is really happening and what makes Darien so dangerous?

Chapter 9

Corly sat on the edge of her pallet and brooded in total darkness. She had a lot to dissect after what Regam had told her. He had only spoken a bit more about Darien and Oltan, but informed her he would go into further detail once she had recovered some.

Everything she had been told was so shocking, terrifying and overwhelming. It felt like her entire world had been pulled out from under her just when things were beginning to stabilize a bit. She scrunched her nose in frustration and shivered at the implications of the information she had received. Trying to make sense of the day she flopped down backwards and replayed events in her head.

She knew Lord Regam had informed her of something important and was thankful he had done so, but she still didn't understand what could have caused Darien to do something so reckless. Grumbling incoherently about the information she had been exposed to, she threw her arms out wide and screamed at the ceiling, letting out some of the confusion, anger and grief residing within.

She began crying in earnest, but at least this time she was

able to control herself a bit unlike earlier when she had dissolved into a sobbing pile of goo.

What upset her the most, besides the news of Aditsan's death, was that she wasn't even allowed to feel joy at the news Darien was alive since he apparently was the one who killed the first real friend she had made since her rescue.

She had told Regam she would keep up with all of her studies and training, but how was she supposed to focus on that promise knowing Darien was somewhere out there fighting against the very people he should be taking refuge with?

Once her mind clamped onto something she didn't like letting it go so despite the tears and mucus running down her face she tried to think about what might have happened with Darien that night in the village. It also gave her a sense of focus and allowed her to lessen the feelings of grief and confusion she had been trying to navigate.

The last thing she remembered before beginning to clean the ovens at the bakery was Oltan and Mistress Wavely getting into an argument about the strange and aloof visitor who had recently appeared in the village. Shortly after Oltan had left there had been some kind of commotion outside on the village commons. That was when Mistress Wavely had suddenly locked her in the oven she had been cleaning and in a stern, but strained voice told her to keep quiet and stay hidden.

Corly hadn't realized at the time that it would be the last time she would ever see the boisterous baker alive or hear her voice and she sniffled as she wiped her nose on her sleeve. If Elnora had seen her do that there would have been no end to her lecturing, but Corly didn't much care about the etiquette of a proper lady at the moment.

It wasn't long after the oven's door had closed before she lost consciousness so she didn't have much to work with, but she tried to calm herself by working through what Darien's nightly routine would have been. This wasn't difficult for her since she had constantly been by his side their entire lives up until that point.

He most likely had something to eat before complaining about his evening chores for longer than it actually took to complete them. Oltan probably had to force him to wash up before sending him down to the library. Darien would have grumbled about it, but would have been secretly excited to spend some solitary time reading and 'accidently' nodding off.

Knowing him, he would have sat at one of the desks in a huff in order to keep up with appearances even though no one was watching him; he was always doing things like that so he was probably still down there when everything happened.

If what Regam had told her was true about the people who assaulted her village she doubted there was a possibility they would have overlooked something as obviously suspicious as the large outcropping serving as the entrance to the library; especially if the torches had been lit. She supposed that was hit or miss depending on if Darien forgot or not, but she decided that was unimportant although she got annoyed at him for forgetting all the same.

Try as she might she couldn't think of anything obvious, but thanks to always sitting in on Darien's lessons whenever she could over the years she could visualize how Oltan would have taught her how to approach this particular quandary.

She concentrated on the kind, elderly man who had raised Darien and some memories of Oltan resurfaced as she lay there. It had been one of those lessons where Darien had been repeatedly giving an incorrect answer to whatever problem Oltan had presented. She couldn't remember exactly what the problem had been, but she did recall that it hadn't been a word or number problem like the ones Oltan often favored. She couldn't even remember what the answer had been, but what had stuck out to her at the time was what Oltan had explained in a rare display of frustration in his pupil.

"Both of you should understand that when all the obvious solutions to a problem have been exhausted you must then consider other possibilities, then feasible probabilities. Even then you may not come to the correct conclusion. That is when you must consider the unlikely and sometimes in rare cases the impossible, for if nothing else gives you the answer you seek what is left must be correct no matter how impossible or outlandish it may seem."

Darien had been befuddled and it had taken him considerable time to grasp the meaning behind his caretaker's words, but at the time Corly had remained quiet while she contemplated and wondered what they could mean. She at first thought he was saying the impossible could actually happen, but that seemed unlikely considering how intelligent Oltan was. Eventually she came to the conclusion the entire point of the lesson had been to emphasize the importance of looking at problems from an unlikely perspective in the hopes of gleaning an answer where traditional thinking was rendered moot. Oltan had been a proponent of employing as many different methods of thought as possible where these types of problems were concerned while Darien had been like a raging farm animal blindly bashing forward in the hopes of achieving success. It had always driven her crazy, but at least when it came to reading and self-study he had been relatively focused, at least as long as the subject matter held his interest.

Closing her eyes and hiccupping a bit, Corly stilled the chaos in her mind and heart.

What could have caused the attackers to miss the library?

It was the only thing that made sense to her. The attackers had to have either missed the library for some reason or ignored it completely. Despite how far removed from the rest of the village it was, the outcropping marking its entrance was rather pronounced and it should have been obvious to anyone seeing it, even for the first time, that there was *something* worth investigating there.

If the people who destroyed her home were as ruthless and thorough as Regam implied then surely they would have checked all the way out where Darien and Oltan had their cottage.

If so, then how could Darien have possibly survived? There was only one entrance and exit so he couldn't have escaped and it's not like he could fight through a group of bloodthirsty maniacs or that he was skilled enough to negotiate so that left him somehow evading their notice.

Assuming he had been down in the library would mean there must have been some reason for the attackers to have overlooked the library itself.

Corly scrunched up her nose and forced her brain to work overtime.

How would Darien hide from the people who attacked us? There're only three small rooms in the library besides the main chamber so it's not like there's anywhere for him to go is there?

She tried to recall if Oltan or Darien had ever mentioned any type of escape tunnel or hidden rooms, but came up empty. Even if Oltan had kept it a secret she and Darien had spent so much time there that she was sure at least one of them would have discovered it. Not to mention Darien would surely have told her about it if he had found one on his own.

Ruling out a hidden passage, especially since it would have been in Oltan's nature to have them seek it out under the guise of a lesson had it actually existed, she switched her line of thought.

Since there was nowhere to hide and nowhere to escape to, then what else is there? Was there a way to make people not notice the library entirely? Is that even possible?

How would Oltan go about hiding the library from people? He must have had only a little time to do it so it had to be something that could be done quickly and discreetly. The outcropping is pretty obvious even from a little distance away so anyone would approach it to investigate. Did he put a canvas or something over it? No, that can't be right.

Thinking so hard about this after enduring the extreme emotional swings from the last several hours was starting to make her head throb, but she forced herself to think things through. She *had* to know how Darien survived and why he was now going around killing people. She never would have guessed that Darien had it in him to harm another person, let alone murder someone. It just didn't make any sense. None of what Lord Regam had told her today had made much sense, but she was determined to find some kind of thread that could possibly tie everything together; at least where Darien was concerned. Not to mention what Lord Regam had said about Darien being more than she thought he was and somehow involved in the attack on their village.

Corly ran through what she knew again in the hopes of finding something she might have overlooked. There was no secret escape route and the library was impossible to miss despite being rather far away from the bustle of the village as Darien and Oltan's place was. Knowing Darien, he would have been oblivious to anything else going on outside assuming he hadn't sat down and promptly fallen asleep. A group of unknown people had attacked their village and pillaged, rampaged and burnt it to the ground, but somehow only she and Darien had survived.

In Corly's case, her survival was at worst an accident and at best a miracle. She paused in her thoughts as she considered the circumstances around her rescue.

If I made it out alive because I was locked in one of those large ovens then is it possible something similar happened at the library?

Her mode of thought shifted from Darien back to Oltan. It would have been very much in Oltan's nature to have a hidden trick or two in regards to the library. She could just imagine him eagerly awaiting for one of them to discover these tricks and heartily laughing at them with his usual warm rasp. Knowing him there had probably been plenty of hints they hadn't picked up on and had gone unnoticed over the years.

She continued to assess Darien, Oltan and even Oltan's pet pig Beatty that Darien always complained about. Oltan had loved that pig and always called her a 'true friend', but never really explained in detail what he meant by that. Oltan would occasionally speak about needing to remember things from the past as those lessons allowed him to live as a better person in the present day.

She had a sudden very fuzzy memory of a day back when she had still been little and Oltan had invited her to carve her initials into the wall of the library's entrance upon her first visit, something every child who visited for the first time was invited to do.

She remembered being very happy there was space near where Darien's initials had been and tried her absolute best to make her letters as neat as possible just as Oltan had shown her. It had been the first letters Oltan had taught her and it hadn't been much longer afterwards she had asked Oltan to teach her the same letters and numbers as he was teaching Darien.

Once she had completed her carving she vaguely recalled Oltan saying something about how it would always serve as a way to 'remember something special' in her life and that he was happy that 'everyone who comes here is an important part of our community and helps to keep us safe.'

Oltan had grown wistful at these words and had been staring off into the upper reaches of the outcropping hanging out over the top of the library. She hadn't been paying too close attention then, but maybe he was looking at something else. Maybe something that had to do with the words he spoke at the time?

What if he meant what he said literally?

Oltan had always been the type of person who enjoyed teaching her and Darien with unbridled enthusiasm, but he was also prone to teaching them abstract concepts in a variety of ways and Corly couldn't shake the feeling she was onto something important with this line of thought.

What would reminders, knowledge, tricks and Oltan's love of each of them have in common with a way to make sure the library could go unnoticed if necessary? I guess maybe if that oversized doorway wasn't there then maybe…

Corly sat up in sudden excitement and had to take a moment to catch herself as her vision briefly swam. She was sure she had just solved the riddle!

If the entrance was blocked up somehow and made to look like the rest of the outcropping it probably wouldn't look like anything other than a natural formation! That has *to be it!*

The more she thought about it the surer of it she became. Corly didn't spend time on solving the how or the why of it, she would save that for later, but she felt an immense amount of satisfaction knowing she had solved one of Oltan's biggest riddles. She fervently wished she could see the look of surprise and pride on Oltan's face and hear his words of praise, but she knew that was impossible.

Flopping back down onto her pallet Corly sighed and resolved to ask Lord Regam some more pointed questions about everything that had happened the first chance she got. Her revelation wasn't enough to quell the turmoil in her mind, but it gave her enough motivation to finally get some sleep. She softly whispered a prayer to any Godling who might be listening for Aditsan's soul to rest easy and fell into an exhausted slumber.

Corly tried to open her eyes, but they were so heavy her eyelids refused to obey. Oddly enough she didn't feel very alarmed by this discovery, especially since she could already see. Briefly considering if she had really even had eyes in the first place, she ultimately decided it didn't matter.

She looked at her surroundings, but quickly realized all

around her was pitch blackness. At first she felt at peace and calm despite the stillness, but soon a strong feeling of fear began to gnaw at her from within and quickly turned to terror. An indescribable cold welled up from within her and she wordlessly shouted and flailed about for help from anyone, anything in order to free her from the soul chilling fear creeping into her very essence. She was overcome with despair by the notion there was no help to be had and no-one could hear her soundless screams in this space filled with emptiness and fear.

Corly continued to scream, but no sound was forthcoming. She wanted to cry, but tears would not fall from formless eyes. Panic wracked her as her non-existent heart hammered in her chest so quickly she thought it might burst.

Her mind was unraveling and it became harder to breathe as she gasped for air to fill lungs that may or may not have ever existed. An absolute certainty that her death was imminent caused all of the frustrations of her life to well up and overflow into the core of her ethereal being. She wanted to scream, to sob, tear out her hair and beg whatever Gods or Godlings listening to spare her, lend her aid and relieve her from her suffering. She had too much left to do!

Her silent, desperate pleas went unanswered as a cold, terrifying wave of darkness crept into her formless body and threatened to overwhelm her; smothering her into oblivion. Before her mind completely shut down from her fear, the last thing she saw was a pair of discolored reptilian eyes rife with madness floating in the darkness and staring a petrifying hole into her very soul.

'Mai, sha. This ain't no place for you.'

Something unseen violently tugged at her and Corly screamed, bolting upright in her pallet. Her eyes rolled in her head as she was still shrouded in darkness and thought she had gone blind. Bedclothes slick with sweat clung tightly to her small frame and she heaved ragged breaths, trying to suck in as much air as she could. Feeling the rawness of her throat, she gasped for each breath and it took a moment for her to realize the wetness of the tears staining her face.

It took several moments for her heart and mind to calm down as her eyes slowly adjusted to the faint light of the moon filtering in from outside. Even after finally regaining a semblance of control over herself, Corly spent a great deal of time rocking back and forth with arms wrapped tightly around her knees and praying for morning to come. She found no sleep for the remainder of the night.

"Eyes staring at you and floating in the dark? Is that the excuse I am hearing for you nodding off during your lessons!? That is the most preposterous thing I have ever heard!" Elnora snapped at her, whipping down her pointer onto Corly's desk for emphasis.

The resounding crack would have normally made Corly jump, but today she simply hadn't the energy to do much more than move sluggishly from one place to another.

Her eyes were sunken dark circles and she felt like she had been carrying a large sack of grain upon her back the entire day. Corly's lack of focus and obvious exhaustion had quickly caused Elnora to cease the current lesson and chastise her thoroughly for not taking care of her body properly. Corly didn't have the energy to argue after tiredly explaining what she had experienced the night prior so she just sat there with a blank look and endured Elnora's admonishment.

Corly's eyes glazed over and Elnora's voice became no more than a monotone buzzing in the background of her mind. She wasn't sure how long she sat in that state as Elnora suddenly whacked her so hard across the knuckles blood seeped out from broken skin. Even then Corly only let out a small whimper as she was brought back to the reality she had been trying to escape from.

"Really now child! You will listen to me when I am speaking and will respond when prompted! I am not lecturing for charity's sake and am only doing so at Lord Regam's order. I am starting to think my time is being wasted so stop with the blather about floating eyes and how tired you are and whatnot!"

Corly tried to pull herself together as she knew she sounded insane, but she couldn't un-experience the terrifying ordeal and couldn't shake the pall it had cast over her. Thankfully she was saved from further scolding by the timely appearance of Lord Regam.

At first Corly thought through the fog in her mind she was going to have to try to endure her daily training in her befuddled state, which would have amounted to little more than a savage thrashing, but Regam surprised her and Elnora both.

"Her lesson ends here. I must speak with her at the king's behest."

Elnora opened her mouth to protest, but quickly snapped it shut at mention of the king and bowed deeply in acquiescence.

"Come with me."

Corly mutely nodded and slid clumsily out of her seat to fall in step behind Regam as best she could. She kept her eyes fixated on Regam's back in order to focus, but her limbs were so heavy it was like she was being weighed down by bags of sand. Corly was in such a funk she didn't even think to ask as to why he had ended her lesson prematurely or why the king had issued him this task. She was even more confused when he suddenly stopped and turned on her once they had reached the small room Corly often used for changing before and after lessons depending on her schedule for that day. He grabbed her by the shoulder and forcefully sat her down on one of the padded wooden benches along the wall and said something.

She blinked a few times in confusion as she heard him speak, but his voice sounded hollow and echoing from a distance. He barked the command at her again and muscle memory took over as her conditioning to respond kicked in and she did as she was bid.

"Close your eyes and relax your body as you focus solely on my voice. Know that no harm can come to you in this moment and carefully recount what you saw, felt and experienced last night. Do not leave out any detail, no matter how insignificant."

Corly quailed at the thought of recounting something so horrific, but Regam firmly held her shoulder and continued speaking in a soft, reassuring voice until she did as she was bid. Regam assured her again she was safe in his presence and she found herself somehow finding the voice to express the events of the previous night.

Her voice warbled and broke as she recounted the darkness and despair threatening to swallow her up.

"At first I thought it was just dark, but it was more like it was a place devoid of light. It was like I didn't exist, but existed at the same time. I dunno how else to explain it. I didn't have a physical body, but I sort of did anyway. At first, I didn't really feel anything, but then I saw those…those eyes. I've never felt more terrified of something in my entire life. Everything felt cold and empty and I was sure I was about to.."

"Die?" Regam prompted.

Corly shook her head. "No, more like…consumed."

"I see. Continue."

Despite having to collect herself several times, she eventually made it to the end where those haunting eyes glared menacingly at her from within the darkness.

Regam remained silent throughout most of her retelling and graciously allowed her to take the time she needed to tell all she had experienced in full. Regam never once expressed doubt, nor did he scold her as Elnora had done. He simply listened, uttered reassurances when needed and took her words at value. When she had finished he instructed her to return to her pallet and sleep for a time and that he would remain by her bedside as she did so and that there would be nothing for her to fear.

Corly wasn't sure how returning to the place where she had had that horrific ordeal could possibly be beneficial, but the retelling of her terror had taken all of her body's remaining stamina and she found her eyelids slowly closing shut.

A short time later she found herself waking from a thankfully dreamless slumber and Lord Regam still sitting on the edge of her pallet as promised. Her village sensibilities warred with her relief at his presence while she slept, but she figured that in this case it was for her own safety so it was okay. She also chose to ignore the fact he had to have carried her sleeping form all the way back to her barracks.

"Did you experience anything out of the ordinary?"

Corly stretched and took a moment to collect herself as she slowly sat up. She gave it careful thought before answering.

"No, but 'good morning' would usually be the proper thing to say. Well, seeing as it's late afternoon I'll have to give it a pass."

Corly felt much more like her normal self and tried to assuage Lord Regam's concern with some light humor, but he only stared at her with those cold eyes of his.

Would it kill him to smile once in a while? She wouldn't ever ask him that out loud though so she quickly changed to a more serious tone. "Uhhhh, I mean there wasn't anything like what happened last night. I don't even remember if I had any dreams or not. I feel much better now. Thank you."

"Since you have sufficiently recovered then change into the clothes prepared for you in the wardrobe and meet me outside."

Corly froze and swallowed hard as she nodded. The tone of his voice was slightly more strained than normal and she worried over what might have set someone as unflappable as him on edge, but he silently got up and left the room so she jumped up and went to the wardrobe tucked into the corner. Normally she didn't bother with the wardrobe during her daily routine as it only contained one singular outfit that had been painstakingly put together on the chance she would get summoned into King Bamaul's presence a second time. Being told to change into this outfit only meant one thing; she was once again being summoned before the king.

After her first visit Doris had mentioned no-one besides Regam and servants of the throne room wore the same outfit before the monarch a second time so an entire new outfit had been tailored to her dimensions in case such an event happened again. This one was just as elaborate as the first and just as much of a pain to properly change into. This outfit at least had a kirtle over the chemise so it was easy enough to slip into, but the embroidery, buttons and ribbon on the light outer gown were just as ostentatious as the last. The light pink color at least somewhat matched her ribbon so she chose to focus on that rather than how *hot* it was wearing so many layers.

Her thoughts of Doris must have summoned the insufferable woman by magic as she appeared without so much as a knock. Corly tuned out the prattle and rambling coming out of Doris, although she was thankful for the help with the more intricate parts of the dress.

A short time later Corly found herself once again waiting to be led into the throne room for an audience with the king.

She had carried the shiny black shoes in her hands while she walked so as not to sully them, a very surreal experience to be so dressed up while still wearing her leather boots, and now had a servant hurriedly changing them out for her.

As the woman did so Regam calmly discussed the actions she should take during this audience with King Bamaul.

"Remember to never raise your head and remain absolutely still. Do not speak or make a sound unless explicitly told to do so and do not fail to speak in proper honorifics if you value your life. You will end up recounting every moment of your experience when prompted without exaggeration or preamble so prepare yourself for that. Keep your recounting succinct and direct. Do not make the same mistake as your previous audience. When you have finished, remain silent and assume the first question asked to be rhetoric in nature. Afterwards he will then let you know which questions to answer directly, although it will most likely not be in the most pleasant of ways. This is imperative. You do not realize it now, but you have just become one of the most important people in this kingdom."

Corly gawked at Regam's final piece of information. She felt like he had just struck her flush in the face with a brick.

"What!?"

Regam stared at her for a few moments while she reeled from this sudden information. The servant finished changing and inspecting her footwear, helped her to her feet and bowed to Lord Regam before silently and quickly departing.

"More will be divulged during your audience. I have already been debriefed, but the king wished to speak with you personally. So shut your mouth and get a hold of yourself!"

Corly snapped her mouth shut. Her head was spinning, but she did her best to pull herself together and took a deep breath. She had already been concerned about appearing before King Bamaul again and now Lord Regam had just casually dropped something on her so outlandish that it couldn't possibly be true.

Sooner than she was ready Corly found herself once again kneeling nervously before the enigmatic monarch of her nation.

Strangely enough, there were no others present besides the king, Lord Regam and herself. No guards knelt reverently along the walls and not even the herald remained to announce them. A fleeting thought about ruining her fancy clothing by kneeling on such a filthy floor ran through her mind, but she shook it off and tried to concentrate.

Instead, she focused on the floor beneath her and forced herself to recall every minute detail of that terrifying experience she had endured. She was concerned the volatile monarch might find some fault with her or find her mentally defective and decide to get rid of her right then and there. She suppressed a shiver at the thought.

There was also the incredible bit of information Lord Regam decided to drop on her about becoming one of the most important people in the kingdom, which both baffled and terrified her. Her imagination had been running a bit wild as she knelt, but her current situation forced her to put those wild suppositions aside.

The king had been sitting silently on his throne for several tense minutes. The steady clicking of his strange onyx bracelet ominously filled the room as he carefully ran his finger over the filament of silver embedded in its center.

Just when she was beginning to think the king may not have even registered her presence he finally spoke.

"You have seen and experienced something few in the history of this world even brush upon the fringes of," he said in a tense voice. His words came out immensely strained, but Corly couldn't even begin to guess as to why that would be.

She remained silent, remembering Lord Regam's instructions to not speak or even move unless explicitly told to do so. King Bamaul lapsed back into silence as Corly tried to ignore the hollow pit forming in her stomach.

A few more minutes passed before the monarch began to speak again, this time in earnest.

"A sense of detachment from the physical realm in a void of blackness and pair of eyes with a reptilian visage floating in said darkness. All while producing an indescribable feeling of absolute terror and fear. This is an incredibly rare occurrence and one someone such as you would usually never qualify for. I have already spoken about this matter with Regam at length, but I have made the decision to inform you of a bit more. This is no small matter and will change your life drastically in the months to come. Would you hear more of this? You may both respond and move."

"Yes, your majesty," Corly immediately responded. Despite her concerns and trepidation, she kept in mind Lord Regam's prior warnings so as to avoid King Bamaul's wrath. She had no idea what she was about to be thrust into this time, but it was far too late to back down now. Additionally, she didn't want to take the chance of answering in the negative and potentially angering the king, so answering favorably was really her only option.

Nervously swallowing a lump in her throat, her answer hung in the air between herself and the monarch. It was only a few seconds before he continued on, but to Corly it felt like several lifetimes, all with unpleasant ends, had played out before her eyes. What he said next however, grabbed her full attention.

"What I am about to bestow upon you in terms of knowledge concerns both your erstwhile mentor and young interest of the heart. You will not be pleased."

Corly felt a chill run down her spine at the obvious venom with which he spoke.

What could my dream have to do with Oltan and Darien? Does it have something to do with why Darien killed Aditsan?

While her thoughts ran rampant with questions and speculation the king suddenly switched topics and Corly had to force herself to pay attention.

"How much information do you possess of an event known as 'The Unification'? You may speak at will without fear of reprisal."

"Some, your majesty, but only what little was taught to me by Oltan."

"I see. Then do you perhaps know of 'The Early Dawn'? Speak."

"No, your majesty."

Corly was thankful for once that she was asked a question with an uncomplicated answer as she had never heard the term before and had no clue what it might mean.

"Interesting. I had thought you would have at least an inkling considering your recent experiences, but no matter for it changes nothing."

Bamaul lapsed back into silence while Corly's mind

raced. She had already had only a tenuous grasp on the goings on around her, but the king's questions had caused her to lose even that.

Wracking her brain for any bit of information she might have heard over the years mentioning this 'Early Dawn', she came up empty as nothing came to mind. Corly heard the king slowly stand from the throne and held herself rigidly still despite the creeping terror of what this could mean, but the monarch simply moved to the side of the room to stare out one of the large openings along the far side.

Lord Regam then spoke in the king's place.

"You know only a part of the beginnings of this world, the Unification and the Two Fallen Gods. However, few remain who know of this world's true beginning; events that took place in antiquity even before Luxes and Tenebrae came to prominence."

Corly had never heard of such a thing, not even in passing, from any of Oltan's lectures on religion. He never spoke much about it in the first place, but what Lord Regam was saying seemed off. The first thought that came to mind was *That's blasphemy!* but she wasn't foolish enough to voice such doubts aloud.

Regam must have picked up on her confusion and expanded on this newest revelation.

"There are those in the world, Haatal Peyeiza among them, who have carefully and painstakingly studied the making and true beginning of this world for many years. Over time these people have discovered miniscule scraps of information buried deep in the reserves of the world that when pieced together begin to form a different portrait of this world's origins; even from before the time of the Two Fallen Gods.

"Artifacts discovered deep within the bowels of the earth, patches of faded manuscripts and parchments, oral traditions passed down generation to generation of people in the far corners of the world. All of these weave a tapestry of information that speaks of the 'Early Dawn' his majesty mentioned. We have also been able to discern that among this period of time is when the term 'Ryudojin' first appeared."

Now *that* was a term she had heard before. Darien had mentioned something about it a few days before the incident at Village Breathwynd. He had seemed oddly enthusiastic about it, but Corly had chalked it up to him being excited about something new about dragons he had found during the course of his self-study. She never understood how boys could get so excited over something so obscure.

She had ignored him at the time, but the more she thought about it the more it seemed odd just how excited he had been. Corly had thought it was due to his current fascination with dragons and that it would pass just like other things he would get excited about and then forget when something else captured his attention.

Now she found herself furiously going through memories to see if there had been anything different at that time compared to all the others, but wasn't able to come up with anything.

Regam paused when he saw the contemplative look on Corly's face, but when nothing more was forthcoming he continued.

"These Ryudojin were part of the 'Early Dawn' of the world as I have already said. Incidentally, that woman we encountered in the Grove during our journey here is much the same."

"She's one of these Ryudojin too?"

Corly was startled, but Regam shook his head.

"No. She is something far more primal and volatile than your young friend. Many over the years have even worshiped her as a Goddess at times, not that that meant much to her."

"What does all of this mean exactly?" Corly was still trying to make sense of everything where Darien was concerned and all of this Early Dawn talk was making her head spin.

"It means there are still forces in this world that have existed even before the rise of Luxes and Tenebrae. Most of them keep to themselves and have no bearing on the world as it sits at the moment. Others are more active and far, far more dangerous. You yourself saw what that creature from the Grove is capable of."

Corly shuddered and hugged herself at the memory of her trip through the Grove. Between the breathing, person-eating trees, disappearing people and the stunningly beautiful naked woman who seemed powerful enough to kill them without much effort she had had enough of that place for a lifetime.

"Then what does she want if people worshiping her doesn't mean anything to her?"

"To bring chaos and destruction to the modern world and return it to its primal roots. As for her motivation for doing so I cannot say much more than that she herself worships the Elder dragons as its 'true rulers', although we have yet to discern exactly why this is and what it truly means."

Corly's face twisted into a frown. "So what does all of this Early Dawn stuff have to do with Darien?"

Regam glared at her so intensely Corly felt like he was weighing the value of her life and inadvertently shrunk further into herself.

"We are fairly certain Darien is one of the Ryudojin, perhaps even the last of his kind. Those with the power of the Ryudojin are bestowed with incredible, and wildly destructive, power and abilities of dragonkind. It was thought none left existed, although over the centuries there have been attempts to artificially recreate them, but all efforts have so far been for naught."

"Why would anyone want to recreate something so horrific!?" Corly blurted out.

Regam turned to look off into the distance with a troubled look on his face. It was one of the few times Corly had seen anything like an actual display of emotion from him so she tried her hardest to pay attention.

"Many times in order to negotiate with those in possession

of great power you must present a front of equal strength to even be considered. It is an unfortunate necessity, but it is the way of the current world."

Corly's eyes narrowed at Lord Regam's phrasing. "Does that mean even we have...?"

Lord Regam nodded. "For a time yes, but the results have never been positive at best and catastrophic at worst. Believe me when I tell you at the time we felt it was both necessary and the best option to protect what we have from those who wish us harm and to reclaim what we have had stolen from us. Now we have other ways of holding an equal footing with those who possess the power of the Early Dawn. Like most normal human beings we learn from our mistakes and progress in what we deem to be the most efficient manner."

"What about all those people that were involved in such things before? What happened to them?" Corly knew the answer before he even answered, but she needed to hear it directly from Lord Regam.

"Much like those from the incident in the Grove they all gave themselves over willingly, fully aware of the details and risks involved."

Corly let out a sad sigh. It pained her to hear just how much Regam and his people had suffered and endured, but it still didn't explain Darien's role in things.

"And you said that Darien is one of these...?"

"Ryudojin."

"Ryudojin. Right, but I've known him my entire life and

there was never anything special or powerful about him other than being a little clumsy and awkward."

The last part of what she said had nothing to do with the current topic of conversation, but Darien's lack of notice in her interest over the years until recently still rankled her.

"It is possible for them to hide or 'cloak' their particular powers and characteristics. Now that he and those he has taken shelter with are openly opposing us I am sure you will find his current appearance unsettling to say the least."

A cold sweat formed along Corly's brow. "What do you mean?"

"Those who possess a Ryudojin's abilities maintain certain characteristics of their bonded dragon since they are bound to each other for the entirety of their lifetime."

He held up a hand to forestall more questions. "We have found in records this may take form in a myriad of ways. A tongue that is unnaturally forked, wings growing from the shoulders, nails like elongated talons or the eyes of a reptile glittering in the night. It takes many shapes. As to how your young friend was able to cloak his trait from those around him for so long was most likely due to the one who sheltered him in that remote village.

"Oltan!? That can't be true! He was such a kind person! I spent almost as much time with him as I did with Darien!"

Regam nodded. "Your Oltan and the Oltan I know are two much different people I am afraid."

"Two different people? What do you mean?"

"Oltan once worked in this very castle under the

pretender line of kings as the head of an experimental
department known as The Interspecies Relations
Development Department - Mythical Division. He was also
at one point involved in those experiments I spoke of earlier.
Once King Bamaul returned the rightful blood to the throne
Oltan vanished and was thought to have most likely perished
in his flight until rather recently. The kindly old man you
knew was no more than a clever facade. What kind of
person would cultivate ancient knowledge and power in his
young ward without an ulterior motive? We have spoken
before many times about this 'library' and his 'lessons' and
what they often entailed. Did they ever seem to be necessary
past learning the basics of reading, writing and common
numbers? I could even argue that reading and writing
wasn't even necessary in a place like that village. Did none
of it ever seem strange to you?"

Corly considered her history with Oltan for a time before
answering. "Not really. I was so concerned with keeping up
with Darien I just went along with it and thought it was what
someone from a bigger town or city would do and we all
knew that Oltan hadn't always been a resident of Village
Breathwynd."

Now that Lord Regam had divulged so much information
she was finally starting to realize just how truly odd the
education Oltan provided was. Not to mention how anti
King Bamaul he had always been. The king was scary as all
the Hells combined, but Lord Regam had assured her he was
the true monarch and that the previous King Tammaz had

been part of a line of usurper kings. He hadn't given her the full history yet, but had mentioned parts of it would be covered by Elnora during her education soon.

Thinking about it closely, what Lord Regam was saying did make sense in a way and answered some questions about Darien and Oltan she hadn't been aware she even had.

All this new information was making her head hurt and her heart ache. Today had been a whirlwind as it was and she felt the need to shut down and let her future self worry about things, but she knew Lord Regam would never allow for that.

"This is a lot to take in on top of the shocking news about Aditsan, but I assure you all the knowledge you have gained is necessary for you to fully understand what is happening around you and will aid you in the future. I have mentioned to you about your potential and that still holds true. I see the foundation of knowledge Oltan provided, no matter the nefarious reasons for doing so, and desire to build upon it so you will become a powerful asset to not just our cause and country, but the rest of the world as well."

It wasn't the first time Lord Regam had mentioned something like this, but she had a different question on her mind.

"So why would Oltan go so far as to include me in those lessons if they were supposed to be just for Darien?"

"That I cannot know for certain, but I can hazard a guess it was simply easier for him rather than to have to constantly turn you away and arouse any modicum of suspicion even in one so young. He has always been rather cautious and meticulous so it would be in character for him. Now those lessons have become an opportunity for you to grow even further than you already have. This is why you were assigned exclusively to Elnora. Believe it or not, she is not only the best educator here among the castle staff, but once was even subordinate to Oltan so her teaching methods should have been easy for you to adapt to."

This was true. Despite her harsh nature and the physical punishment Elnora's lessons had been relatively easy to process and understand. She supposed it was a minor blessing she was able to receive guidance from someone somewhat similar in method if not in execution.

King Bamaul finally spoke again. "The old man's reasons are as varied as they are nefarious. Few alive today are even aware there was a period in history that existed before the rise of Luxes and Tenebrae. A period of primal forces running rampant and chaos fueling the world far before the coming of men. This period of time is what came to be called the 'Early Dawn' of our world.

Those beings that rose to prominence at the height of that millennia are whom we refer to as dragonkindred. Creatures that are far, far more than what few texts remain will discuss or lay claim to as fact and capable of astonishing feats.

There are many even now who still reside in this world who revere the few remaining Elder dragons as literal Gods and view any others, including the Godlings and even Luxes and Tenebrae, as inferior imposters to the throne of the world.

Their machinations, exploits and irregularities have greatly changed the landscape of the world over the centuries and were the ones truly responsible for the downfall of the Two Fallen Gods and all the chaos that ensued. Responsible for the people who lost their way, their culture, lands and homes after the violent changes in the natural world caused by the Unification that followed. Even Regam's own ancestors were those who were displaced. To this day there are regions of the world that still have not completely recovered."

Corly didn't move as she absorbed all of this stunning amount of information. She understood none of this should be mentioned outside of Lord Regam or the king and knew to choose her moments of speaking carefully despite being given leave. She didn't want to repeat her mistake from her previous audience and knew the monarch could change demeanors on a whim. A wrong move here after learning of something so important could result in any number of unpleasant outcomes, no matter how 'important' she herself had become.

The king continued. "One such irregularity occurring over the centuries is what your young friend Darien has found himself embroiled in."

Corly's mind was racing while she tried her best to keep up with the massive amount of knowledge being imparted. She still didn't understand what any of this had to do with her, but she remained patient despite the pain in her knees from kneeling for so long. She had so many questions, but remained quiet; Godlings only knew what would happen if the king thought she was trying to interrupt him.

"These irregularities are often initiated by their chosen surrogates. You have already been familiarized with the term 'Ryudojin' correct?" Bamaul paused for a response and Corly quickly answered.

"Yes, your Majesty." *Did he forget we already covered that?* Corly briefly wondered just what was happening inside the monarch's head, but quickly stamped out such a dangerous line of thought.

"Good. These surrogates and the Ryudojin are one and the same and are the ones who have inherited a portion of the primal essence of their associated dragon. However, wherever a Ryudojin appears you can be assured that catastrophe is bound to follow.

I believe you have already borne witness to such an event at your village and even here at the castle, although smaller in scale. I can assure you there will be much more to follow should the tide of the Early Dawn not be stemmed, and quickly."

Corly still wasn't sure what exactly was expected of her or why she was important, but she kept her mouth shut and ears open. She had learned a long time ago that listening to not only what was being said, but *how* it was being said could sometimes make a world of difference.

She was definitely going to have to ask Lord Regam for

even more of an in-depth explanation later, but she tried her best to keep up with the king's story. It was possible that none of this was even true since it was rumored that the king's increasing madness often resulted in him living in his own version of reality. She wisely kept this thought to herself.

"You are aware of the Grove of course, having lived in such proximity."

"Yes, your Majesty."

"Legend goes that what is now the Grove was once the point of separation between the two halves of the world before the Unification, but that is only a portion of the truth. The Grove, even unto this day has remained a place of power, mystery, wonder, terror and tragedy in even counts. Do you know why the Grove came to be such a place?"

"She does not, your Majesty," Lord Regam interjected. She had been told that he might interject on her behalf from time to time so that she would not be seen as overstepping even with leave to speak. Corly was grateful for his timing as she was terrified of faltering in even the slightest way.

"I see. We have learned through years of difficult, dangerous and arduous research that the reason this area had been utilized as the Dividing Line was because it is the center of the tempest that spawned the chaotic powers of the Early Dawn. From what we have learned the Two Fallen Gods felt it an appropriate place to separate the world's population so they both could sustain themselves without conflict. This agreement obviously ran its course at some point for reasons stated previously, but what is fact is that their battle and subsequent pseudo-deaths triggered a transformation resulting in a combination of the chaotic and primal with the more mundane nature of the world. This…Darien? He is one with the Grove we could say. It is best if you no longer consider him to be human."

What? What is he talking about?

"Speak with Regam later about further details, but you must be prepared for anything those of the Early Dawn may send your way for they all share one common goal; to plunge this world back into the primal age where the Elder dragons ruled over chaos as the True Gods and utilized all lower life as sustenance. The next time you meet this Darien he will no longer be the person you thought you knew and *will* attempt to devour you if you stand in his way.

Had she been told all of this just a few days ago Corly never would have believed the adorably awkward boy from Village Breathwynd who always had his heart in the right place would ever be capable of even thinking about harming her, but after learning about his role in Aditsan's death and what King Bamaul was telling her she was no longer sure.

Another thing the king had said that caught her attention was the mention of 'sustenance'. She made a mental note to ask Lord Regam about it later and resisted an ominous shudder at what it could entail.

"Needless to say your life has taken an even darker turn with your recent vision. It implies the enemies of humanity itself have their eyes on you and you must rise up to meet them in order to retain the peace these lands now enjoy. If you do not then who can say how many other Breathwynds there will be in the coming days?"

His words struck a chord within Corly. Until now she had just been doing her best to follow along and not incur the monarch's wrath, but what he said had some merit to it if the rest could be believed.

"Besides," the king continued. "The fact you even received this vision shows that your former friend has completely given up his humanity and has set his eyes upon one he is most familiar with in terms of aura consumption."

"Your Majesty, the girl has not received education about that concept as of yet. This will be rectified accordingly."

Lord Regam again saved her from acting on her confusion at the term 'aura consumption'.

"She has received at least some knowledge of aura and the like during her assigned lessons I presume?"

"Yes, your Majesty."

It was true Elnora had briefly touched upon the topic of the aura everyone supposedly possessed here and there, but had always quickly moved on saying there would be time later and there were other things she needed to understand to perfection first so her exposure had been rudimentary at best.

She was aware from these self-same lessons, not to mention all the times Darien would ramble on incessantly about dragons, that people associated with dragons had worked for the king of Katama a very long time ago without problem, so where did all this talk about being the 'enemies of humanity' come from?

She was sure Lord Regam would answer her questions later, but right now she was sorely confused. Her aching knees and back weren't helping matters either.

The king must have grasped Corly's confusion. Luckily, she received an explanation rather than condemnation.

"It is rather complex, but those like the Ryudojin cannot survive without feeding on the auras that all sentient beings possess. The stronger the aura, the greater the benefit and the longer they can thrive before needing to siphon away another. Unfortunately, this process is rather unsettling and not a little painful for the victim and the outcome is almost always the loss of life. It is not uncommon for those afflicted to lose their sanity before the end, which could be considered a mercy all things considered."

Corly suppressed another shiver. The thought of Darien being some sort of magical being of death and destruction incarnate threatened to tear her heart in two. It also made the vision she had seen make a little more sense. The feeling of terror and foreboding she had felt at the time was something she never wanted to experience again. She just wasn't sure what was expected of her in this situation.

The king finally turned away from the window and stood before Corly. All she could see was the tips of his boots, but it was enough to make her send a prayer for safety up to the Godlings.

"As of this moment the boy you knew is dead. He is not

only the enemy of our country, but of all humanity. You will act in accordance with this. You are dismissed. Regam will give you further instruction and education in this matter."

Corly was relieved she had made it through another audience unscathed, but still was uncertain of her exact role.

Once they were free of the king's terrifying presence Corly felt like a weight of an indescribable magnitude had been lifted off her shoulders. However, that feeling would be short-lived.

Walking the halls of the castle, Corly a step behind, Lord Regam began to explain in greater detail what the king's words had meant.

"I am sure you find all of this rather overwhelming, but you do not have any time for confusion or doubt to cloud your mind so I will not tolerate any indecision in the coming days."

Corly's sense of foreboding increased again at Lord Regam's words, but she remained silent.

"You will soon find yourself faced with difficult choices. At least they may seem difficult to one unaccustomed, but I assure you what his majesty spoke about rings true. I will tell you again your former friend is no longer the person you knew. Should you meet in the future he *will* do everything in his power to extinguish your existence. You must be prepared both physically and mentally for that eventuality."

Corly didn't know what to say. She felt an indescribable sadness knowing what had befallen Darien. Her elation when she learned he had survived had immediately been tempered with the news of Aditsan's death and now this. She felt like the world had suddenly sped up around her and was threatening to leave her behind. There was so much information to digest that she knew it would take considerable effort to keep from being swept away by it all. Steeling herself for what she was sure would be some unpleasant days ahead, she vowed to protect the innocent people with all her might so there would never be another Breathwynd. She would train, study and work even harder than ever and rededicate herself to proving her worth. Failing to do so would be sure to bring Lord Regam's ire upon her, but she still had so many questions.

"You seem as if you have some concerns."

"Well, it's just that there are a lot of rumors about King Bamaul, even in Breathwynd. None of them are very flattering either. I never really thought it mattered being so remote, but now it is all too real. I don't know what to believe or what to expect."

Corly's concerns came out in a rush. She was so nervous she tripped over herself a few times, but managed to convey her fears.

"I've never even been told why King Bamaul took the throne or why some say he is the true king while others say he's not. Didn't King Tammaz's family rule over Katama for many generations?"

Regam let her finish speaking before quietly leading her outside to where several Bloodsetters were drilling in their own private yard. He spent a few minutes silently looking over his men and Corly knew better than to try to interrupt.

"This land has a longer and even more storied history than many know. His majesty's right to rule is tied to that unknown history, but there is not more I can speak of to you at this time. As for why we support his majesty and recognize his claim is partly because we are aware of this history and that we will be compensated by having what was taken by that fool Tammaz's ancestors returned to us in the end."

Corly scrunched up her nose at Regam's explanation. "They stole something?"

She had never heard about anything like this, even from Oltan. It sounded more complicated than she felt comfortable dealing with, but she *did* ask.

Regam nodded. "Our people once laid claim to the lands south of the Grove. That was a far more chaotic period in history, but it is our ancestral home. We were...forcibly removed from it after a certain event."

"What event?" Corly was wildly confused, but noticed the slight tightening of Regam's fists as he spoke.

"I have already informed you of more than you need to be aware of for now. Come. We have other matters to attend to."

"Well alright, but I still think I should know more about this and what it has to do with Oltan and Darien. It just seems so outlandish."

Regam didn't answer, but inwardly he reveled at the progress he was making in the girl's indoctrination. Bamaul had agreed that the time to expose her to the darker elements of their country's history was at hand and there was still much left to do.

Chapter 10

Regam kept himself from smiling. After their conversation about the displacement of his people and Bamaul's right to rule the girl had finally broken the way he wanted and asked for a detailed explanation about her erstwhile friend and lover. All he had to do now was guide her along the intended path and the bait for their enemies would be set. The old man would surely love to hear that the child was firmly under their control and soon the boy would follow suit. Aditsan's death had been a blessing despite the pain of losing one of his most trusted subordinates, but that death would not go in vain as it had accelerated his plans for the girl and made her even more malleable. Once Gelas and the handler he had been paired with were fully capable of deployment all the relevant pieces would be in place to bring low Philip Lockhart and those few remaining who followed him.

The girl had had a rather predictable outburst at the news the boy was alive, but he had been pleasantly surprised at just how close the connection between the two of them actually was. He had assumed they were at least acquainted based on Aditsan's reports and as small as the pissant village was, but discovering they were erstwhile lovers was wholly unexpected. Despite the old man having cleverly concealed this from him until now, things couldn't have aligned more perfectly.

He was currently leading the girl to their next destination, a critical and necessary juncture in the girl's "education". It was somewhat of a risk due to the unpredictable nature of the one they were on the way to meet, but Bamaul had authorized it once Regam had explained his reasoning for wanting to expose the girl to such a volatile situation.

She had remained obediently silent since her audience with King Bamaul other than an occasional sigh or sniffle. He hoped she would be able to suppress her emotions better in the coming days as it annoyed him to no end to see such weakness in one under his tutelage.

However, the silence was more than welcome after her outburst when he had broken the news about Aditsan. Striding confidently through the bustling activity of the castle grounds, servants, pages and carriers alike gave the chief of the Bloodsetters a wide berth while still showing him proper deference.

Making his way into the castle interior he continued to lead the girl through the great halls, the only sounds accompanying them being the heels of their boots softly echoing off the stone floor.

Eventually they made their way to the shamanic order occupied by Peyeiza and his acolytes. Thankfully they were not entering the shamanic den itself, there was no knowing how the girl and her delicate sensibilities would react to the various effects found inside, but an area just adjacent to it. To most the area of stone adjoining the left side of the shaman's entrance looked like any other part of the castle, but it was in fact much different.

Regam removed a paper talisman from a pouch he kept securely sewn into his tunic and affixed it vertically to the wall. Stepping back a few paces he placed a hand on the girl and moved her safely behind him. Uttering a few words in the Golden Tongue, a rune similar to those from the ritual Peyeiza conducted on Gelas flashed to life with a bluish light before fading. The talisman quickly turned to ash and the embers vanished before even falling to the floor.

A soft and ethereal 'vrrr' filled the air and an outline of a door slowly formed. Confidently pushing lightly caused it to sink into the wall and slide to the left just enough to allow passage for a single person. He entered the portal without hesitation, knowing the girl would obediently follow. The door quietly and quickly closed behind them in the same manner it had opened and melded back into the stone.

The girl had been mostly indoctrinated in the way he had foresaw up until this juncture, but this particular sequence of events, starting with the news of her once-lover, would undoubtedly cause her full commitment to their cause should she still harbor any lingering doubts.

Another small sniffle from behind confirmed his thoughts. The girl might be experiencing a tumult of emotions, but her penchant for curiosity and determination to prove her worth always won out. Regam had consistently used these characteristics to his advantage, no matter how annoying the brat could be at times.

"Stay close to me and do not stray even an inch no matter what. Take hold of my hand if you must, but heed my warning to stay strictly by my side, else I cannot guarantee your life or safety." The girl's eyes grew wide and she nodded before tightly gripping the back of his tunic and pressing close.

Not bothering to bring a torch or other source of light Regam made his way through a convoluted series of twists and turns leading further and further down into the bowels of the castle known to only a few.

Each passage had a slightly different pale hue to it than the last and even Regam did not know the true source of the ethereal flickering light other than it was the finalized work of Peyeiza and his forebears who had worked under Tammaz. The rank smell of mildew assaulted his senses and the only sound either of them made was the girl's heavy breathing as she tried to control her nerves.

With practiced precision Regam continued on in the minimal light. A wrong turn or misstep at any juncture would bring about a great deal of misfortune and pain before ultimately resulting in a violent and painful death no matter their allegiance to Bamaul or the Bloodsetters. Regam had had Peyeiza lead him through this deathly maze a multitude of times, some of which he spent blindfolded, before he was capable of navigating it himself and was confident there were no others, save for perhaps the king, who could do the same.

Walking slowly and carefully, he mapped out the proper route in his head. Despite his confidence he was no fool and took proper precautions against the dangers around them. Vivid memories of test subjects composed of prisoners, prompted by promises of freedom should they succeed in reaching the end, released into the maze in order to test the shaman's new 'safety measures' were enough to burn caution into anyone's soul.

After more than twenty minutes of walking in silence they suddenly could hear a low, indecipherable moaning coming from somewhere within the darkness ahead. The girl's hand tightened on the back of his tunic, but he continued to stride forward. He would discipline her later for such an act, but it was far more important to remain silent and approach with caution as they were almost to their destination.

They smelled the target of their excursion before they saw him. The girl let out an audible "ugh." as the moaning turned into a faint muttering coming from somewhere ahead, but Regam knew even if they had several knowledgeable scholars listening intently to every word they would never decipher most of what was uttered.

The final stretch leading to their destination yawned out before him; a long tunnel with sheer walls bathed in a pale green light and a floor shining brilliantly with an ethereal gleam. This floor rejected any marking or mar and remained pristine no matter what it had been subjected to during testing. It was supposedly made from some lost ore long forgotten by the rest of the world save maybe by those like Peyeiza.

Regam understood from the several long lectures Peyeiza had subjected him to, not to mention those that had been used to test the defenses, that this tunnel only looked innocuous. It was in fact a hallway of utter terror one must tread carefully less they become nothing more than a pile of flesh and bone; and that was if they were lucky.

Regam suddenly stopped in his tracks and to the girl's credit she also came to a halt without asking any questions or making a sound. It seemed she inherently understood the gravity of their situation.

Removing another small pouch from within the folds of his tunic, Regam lightly sprinkled a negligible amount of soft white powder before him and gently blew on the tiny shimmering particles dancing and floating on the air. It took a few moments for anything to occur, but slowly the tiny specks of light slowed and stretched outwards down the passage. Suddenly the specks shot away down the hall at incredible speed with a low-pitched keening that unnerved even him; it had the feel of the unnatural to it.

The effects of the pouch were time-limited so Regam quickly walked the corridor while almost pulling the girl along behind him.

"Be quick on your feet and forget your trepidation. Our life, health and safety are currently on a limited timer. Do as you are told without question or complaint lest you cost us our lives, understood?"

To the girl's credit she was able to voice her understanding despite her obvious fear, but Regam was sure a torrent of questions would follow later; the girl often seemed desperate to devour knowledge for some reason. Once their current task was complete Regam was sure to field a multitude of inquiries and he would have to craft some careful answers.

The keening of dissipated particles added an ethereal feel to their surroundings as the walls pulsed with a soft green light as they passed. They soon came to a halt before another door that only Regam, Peyeiza and Bamaul understood how to safely open. It was somewhat similar to the one leading to the old man's cage, but required no key.

The portal itself was not so much a door as a tall rectangle of utter and complete darkness. Peyeiza had once named it the 'Door of Nothing' despite the low muttering that could still be heard lightly echoing throughout the corridor and Regam found it to be an apt term. The door radiated stillness as if the very nature of the world ceased to exist within its frame. No movement could be seen within the onyx veil and within that stillness resided a finality that unnerved even the stoutest of heart.

Regam felt the girl tense up behind him, but she held firm and kept her emotions in check. Plunging two fingers into the stillness of the void, he heard an audible gasp from the girl when the door sucked his fingers in until he began to slowly trace them along the 'tracks' he felt within. He wasn't exactly sure what these 'tracks' even were, but he felt the term was as good as any for the sensation he was experiencing. More importantly, there was only one correct pathway that would allow them entry. Any slip-up or mistake in the slightest would lead to an unfortunate fate. There had been any number of casualties among the prisoners used during experimentation that had led to death, dismemberment, madness and even a few who seemed to inexplicably blink out of existence.

Regam paid those incidents no mind at the moment, not that such a fate didn't concern him, but this task required his full concentration. One wrong movement, twitch of a finger or brushing up against the side of the wrong track would trigger any number of effects.

Working with a practiced hand Regam ignored the muttering rising in intensity around them. Small beads of sweat broke out on his forehead and he closed his eyes lest the salty drops distract him.

He knew his attempt to unlock the door had borne fruit when it vanished out of existence, leaving his outstretched hand hanging in the air. Standing before them was an opaque opening swirling and sparkling within its confines. Slowly and carefully retracting his hand, he waited a few moments for the tingling feeling of something unseen coating his hand to vanish before grabbing the girl and stepping through, pulling her along behind him. They both instantly felt their stomachs lurch as if they had been pulled violently sideways and the girl stumbled into him on the suddenly uneven terrain.

Rubble and ruin surrounded them on all sides as a testament to some long-forgotten race. There were broken carvings and statues of unknown people and beings lost to time with torn and rotting tapestries barely more than a tatter of threads hanging loosely from the walls. Broken, cracked flagstones marred the floor and looked as if some massive force had heaved them upwards from underground.

It had been theorized that this had once been the throne room of a forgotten king from a long-forgotten race based on the shattered remnants of the throne sitting upon a raised dais on the far side, but none of that was remarkable compared to what they had come there for.

Looking back Regam verified the opaque opening still remained, as it was now their only means of exit. As far as he was aware there were no other entrances or exits to this room and he dared not try to explore as they had verified unknown dangers lurked even here in the darkened corners filled with crumbled pillars and shattered artifacts.

As with the previous hallways there was no evident light source, manmade or otherwise, yet the room was as bright as midday. However, that wasn't what grabbed their attention. In the very center of the room upon a slightly raised platform sat a large cage approximately six feet by six feet with thick sturdy bars made from some unknown metal lost to the ravages of time.

When he had once asked Peyeiza how they could go about testing the properties of this metal in hopes of discovering its origins and uses in order to harness a new power the Haatal had simply answered 'We don't.' Since the shaman had seemed rather terrified of the prospect Regam had chosen to heed the words of someone far more experienced and informed than he for the time being.

Approaching the cage, the source of the incoherent rambling became apparent as a large lump of flesh and bone unfolded bent limbs and bowed back to stand up. A hunched back accompanied long and spindly limbs hanging down at its sides. Knobby elbows and knees gave a malnourished, gaunt appearance and filthy disheveled hair flowed from its head to its face in a grotesque imitation of a beard. Red-rimmed and yellowed eyes stared balefully at them as the occupant tightly gripped the bars of its cage with cracked and grimy hands crowned with brittle fingernails chipped with age.

However, the most remarkable thing about the thing's appearance was the tiny scrawls tattooed deeply into its skin and covering nearly every inch of its back, shoulders and legs. Similar etchings appeared on his torso in a pattern spiraling outward, but were less in number than the rest of his body. Looking closely with a practiced eye Regam was chagrined to find that new additions had been added to the miniscule markings. Had he not thoroughly studied the manuscripts Peyeiza had given him access to and gained a modicum of understanding of what these markings represented he never would have noticed, but his keen eyesight and meticulous power of observation when it came to these visits made it easy to discern.

At first glance one might assume the cage's occupant was some rare or unknown beast, but Regam knew better despite the acrid and foul stench of unwashed skin and bodily expulsions assaulting their senses. Uncleaned feces and urine stains littered the cage and Regam frowned beneath his Makavai.

Surely there must be some useless soul Peyeiza could spare to clean this cage more than once a year. He understood that doing so was incredibly dangerous and took much time and effort, but it would make things a little less unpleasant.

The man was unclothed and all attempts to clothe or bathe him over the years had always ended with disastrous results. Whether those results were due to the man in the cage or those horrors lurking in the shadows was unknown even to Peyeiza and Regam had no intentions of investigating further.

The shaman had once proposed a somewhat outlandish theory, but Regam had seen enough in his lifetime to give credence to almost anything so he took even that particular theory into account when interacting with this 'person'. He wasn't even sure if 'person' was the correct term considering the occupant's nature and appearance, not to mention the how and the why it was here in the first place.

The muttering continued even when Regam stood before the man, or what once passed for a man, making sure to stand just out of arm's reach as its voice rose in pitch and intensity until it was shouting. The girl recoiled at the sudden outburst, but Regam decided a bit of leniency here at her cowardice would be effective for their future discussion.

As soon as their presence finally registered on the occupant it increased the fervor and ferocity of its screaming babble. To her credit the girl remained quiet despite her trepidation, but she no longer shrunk back behind him; Regam supposed he should give her some credit for that.

The thing continued its fervent pace for a few moments before throwing itself violently against the cage, flailing its arms and legs in an attempt to reach its observers and slamming full force into the metallic bars. Spittle from the man's ranting flecked into Regam's face, but he remained silent and immobile while the incoherent screaming continued.

Regam forcibly pulled the girl to stand at his side and the man grew quiet for a few moments before launching into another series of incomprehensible screeches. The girl flinched at the rapid changes in the occupant's behavior, but held her ground.

After another few minutes of silence on their end the girl finally grew bold enough to ask a question despite the noise.

"Lord Regam, who or what exactly is this? Why is he here? *Where* is here? Why are *we* here? Was this really what you wanted to show me? What does it have to do with Aditsan and Darien and all that 'Early Dawn' stuff?"

She had to raise her voice a bit to be heard above the din, but Regam took each question in stride. *Once this child gets rolling with questions she never ceases. I suppose her curiosity is a good thing in terms of her growth, but I should answer these questions carefully. I do not want her getting too curious.*

"I will answer your questions, and in order, but I must ask you a question so I can first discern the depths of your understanding."

The girl set her mouth in a way Regam had come to recognize meant she was annoyed, but that was unimportant.

"What do you know of the Two Fallen Gods and the one who witnessed both their battle and their end?"

The girl frowned and began to bite the nail of her thumb, but he could tell she was thinking things through as she had been taught in order to provide a coherent and well-thought answer so he waited patiently for her to plumb the depths of her memory. Elnora had specifically been told not to broach this particular subject during the girl's lessons in anticipation of the possibility of bringing her here so whatever knowledge she possessed would be organic. He was curious to see what she knew and was just as sure whatever she did know would be incomplete or corrupted based on her limited knowledge of the wider world.

Considering she spent a good amount of time around the old man until they had finally located him he was sure she must have some knowledge on the subject, he just needed to ascertain what the extent of that knowledge was.

The girl continued to think as the screaming abated a bit, now wholly absorbed in her thoughts and completely ignoring the caged abomination like it wasn't even there. Regam had to admit her adaptability was rather impressive.

Eventually she began to speak in the tone of a student recalling a lesson at her instructor's request, a habit borne of the old man and Elnora both Regam was sure.

"Oltan used to teach only a little about it. He was strangely mum about that topic a lot of the time. It made us curious so Darien and I usually had to pester him quite a bit to get anything more than just the basics, which was weird for him. He was the type of teacher who usually pushed us to learn as much as we could about any given topic, but he shied away from that one."

"The two of us spent a good amount of time searching the library, but didn't find much more than what Oltan had already been willing to teach us."

"What do you know?" Regam was getting impatient at the lengthy exposition, but waited for the girl to continue.

"Well, supposedly there used to be only two Gods instead of the Godlings, Luxes the God of Light and Tenebrae the God of Darkness. The world was evenly separated by the 'Dividing Line' where worshippers of Luxes lived on one side while those who worshiped Tenebrae lived on the other. As far as I can remember there was something about the two Gods almost never having contact with each other for some reason."

"Is that the extent of your knowledge?"

The girl shook her head, causing her ridiculous braids to flail about.

"Uhhh, something eventually happened that made the Two Gods angry and they got into a fight where they destroyed each other which created the Godlings and caused the 'Unification' of the two separate halves of the world. I don't think I know anything more than that since Darien didn't always share everything from his studies. He'd rather complain about them more than anything."

Regam remained silent at her words for a time as the man in the cage stopped screeching and instead began moaning and wailing in earnest while yanking at the tangled mess of hair on his head and face.

"You have the general story told to the people around the region more or less correct. What do you know of the one known as 'The Witness'?"

The girl scrunched her nose up as she thought.

"Um, something about a person who watched them fight. I don't really know to be honest."

"I see."

Continuing to stare at the raving man in the cage Regam mulled over his options. The girl was rather intelligent and inquisitive despite being a simple village brat so he felt that telling her most of the truth would be the best course of action. It wouldn't do for her to acquire conflicting information later and lead her to question the information he was about to give her.

"You are correct that there was a person who witnessed the clash of the Two Fallen Gods during the lengthy battle that lasted for generations. A single, solitary soul chosen either by fate, chance, circumstance or maybe even the Gods themselves who witnessed the end of the beginnings of this world. However, there are several pieces of information unknown to all but a few."

The girl nodded, but remained mute and patiently waited for Regam to continue.

"There are many rumors and inconsistencies about what happened to that individual and what occurred once the battle between Gods ended beyond the creation of those so-called Godlings. Most agree this person simply passed after his discovery by those who eventually found him. The story often refers to him as having lost his sanity and only speaking of the events he witnessed verbatim time after time before finally expiring, his task complete. However, this is not entirely accurate."

He glanced down at the girl again and could see her concentrating on this new information and a surprised look came over her when she came to the rather obvious conclusion.

"Is this person the Witness!? How could he possibly still be alive!?" she exclaimed in shock.

Regam nodded and the girl's mouth hung agape in awe as she stared at the inhuman being within the cage. Strangely enough the man stopped his screaming and yelling at that moment and stood mutely staring at the two of them, still tightly gripping the bars of his prison. Regam took note of his silence and began counting down in his head. The effects of the particles from earlier had finally reached the caged man and their time was now extremely precious.

"How is that even possible?" she asked, her confusion plainly evident.

"No one truly knows. Perhaps he still has some unknown part to play in the battle of the Gods that is far above the realm of our own understanding. What we do know is that he is still alive although he is less than sane as you can see. He is also one of my people."

"What!?"

Regam felt a little irritated at how incredulous the girl was, but he pushed that emotion aside and carried on with his explanation.

"Look upon him carefully and without revulsion and tell me what you see."

The girl had been doing her best to avoid looking directly at the Witness since their arrival, but now he forced her to gaze upon his exposed flesh. There was a good reason for this, but it was also far past time she learned to leave all of her past village bumpkin sensibilities behind.

When the girl hesitated he quickly and forcefully grabbed her by the top of her head and thrust her forward until she was just out of the caged man's reach. She let out a small yelp, but he paid her discomfort no mind.

After a few moments of forced proximity to the silent Witness he released his grip and set her back a pace.

Watching her wipe the perspiration from her face he asked her what she had learned and urged her to be quick in her response.

She took another moment to compose herself before staring a hole through the Witness, now muttering to himself and huddling in the far corner of the cage.

"I couldn't understand any of what he was saying before and the stench made me want to vomit."

Regam wanted to gut her then and there for wasting time, but stilled his hand and waited for her to continue. He was sure she had more to say than something so blatantly obvious.

The girl looked up at Regam and asked the question he had been hoping to hear.

"Are those some kind of words or symbols covering him? It was hard to tell because I thought it was just filth at first, but after getting a closer look it might have been some kind of writing. I couldn't read it though."

"You have keen eyes."

Regam was glad the time and investment spent on the girl was showing progress in how her mind worked as well as her physical and social abilities. Others who had been brought here in the past made no notice of this anomaly of the Witness's anatomy; not that many of them lived long afterwards.

"It is the written form of what is the true and original language of this world and our people. It has not been spoken or written with any true fluency in centuries and the few shamans who have come here in attempts to glean understanding have walked away with little success. What we do know and understand due to one of the few and extremely rare occurrences of lucidity the Witness has had is that they are the names of every one of our people who have fallen in battle on our homeland soil."

The girl had a perplexed look on her face as she asked another obvious question.

"How would anyone know? He could be lying or still just raving since no-one can read or write that language anymore. How could anyone verify that?"

Regam folded his arms and stared at the muttering Witness.

"That is an excellent point. However, Peyeiza has made some…impressive strides in verifying this information over the past several years. I'm sure I don't have to tell you how that was accomplished considering what you yourself witnessed back at the Grove."

He shifted his gaze sideways to check the girl's reaction. From the look on her face he could tell she had come to the correct realization, but was none too pleased about it.

"Why do so many of your people sacrifice themselves so easily for such things? Won't your people eventually die out or…or end up like Aditsan?"

The girl's question was tinged with sadness, grief and no little anger, but Regam didn't hold that against her. On the contrary she was rather playing right into his hands.

"It is because our goal is that worthwhile, the reward so great and important that it is the noblest pursuit of all of our people. There is no one amongst the Bloodsetters or shamans who would not willingly give our lives in this task for we know that we do not have to absolutely be the ones to reap the benefits. Myself, Peyeiza and every last one of us understand the sacrifices that must be made even if it means leaving this mortal world behind for our future generations to inherit. And we are by no means the entirety of our people as you have already seen. As long as our people reclaim our place in the light then we know our souls will be welcomed home by the Mother. Even I would willingly head into the warmth of the bosom of the Mother should it ever become a necessity.

"But what do these names have to do with that?"

At her question the Witness suddenly unfurled from his corner and stood in the middle of his cage. Looking upward at something only he could see the man opened his mouth in a silent scream.

Regam considered how to answer the girl's question carefully. Even he and Peyeiza were not entirely sure about what little had been gleaned from the Witness's lucid moments and most of that had never gone further than the verification of the markings and that they served as a living memorial to the memories of his fallen brethren.

"Look closely at him again. We believe it is a sign that those who have passed from this world into the bosom of the Mother are held in memoriam for a purpose beyond our comprehension at the moment. What we do know is that the first step is reclaiming the remaining lands that had once been stolen from us."

While Regam spoke, the girl did as she had been instructed and gazed intently at the decrepit man in the cage. At first nothing happened, but she squinted when she noticed some movement along his skin. It started as a small ripple in the air around him before turning into a swirl of what looked like ink. The ripple dissipated and the girl shivered as the Witness's skin crawled and undulated for a few moments. When all was still again small rivulets of blood ran down the grimy abdomen of the Witness, but Corly couldn't quite discern what had changed.

Regam answered for her as if he could read her thoughts. "Aditsan's name and the names of the others that fell during the last campaign are now registered. Never forget the sight you just saw nor forget the sacrifice he and the others made, for they were made for us."

Regam paused for a moment of gravity and to gauge the girl's reaction and decided to continue on with what he had been saying as she looked to be completely invested.

"The reason we have been slowly and with painstaking care crafting plans and enacting them under King Bamaul is partially due to caution where the Witness is concerned."

"What does that mean?"

The girl's face morphed into a look of confusion, but Regam continued as if he hadn't been interrupted. He did wish that she would stop asking questions now that she had asked the most important one since their time was running short, but he outwardly maintained his composure while continuing to count down in his head.

"Those rare times he seems to regain clarity have been riddled with certain inconsistencies."

He held up a hand to forestall any more questions. Once the girl got her teeth into something she had a tenacity impressive for one her age, but he needed to finish things here quickly before the effects of the powder expired; not even he would be able to keep them both safe then.

"The foremost of these inconsistencies is that he sometimes speaks in a voice seemingly not his own. We have yet to ascertain if the words he speaks at those times are his own or at the will and behest of some unseen power."

The girl obviously didn't understand what he meant, but that was inconsequential in terms of her place in the grand scheme of the universe. Suddenly, the Witness stood up straight and looked at the two of them as if truly seeing them for the first time, clarity clearly evident in his eyes. Regam knew what was occurring and although the man wasn't currently dangerous his demeanor was a harbinger of the end of the powder's effect. The Witness began to speak in a clear and powerful voice.

"Lo! Here was the determined place and the determined time where supremacy over the land shall be founded. Two have rejected the constraints of this world and reach for what each believes to be His and Her right. I am Witness to this for I have seen it since the beginning. Listen unto me and listen well for this is the new history of your world.

For many years did the great Gods wage war upon each other. Neither one ever truly gaining an upper hand. The trees disintegrated and the lakes dried as each fed off the land during their struggle. The land withered under the weight of such power and wrath and such as you see this place now so shall it ever be. Wind and sand and devoid of people save those who will be the riders."

Regam had heard the Witness's sermon before, but Peyeiza would want to know if it deviated any from prior episodes so he paid close attention for any change in wording or inflection.

"For countless years did these Great Gods struggle to destroy one another. The statues that so many sought were cast down and broken into the sands and that place has been shifted. The Balance it was called! The Balance has been broken! But so it has been healed for one reason or another I cannot say? For each God at the exact moment grew tired of the struggle and reached deep within themselves to the place where they had stored the whole of their connection to their people and lashed out with all their might. When the two powers met there was a blinding explosion that rocked the world and both Great Gods fell.

But lo! When the two Great Gods crashed to the earth there was a shimmering as the bodies of each God shattered like glass and sent a mass of glittering fragments violently in every direction. Each shard shifted and radiated under the sunlight, now for the first time in unknown ages beaming unabated through the wind and sand upon the land once known as the Dividing Line. These shards grew in size and shape until each took on the characteristics that look much like you and I, but yet not. When each shard had fully formed there stood the Godlings and it is they who now rule this world."

Regam waited for a precious few moments as the clarity faded from the Witness's eyes. There had been no deviations as far as he could tell, but Peyeiza would still need to be notified. The usual madness quickly returned and the Witness shivered before cackling maniacally, all semblance of sanity having dissipated.

"We have precious little time remaining so we must depart, but never forget what you have seen in these few brief minutes for the Witness is one who not only saw the end of the beginning, but is a harbinger of things to come and is of our own people who will reclaim our place in the world. You are expected to aid us in that task. I need not tell you more than once that this is a secret to be kept to the grave, especially since there are only a handful of people who know of his continued existence."

The girl nodded, although Regam could tell she had far more questions. Her obedience and understanding of her position pleased him. The more of his people and their culture and history she was exposed to the deeper her understanding, gratitude and loyalty grew. Those emotions would be utilized to not only keep the old man in check, but also bring her young friend to his knees at Bamaul's feet. He vowed that until the day she departed from this world or outlived her usefulness, whichever came first, she would serve them until the very end.

Regam smiled coldly. "Let us depart. It is quickly becoming unsafe for us inside this space."

Firmly gripping the girl's hand he led her away from the Witness, who had begun slamming his head against the bars of his cage. Regam grimaced and hurried the girl along through the opaque opening and corridors back to the relative safety of the castle proper.

The girl was slightly out of breath by the time they exited, but she voiced no complaint. It was much better than becoming a victim to the myriad of horrors Peyeiza and his predecessors had created and maintained within that space. Some of the unknowns even stemmed from long before even that pretender Tammaz sat on the throne.

At least part of their pact of false promises was kept by that family of usurpers.

Anger briefly welled up within him at the thought, but he quickly regained control of himself.

He waited for the girl to catch her breath before issuing instructions.

"From here the time spent during your lessons with Elnora will increase. It will take away some from the physical aspect of your training so continue to be vigilant in honing your skills on your own."

"Yes sir!"

Her fervor was a pleasant sight. She had adapted more quickly to her surroundings than he had anticipated, but that just showed how malleable a piece she was. Most children her age would still be a useless mess grieving their loss, but the girl had proven to be a boon exceeding even his initial expectations. Not that he would tell her that. At least not yet.

Regam glanced back at the door now fading from view and thanked the Mother above for the providence allowing Peyeiza to glean the necessity of saving one person from Village Breathwynd.

It had been during one of the Witness's unexpected moments of lucidity when Peyeiza had been present that the shaman learned there was someone within the village where the target of their next search was hiding who must be rescued. Peyeiza had not received a name during the revelation, but that they 'would know when the person is encountered'.

Regam had doubted, but when he had laid eyes on the pathetic, tiny form of what he had at first thought was the girl's corpse he knew; knew in his heart this was the person the Witness had spoken about. A living chain to keep the old man pliant and cooperative as well as a lure to bring her erstwhile friend to Bamaul's feet.

Regam silently praised the Mother for Her blessings and gave penance for his doubts. Because of what the Witness foretold and Peyeiza's untiring efforts the ancient power of what Bamaul sought as the final piece in his ascension was within their grasp. He would let no one interfere with all of their goals coming so close to fruition, no matter whether they be man, dragon, or God.

CHAPTER 11

Clasping his hands behind his back Bamaul stared off into the horizon through one of the large open windows. He consciously avoided caressing his bracelet despite the tugging at his soul to constantly polish and revere the artifact fusing itself to his wrist.

The bells had been quieter than usual after his time with the girl, proving he was slowly, ever so agonizingly slowly, overcoming the adverse effects with which the bracelet was constantly assaulting him. With enough time he would inevitably make the bracelet submit to his will and master its power so he could bring his destiny that much closer to fruition.

The bells in his head clanged loudly in protest for a moment and the bracelet grew unbearably hot, but Bamaul forced these ailments aside with great force of will. Whether the filament of silver embedded deep in the center of the bracelet had a will of its own even Bamaul wasn't sure, but he intended to make that will and that power his own completely before long.

What he *was* sure about were the next steps to be taken

where the girl and her former lover were concerned. His plan for the boy Darien would have to wait for a time, but the sooner they finished the girl's indoctrination the more it would serve his plans. Bamaul's eyes took on a feverish light at the thought of bringing such news to the old man. It was sure to evoke waves of despair in one who once always prattled about optimism and hope so fervently. Staring intently at the setting sun he addressed his ever-faithful head of the Bloodsetters standing at the ready.

"Regam."

"Yes, your majesty?"

"Bloodswear the girl."

Regam remained silent for a brief moment before answering, an act of defiance that would have earned any other in his presence instant death. However, Regam was a trusted, important and invaluable ally who had proven both the worth of his words and strength of arms many times over the years so Bamaul allowed such leeway for him alone.

"Of course."

Bloodswearing the girl would force her to wholly commit to his banner without reservation and with no other recourse than to see their victory through to the end. By all accounts the girl felt more than a little indebted to Regam already, but her confusion about her former friend and lover and the old man was sure to raise some doubts. The death of Regam's subordinate had proven to be a stroke of good fortune; it had sped up the process much more quickly.

He had already taken it upon himself to plant the seeds of

hate and distrust, despite needing to expend some of the hard-earned aura energy stored within that fine silver filament set within his bracelet. It had been unpleasant and more difficult to control than he had anticipated and the ocean of bells in his mind had clanged such a cacophony he felt his soul might explode, but he had endured. The result had been as expected so the pain was more than a fair trade in his mind.

Regam was sure to have his grievances with his orders, but he should be aware of the sacrifices required for accomplishing his goal and what better pawn than an indebted outsider who may not be fully accepted, but usable in so many ways. Her connection to the old man and the boy made the prospect just that much more salivating. He would have to think of a way to mollify Regam somewhat, but that would come after the deed itself was done.

"When?"

Bamaul thought about the mistakes made by Regam's men in their last assignment when they had failed to eliminate the constant thorn in his side that was Philip Lockhart before giving answer. The girl was far from the level qualified to face such a foe and exposing her to the boy at this point would be sure to cause unnecessary complications. A simple excursion involving those unknown to her, preferably foreigners, would be best.

"The girl has had no contact with the people of Het Tapas correct?"

"Correct, your majesty."

"Discover a location of dissenters near our southern border and conduct the next sweep. I am sure there are some locals of descent in the south who would be emboldened enough by the distance between us to give voice to any grievances they may have. Eliminate them as you please, but it is imperative the girl wholeheartedly understands what she is doing is just."

"Your will, your Majesty."

"Make it so as soon as a location is decided upon. I assume you have people in that area already so it shouldn't be too hard to pick a place based on their reports. We will proceed from there as appropriate. You may depart."

Regam bowed and silently left the throne room. Bamaul was sure the leader of the Bloodsetters had some reservations, but this plan was another part of bringing the power of the bracelet and the ancient beings of the world together as one, within him and him alone as they should be.

Regam stalked through the halls, terrified servants bowing deeply and scurrying out of his path to avoid the rage filled visage of the head Bloodsetter.

He wants a woman *to be of the Bloodsworn? Has that artifact finally seized complete control over his mind? Such a thing has never occurred in the history of our people and even if it had she is not close to ready for such a thing. The others will not be pleased when they hear of this, but I have no choice but to follow a direct order from his Majesty. I will have to find a way to keep everyone calm enough to refrain from doing*

or saying anything unnecessary until her ritual is complete.
Even then she will have to be even more isolated from the
others than before. Especially now that Aditsan has been
taken into the bosom of the Mother.

Striding through the halls, the memory of giving Aditsan the mission to get close to the girl came to him almost as a premonition of things to come. The man had been a rare case among the Bloodsetters, Bloodsworn while already wed, and as such had a more amicable demeanor to outsiders the others lacked. It had made him the perfect candidate to 'open up' as a sympathetic figure to the girl and further entwine her in their ways with the faint allure of happiness even in the face of what she viewed as tragedy.

His death had been unexpected and Regam blamed a good portion of it on himself for being careless in sending Aditsan's squad. He had hoped to eliminate Lockhart and the rest all at once, but the boy's presence had been unexpected. What confused him was how such a whelp was able to defeat one of his fully Bloodsworn men when by that messenger's account he had yet to reveal himself as one of the Ryudojin?

Regam supposed the boy must have kept the fact secret, and probably at the old man's direction, before deciding such subterfuge was no longer necessary. He knew the thoughts and concerns on his mind were also unnecessary since he had already received his orders and there was no ignoring them. The brief pause before he gave his reply would have been enough to inform the monarch of his reservations, but even he wouldn't dare give voice to a complaint.

Striding into the central courtyard he discovered the castle guard attempting to drill in formations and doing a sloppier job than usual. The sergeant in charge was barking commands in a falsetto that grated on his ears and was clearly in over his head as many of those commands made little sense. Smoldering on the inside at the sight of such incompetence he almost drew his blade to vent his frustration on the hapless fools pretending to be warriors.

"Sir?"

His hand was stayed by the word of the Bloodsetter he had left stationed there to await his return.

Regam stared balefully at the guards a moment longer before removing his hand from the hilt of his blade.

"We have new orders. Assemble squad 1 and inform them to remain on standby as they await further instructions."

"At once, Lord Regam."

The man ran off to relay his orders and Regam stared at the drilling guards again as if he was scrutinizing their every move, but his mind was elsewhere. However, his presence did not go unnoticed as the sergeant became obviously more agitated and panicked with his cadence and commands. The resulting effect was an even more confused and clustered group of men walking into each other and turning in wrong directions. Many of these men were relatively new, lured by the promise of good pay and security for their families despite the known risks of working within the castle, but there was only so much incompetence that should be tolerated.

Despite his misgivings about the guards and his orders Regam worked out a war within himself and slowly exhaled as he came to terms with how things must be done in the near future. Turning on his heel and walking away he began to put all the pieces of the next sweep together so that the girl would undergo the full experience of what it truly meant to be a Bloodsetter.

"What?" Corly yelped.

"Do not show such surprise! How many times have you been instructed to contain your emotions? This should not come as a shock to you considering all of your training."

Corly had just been informed she would be participating in the Bloodsetter's next mission and she was panicking inside and out.

"I apologize, but why so suddenly? I didn't think I was ready for something like this."

"You are not here to think, only to do what you are told. However, it is true that in terms of combat ability you are lacking when compared to the Bloodsetters who have been serving as your instructors, but in terms of the rank amateurs we are sure to encounter I give you a passing mark, albeit barely."

Lord Regam's words were spoken harshly, but Corly was pretty sure what he said counted as a compliment. She would take what she could get.

"The operation departure time is just before the sun rises so be sure to be ready in all regards for both travel and combat. You have been instructed all this time in combat, etiquette and knowledge by some of the best in those fields so now is the time to show the fruits of your labor. I can assure you that having a prominent role in what is to come over the next few days will go a long way towards the others accepting you in much the same manner as Aditsan."

Lord Regam's words struck a chord at the mention of Aditsan. The kindly face of the Bloodsetter who had been her only friend at the castle came to mind and she struggled to hold back tears. Thankfully she was successful and escaped what would have surely been another reprimand.

"What exactly am I supposed to do?"

"In short whatever you are told, but in terms of our strategy you will be initially responsible as a scout. You and I will approach the target destination ahead of the others to assess the layout and atmosphere. We will be presenting ourselves as an engaged couple traveling to see southern Katama down to Het Tapas so as such you will need to bring appropriate attire for more than just travel and combat."

Corly's mouth hung agape.

"Engaged!?"

Lord Regam glared at her.

"Yes fool! In this particular situation presenting ourselves as such gives the most appropriate excuse for you to be a part of the scout team. Normally one would be sent ahead alone, but you are far from ready for that, nor have you received proper training for it."

"Then why…"

"Because that is what has been decided," Regam snapped.

Corly took a step back at how explosively irritated Lord Regam was, but held tears in check and brought her training to bear.

"I-I understand. I will do my best to not embarrass or disappoint my instructors." She steeled herself from asking any more questions and tried to force her emotions aside in order to focus on her instructions. She didn't like it, but she knew she would have to leave the old Corly from Village Breathwynd behind at some point. No use fighting it any longer.

"Good. I should also inform you of perhaps the most serious aspect of the mission."

Lord Regam paused as if expecting another interruption, but nodded and continued at her silence. "This mission is what is known as a 'sweep'. Its purpose and intent is to discover and eliminate those who plot to oppose King Bamaul's rightful rule over this land. Should they be discovered you will be expected to assist in their termination. Do you understand?"

The blood drained from her face and her throat went dry. A hollow feeling formed in the pit of her stomach and she began to sweat profusely as the insinuation behind Lord Regam's words worked its way through her.

"I-I have to kill someone?"

The words came out as a dry croak and she felt like she might faint. Training was one thing, but to take the life of another human being? She wasn't sure she was even capable of such a thing!

"In the most likely event, yes. I will not lie or play at pretense; it is the most likely scenario based on our intel so you will come to terms with it. I suggest you do so before we reach our destination and not after. It will be much easier for you if you do and I expect as much."

Being given less than a day to get used to the idea of killing another person was less than ideal, but very much in character for Lord Regam. Corly began biting her thumb as she tried to process what these sudden expectations meant for her.

Killing another human being was something that could never be taken back and was an act she probably would never be able to forgive herself for so how should she even begin to prepare for such a thing? Would the Godlings above forgive her, even if her reasons were just and sound as Lord Regam was saying?

Lord Regam's next question broke through her contemplation.

"Has Elnora covered the concept of 'outcome of balance'?"

"No, not at all."

It was a term she had never heard before and she was sure to have remembered if it had ever come up in any of Elnora's lessons. The memory of her teacher's wooden pointer repeatedly thwacking her across the knuckles made her involuntarily wince.

Lord Regam ignored her obvious distress and continued. "It is a term meant to define committing an act that may seem heinous at worst and ambiguous at best, but in the end prevents a greater tragedy from occurring. Do you understand so far?"

"I think so, but not entirely. I am sorry."

"Very well. Take for example an individual who is an everyday normal farmhand. By all accounts he has lived a normal life working the fields, drinking and eating at the local tavern, et cetera. He is to all who know him a normal, hardworking and respectable member of the community. During the course of our mission you are ordered to kill that man. What do you do?"

Corly was sure there was more to the scenario than she had been given, but she couldn't find any reason why that person would have to die.

"I don't understand why."

"Wrong. You kill him. It doesn't matter if you know or understand the reason. This is where 'outcome of balance' comes into play. Now that you have failed to kill that farmhand the very next day he leads a group of dissidents into the village and kills everyone there because he was indeed an enemy of the state playing a role all along. If you had done as you were ordered, this tragedy would never have come to pass. That is 'outcome of balance'. Should you ever fail to find the resolve necessary to do what must be done when it needs to be done then you are the one directly responsible for whatever tragedy occurs later due to your indecision or lack of action."

Corly felt all kinds of conflicting emotions within at Lord Regam's words. She inherently knew killing someone was wrong and would incur the wrath of the Godlings when she is judged in the Next Realm, but Lord Regam made it sound like there would be blood on her hands either way. Trying to think of a counterargument, she dismissed each that came to her as unviable. She wished Oltan was there to give his usual sage advice, but there was no use wishing for the impossible.

Regam waited patiently for her to work through the complex situation for a few minutes, but he spared her no more than that.

"We have precious little time remaining before our departure so I suggest you come to terms with the reality of your situation before then. If it has not already become readily apparent since you arrived here, know that you can no longer cling to the sensibilities and beliefs allowed for a naive country bumpkin. Your life is now entwined with that of our people and our nation so you must completely leave behind who you once were and embrace who you need to become."

Corly felt like she might faint from the weight of Lord Regam's words, but managed to put on a brave front.

"Yes sir."

Regam nodded. "I do not expect you to accept this so

suddenly nor so easily, but you will accept it all the same. It is imperative you do so as many lives rest on our words and actions when conducting a sweep. Prepare yourself however you must. Appropriate attire will be prepared for you upon our departure for both travel and for appearances as my fiancé."

"Yes sir."

Corly found that 'yes sir' was the only reply her brain was capable of evoking and she stood staring at the door for a while after Lord Regam had left the room.

A chill ran down her spine and she resisted a shudder as she lay down upon her pallet without even bothering to change into her nightwear. Wrapping her arms around herself she tried to ignore her cold and clammy hands and closed her eyes in prayer to whatever Godling might be listening.

Please give me the courage to do the right thing and make the right decisions going forward. I don't want to kill anybody, but I don't want people to suffer because I wasn't brave enough to act when I had the chance. I don't know what I should do and I have no time to think about it!

As these troubling thoughts continued unabated in her head, sleep would be a long time coming.

Early the next morning Corly was sure to be awake well before she needed to be despite her lack of sleep. She was already fighting off yawns and her eyelids were so heavy they felt like they had weights attached to them.

She had changed into her normal training attire and made sure she could pack anything she might be told to bring at the last minute. As usual Doris was the first to appear to whisk her away to the outer stabling yard where Lord Regam and the others were already preparing for their departure.

Corly inwardly groaned. Despite Doris having come to fetch her per their usual routine she should have taken the initiative and left on her own and at least brought some additional items from her barracks even though she had been told things would be prepared for her. She instinctively knew she had already fallen a step behind in gaining the favor of the Bloodsetters and vowed to work doubly hard going forward to ensure no further mistakes.

None of the Bloodsetters spared her a glance as Doris plopped Corly's lone sack of belongings at her feet and tittered off to wherever she went at times like this. Steeling herself, she reported to Lord Regam; fully expecting to receive a reprimand for not arriving early.

Lord Regam barely spared her a glance and only pointed at a small wooden cabinet with carrying straps attached to it sitting on the ground nearby. Corly knew this would contain her outfit for her 'fiancé' role so she took extra care when lugging the cabinet over to the horse that had been prepared for her. The last thing she wanted was to ruin the visage of her facade by rumpling or creasing whatever fancy clothing Lord Regam had acquired.

The horse must have sensed her trepidation since it lightly

head-butted her when she went to give it a reassuring pat and get it used to her scent. She smiled and stroked the chestnut mare's snout that sported a beautiful cream slash running up to behind its eyes.

"I'm ok, just a little nervous is all," she said quietly so the others wouldn't overhear. "Let's get along with each other." The horse gave a light snort, but eagerly ate the apple she pulled out of her small sack of supplies and lightly shook its mane.

She was glad her affinity with animals had translated from Breathwynd to the castle since she had thought the only familiar aspect of life at the time of her arrival would behave differently or outright reject her. Thankfully she had learned that animals in general had the same reaction to her here as they had back home. Corly had never had much experience with horses prior to departing Breathwynd, but was happy they accepted her. She finished checking her belongings and giving the horse another once over before receiving the order from Lord Regam to mount.

Regam trod over to give her some last-minute instructions as the others fell into formation awaiting their leader.

"Stay close to me as we still have much to discuss. I hope you have come to terms with the scope and severity of this mission and what it requires of you. If you do not have the resolve to see it through then alternate arrangements will be made, but there will be consequences as such."

Corly took a deep breath. A single night was hardly enough time to adapt to the harsh reality she had been presented with, but looking back at all the training and education she had been subjected to since her arrival she supposed she should have seen something like this coming.

"I understand. I will not disappoint you. Please instruct me well."

"Let us depart then."

Lord Regam spurred his horse forward so suddenly that Corly had to call to bear all of the skills she had learned just in order to keep up with him. The others easily followed suit and Corly again wondered just how she was going to succeed in her role during this mission.

Maybe this won't even be anything major. It's just to check right? It's possible there won't even be any of these 'dissenters' Lord Regam is so worried about. That would be for the best.

Deep down she knew that was just what her heart desired, but her head knew otherwise. Just then her stomach rumbled, reminding her she had yet to eat anything since the previous evening. Reaching into her sack again and pulling out a piece of hardtack she grimaced when she took a bite of the hardened bread. Her jaw was sore by the time she chewed enough to turn it into a palatable mush and frowned as she swallowed. Corly never thought she would miss the tepid stew she had been fed on the road during her travel from Breathwynd to the castle, but here she was. Several of the others had done the same so she was glad she wouldn't be reprimanded for digging into her rations so soon. Taking a drink from her water skin, she mentally prepared herself for a few minutes before urging her mount forward to ride slightly behind Lord Regam and waited for him to acknowledge her.

After riding in silence for a bit Lord Regam finally addressed her.

"Starting from now you will need to act the part of my fiancé as we previously discussed. I had told you to leave the country girl in you behind, but for this operation you will need to draw upon that experience in order to portray a believable front. I assume you are somewhat familiar with the Jarabin people?"

Corly's face twisted in confusion. "No, I am afraid I am not familiar with them." She also wasn't sure how being a former resident of such a remote community as Breathwynd would help her, but she wisely chose to keep that thought to herself.

Lord Regam paused and Corly thought she caught a hint of confusion for a moment before he continued on.

"I see. As we ride, I will explain in detail who they are and what that entails in terms of your actions and behaviors as my fiancé. In short, our story is that I am of the Jarabin marrying someone from outside the tribe for political reasons. The Jarabin are a typically nomadic people who mainly inhabit the plains on the other side of the Breathwynd Mountains so I will be instructing you on their ways and how you should behave as an outsider marrying into the tribe. We will also discuss in detail the area you hail from and why we are in this particular situation so pay close attention."

Corly nodded and continued to religiously chew more of the tasteless hardtack while Lord Regam launched into a diatribe about the meticulous details of the Jarabin people and their way of life. She was shocked to learn there was *anything* over the Breathwynd Mountains, let alone people! It was widely accepted among the villagers that there wasn't anything over past the mountains and who would bother to check anyway?

The sun had risen far overhead by the time they stopped to rest and water the horses and Lord Regam still hadn't finished. Corly's head felt full to bursting with all the information she had been told and was expected to retain.

"As for how you came to be my fiancé, it is imperative you remember you are a child of a prominent noble merchant in the influential town of Northbrush near Pajana's border. Our marriage is political in nature as I said and we are traveling throughout southern Katama as part of the dowry so that a stubborn and spoiled child can 'see the world' before marrying. From now on you should adopt a condescending, arrogant attitude and tone to those around you, especially the residents we will meet, and be more demure, accommodating and respectful when addressing me."

Corly frowned while she took in Lord Regam's instructions. She was still reeling from the information she had received about the Jarabin, especially their liberal views on physical intimacy, so finding the ability to act in a way so wildly different than her usual demeanor in such a short time felt like a daunting task.

"How exactly do I do that?"

Regam looked at her sternly. "It is not that difficult. You see everyone besides me as beneath you and not worth your notice, time or respect. Just being near them is a gracious gift on your part since your status is so high above theirs. It is imperative you act this way in order to incur both loathing and wrath. It will become the catalyst to discovering if there is truth to the information about a dissenter faction forming within the town. Start altering your mindset in this way immediately. The others are aware of your assignment and will not hold you accountable for your words and actions while in the field. However, they *will* hold it against you if you fail to carry out your part to the best of your ability. In fact…"

Lord Regam halted the formation and trailed off, lifting one hand high in the air and wiggling his fingers in a way Corly had learned meant he was communicating with 'the silent language'. She had yet to be taught any of the strange way of communicating, but she was sure it would come in time.

Within moments one of the Bloodsetters came running over and quickly dropped to a knee. "Yes my lord, my lady?"

Corly couldn't hide her surprise at his actions and mode of address. No other Bloodsetter besides Lord Regam and Aditsan ever spoke to her in more than a handful of words outside of her individual training sessions so to be suddenly shown so much deference was startling.

"What...what?"

"What were you just instructed?" Lord Regam snapped. "And close your mouth. A lady would not be staring wide-eyed and slack jawed like a fool!"

Corly snapped her mouth shut and tried to put on a front that felt wildly insincere and inappropriate, but she wanted to do her absolute best with so many people relying on her and with so much at stake.

Bringing some of Elnora's training to bear she straightened her posture and tried to recall some of the other topics of her etiquette lessons. She certainly didn't feel the part, being all dusty from riding in the saddle as she was, but she tried her best.

"Yes. Very well then..."

"His name is unimportant and you do not care or need to know it," Lord Regam instructed her. "Adjust your tone to one haughtier and more arrogant. Tilt your head back while looking down at him since he is only worthy of utter disgust. Once you are dressed the part you will have a hand fan you can use to cover your face as if you are afraid of his very scent getting too close. Think of something you find extremely unpleasant if you need to, but you must drop any hint of an apologetic tone and kindly demeanor for a colder and more disinterested attitude."

Corly thought about what she could do to adopt these mannerisms more efficiently and she came to a conclusion surprisingly quickly. She just had to act like Lord Regam!

She almost smiled at the sheer ridiculousness of the idea, but quickly hid it behind her hand while feigning a cough.

Adopting a stern expression, at least she hoped it was a stern expression, she tilted her head back slightly and stared down her nose at the still kneeling Bloodsetter. Thoughts on how Lord Regam might act and speak ran through her head before she put those thoughts into action. She did, of course, put her own twist on it.

"Ugh. Depart if there is nothing to say. My Lord, is this *thing* truly necessary for our travels? Its presence offends me in both odor and appearance!"

Lord Regam gave a slight nod of approval despite Corly internally screaming at how awful she sounded. Inwardly she prayed the Bloodsetter wouldn't end up hating her despite Lord Regam's assurances.

"I apologize my dear. He is indeed a necessity for our travels as our belongings and stores must be seen to in order to be kept in a presentable condition. Forgive me for that and please tolerate it for some time longer before we return to the border."

Corly had started to take what she thought was a dainty sip of water from her skin and nearly spit it out in an unsightly torrent. She had *never* expected Lord Regam to speak in such a polite and apologetic tone. He even said *please!* Corly was stunned at such a jarring change and she only came back to reality when she heard the normal Lord Regam barking at her.

"Pay attention and do not fall out of your role for even a moment! You must uphold the act even if you are alone! Lives depend on it! Do *not* fail in this task again! Is that understood?"

Corly forced her nerves to settle and tried to slide back into her appointed role.

"Of course my lord. I will not allow such an error to occur a second time. This thing's stench wafting over me seems to have momentarily befuddled my delicate senses."

Corly hoped she sounded like a proper noble lady, like those few she had encountered during her etiquette lessons, but it still made her a bit queasy. Still, she had been given an important role and hoped that maybe the better she was at it then she might be exempted from the more nefarious portion of the mission should that come to pass. It was a faint hope, but she silently clung to it all the same. No doubt Lord Regam would chastise her if he found out so she remained mum on that point.

Lord Regam also fell back into character. "You there! The lady is obviously thirsty! Do you not see her and why have you not aided her with her skin or prepared her tea? Do so and quickly before your head rolls!"

"Yes, my lord," the Bloodsetter mumbled.

Corly had had no idea tea had been an option or that they even had the means to brew it. She wasn't the biggest fan of the bitter liquid, but she could tolerate it some due to her exposure to it during her etiquette lessons. She supposed her current situation was what those lessons were actually for so she pictured in her head how those 'proper' ladies sat, spoke, moved and presented themselves as she waited in order to get into the right frame of mind.

"The tea is pre-prepared so it will only take a little time to heat up to the proper temperature. Please forgive the delay."

Corly was again barely able to cover her surprise at such a drastic change in Lord Regam, but she kept her face passive and murmured a lofty "Quite." like the ladies back at the castle might have done. She definitely wasn't comfortable in her role, but the more she thought about how to act like a combination of Lord Regam and those upper-class women the more she felt like she could get accustomed to it. Now if only her heart would stop fluttering every time Lord Regam spoke in character she might have a little more confidence in herself.

Soon the Bloodsetter returned and again knelt, except this time he proffered a delicate looking cup and saucer filled with lightly steaming tea. Corly initially reached to retrieve them before Regam quickly moved to do so for her and handed it to her directly across the miniscule distance.

"Do not ever try to do anything for yourself. There will always be an attendant for your every need, including myself. Remember this."

Corly nodded that she understood. She had never been waited on hand and foot like this before so the whole experience felt very surreal.

Squaring her shoulders in resolution, she slowly and

daintily sipped her tea like she had been taught and resisted the urge to sigh. It was going to be a *long* few days.

"There it is," Lord Regam spoke as their destination finally came into view. They had camped quite a ways off the main road the night before and now Corly and Lord Regam were astride their mounts on a hill overlooking the industrial town of Cerventa.

The same Bloodsetter who had been working as her exclusive servant stood behind them, ever ready to serve the needs of his false mistress. Corly again hoped the man wouldn't bear any grudges for her words and actions during this mission, but she would worry about that later.

"We will go over the sequence of events again before we head into town."

Lord Regam had dropped his fiancé persona for the moment, but Corly wisely chose not to point that out to him.

"We will enter the town and stay at Sandstone Rest. Vacancy has already been assured and rooms will be ready for us by the time we reach our accommodations due to our associates in the area. You will not drop your persona for even a moment no matter what occurs, even if things get violent before we anticipate it. Only when dissenters are confirmed and targeted for elimination or in the defense of your own life may you act otherwise. Is that understood?"

Swallowing a lump in her throat, she nodded. She still held out hope that everything would end up fine, but she had had a hollow feeling in the pit of her gut ever since the night before their departure.

"If you have not prepared yourself for what is expected of you by now you should do so while you change. Before you make any mistakes or express any misgivings, yes I mean here and yes, I mean now. He will assist you so you should discard any lingering notions of backwoods propriety or modesty. Our mission is of the utmost importance and all of us *will* fulfill our roles without exception no matter what circumstances arise. Is that clear?"

Trying *very* hard to stay in character Corly was barely able to emit a "Yes, m'lord." before her servant aided her dismount. Heart pounding heavily in her chest at the notion of brazenly changing out in the open like this, she supposed she should have seen it coming based on all of her previous interactions with the Bloodsetters.

The Bloodsetter had already laid out a large blanket and had been unpacking her clothing from the black wooden cabinet he had been carrying strapped to his back the entire trip. Corly resisted the urge to apologize for the amount of work that was involved in piecing together the noble outfit laid out for her. Her face went flush and she started to sweat nervously as the Bloodsetter motioned for her to begin undressing from the comfortable, but road-stained clothing she had been traveling in up until now. She was also not a fan of how she smelled at the moment, but Lord Regam had assuaged her concerns by mentioning she would be able to wash up to her heart's content once they reached their inn so she had to endure it until then.

Taking a deep, resolute breath she began the mortifying process of changing her clothing as the Bloodsetter assisted her while Lord Regam stared balefully out over the town.

A short while later a still mortified Corly and Lord Regam slowly approached Cerventa on horseback with her manservant tagging along a little distance behind. Several locals paused to stare at the newcomers in curiosity, but no groups gathered or made much of a fuss about them like what would have happened back in Breathwynd.

Corly, constantly reminding herself of the part she was playing, removed her ornate and large brimmed hat designed to shield her from the sun's rays and lazily fanned herself.

"My Lord, it is much too hot for further travel, but is this *really* where we shall be staying? I was so looking forward to more lavish and civilized accommodations."

She felt absolutely awful for saying such terrible things and the looks on the faces of those who heard her as they plodded along the major roadway into town made her want to beg for their forgiveness, but she had promised not to break character no matter what so all she could do was endure.

Thankfully Regam took charge before she could falter. "You there! Find us appropriate accommodation for the young lady. My delicate bride-to-be is both weary and parched from our travels. Be quick about it!"

The manservant slightly bowed and placed his thumb and forefinger to his brow in a show of both understanding and subservience. Those around them clearly felt sorry for the man and the few whispers reaching Corly's ear confirmed her thoughts. Lord Regam quickly silenced those by glaring at several of the townsfolk with his hand held tightly to the pommel of his sword.

While they waited, they were eventually approached by an officious looking individual with an obviously strained smile on his face. The slightly overweight man sported a well-tailored suit rather than the simple tunic and leggings most of the townsfolk wore and had a silver clasp holding together a leather belt rather than the rope belts most of the men sported. A thick mustache and beard was sprinkled with silver and gray and a small set of spectacles rested upon the ridge of his nose. It was obvious he had dressed up in a hurry as he was slightly out of breath and red in the face, but he gave off an earnest and polite air.

The man doffed his cap and gave them a slight bow while most of the townsfolk who had listened in on their earlier remarks began to shy away and go about their business.

"Good day to you both. I am Famil, the current mayor. How may I be of service this day my Lord and Lady...?"

Someone must have gone ahead and informed him that some important looking people had arrived and should probably be greeted. Corly didn't envy the man, who was clearly nervous, but she didn't dare drop the act.

"Yes. I am Lord Castena of the Nahodine tribe of the Jarabin and this is Lady Carabelle from the town of Northbrush. I am sure you are aware of the significance of each, but I will put that aside for now. Before our upcoming nuptials my bride-to-be absolutely insisted on seeing various parts of southern Katama before she officially joins my tribe. Please indulge us for a time."

The man obviously had no idea what the 'significance' of the Nahodine tribe or town of Northbrush was, but he bobbed his head in feigned understanding all the same. Corly herself was only vaguely aware of things based on what Lord Regam had told her during her briefing, but basically it was a political marriage between an affluent border town and the prominent Jarabin tribe of that area. She didn't know why it was supposed to be important, but she guessed she didn't need to know that much otherwise Lord Regam would have told her.

Famil glanced over at her for just a brief moment while she did her best to feign indifference and acting annoyed before returning to his conversation with Lord Regam.

"Ahhh, yes, yes. Congratulations on your upcoming nuptials. I am afraid we have little interaction with the nobility, but we welcome you and will do our best to accommodate you and make your stay as pleasant and enjoyable as possible."

"My thanks. My young fiancé is quite tired so I hope your hotel...or inn I assume will be enough to allow her adequate rest." Regam made a show of looking around the town in slight disapproval before changing his wording from 'hotel' to 'inn' and the insinuation was obviously not lost on poor Famil.

"You are correct my lord. There are no hotels or the like here. However, our best inn is extremely clean, serviceable and reliable with courteous, informed and well-mannered staff. I am confident you will find it acceptable and enjoy your stay."

Corly would have been more than fine with a straw pallet and a coarse woolen blanket like she had used back in Breathwynd, but she couldn't say that here.

"I'm sure your attendant has been directed to our best establishment by now. Would you allow me to escort you there?"

Famil was sweating so much Corly thought he might pass out and the pained smile on his face made it evident he wished to be anywhere else but there.

"That is acceptable."

Famil almost flinched in regret, but kept to his word and guided them effortlessly through the minor throng of residents. It wasn't all too difficult being on horseback as they were and Corly felt like she might die from the embarrassment of the stares and whispers.

They remained in an awkward silence until finally reaching the aforementioned inn. Famil had been correct in his description as the two-story structure appeared clean, well-maintained and even had an employee outside sweeping the walkway approaching the small wooden porch at the entrance.

Famil gave them another small bow. "Another employee will be here to assist you with your lodging and any

additional luggage you may have, but for now please allow
Arilea here to handle your mounts and any questions you
may have about your stay."

Regam nodded at the man and even thanked him for his
time as Arilea put aside her broom and approached them
with a beaming smile.

"Hello there and welcome to Sandstone Rest! What can I
do ya for?"

The girl was the complete opposite of Famil. She had
blonde hair tied up in a kerchief, sparkling blue eyes and a
bright dazzling smile. A light dusting of freckles across her
nose completed the look of someone you would instinctively
want to be friends with. Normally Corly would have
immediately tried to do so, but Lord Regam had already
coached her with how to act in this exact situation.

"If we encounter any young woman who is conventionally
attractive and seemingly popular in town it is *imperative* you
treat her coldly and with obvious disdain. Your role is such
that any who seem to be any kind of threat to you, socially or
otherwise, be dismissed as less than."

It was scary how stunningly accurate some of Lord
Regam's predictions could be. She sniffed derisively and
looked away while poorly hiding a frown behind her hand-
fan like she had been shown. A flicker of uncertainty
crossed Arilea's face, but she quickly recovered.

"Well then, we can get you and your lovely wife sorted
and set right quick if you could follow Merille...now where is
that girl? Merille!" Arilea shouted. "We have guests!" The

aforementioned Merille suddenly exploded out the front door looking just as disheveled as Arilea was put together and hurriedly came to a stop before giving a lopsided salute. "Sorry ma'am! I'm here!" A crooked grin flashed across Merille's face that when combined with her close-cropped raven dark hair and small facial features gave her an impish look. There was no telling how much trouble this girl caused, but to Corly she seemed spirited and someone who always tried her best.

"I keep telling you that you don't have to salute. This is an inn, not the army! Anyways, the Lord and Lady here need to be seen to the best rooms we have. Just register them at the desk and then bring them to the same rooms as that nice quiet man from a short time ago."

"Yes! I can do that right away!"

Corly also got the impression Merille was the excitable sort and not a little out of her element, but her heart went out to someone who was obviously trying so hard.

"Now then, me an' one of our boys will be taking care of your mounts so no worries there you can be sure. Just follow Merille here and she'll take care of you as you and your lovely wife settle in for your stay."

"Fiancé."

"Pardon?"

"Lady Carabelle is my fiancé. We are not currently wed, but will be when our travels end. I assume we have been assigned two rooms as her manservant will also be staying with her."

"Understood! Be assured we have already prepared our cleanest and most inviting lodgings! You'll find no lack of comfort here! Beds are clean, free of lice and aired out daily. Meals are always included daily too! I can't say there's much in the ways of entertainment for someone used to a much larger city, but there is a small market and various local shops and the like to explore. I'm sure both of you will be able to find something to your liking! Well then, please follow Merille and leave the horses to me!"

Corly heaved a genuine sigh. Not because she was staying in character, but because she was genuinely depressed at how poorly she was expected to treat someone who was so positive, upbeat and likable. Thankfully it came across as annoyance to those within earshot as they dismounted and passed the reins to Arilea, who summarily began to lead the horses to the rear of the inn.

After her manservant had helped her down from her mount Corly lazily fanned herself in an attempt to keep from gawking at all the new sights and sounds around her. It reminded her so much of Village Breathwynd that it made her heart ache.

However, she didn't have much time to reminisce as Lord Regam elegantly linked arms and escorted her along behind Merille. She had to admit he made quite the debonair figure in his neatly tailored clothing. She was reminded of just how muscular and terribly strong he was as they walked and it wasn't as if he was a bad-looking man, in fact at the moment he looked rather dashing. It was just the knowledge of his

demeanor and usual manner of dress keeping her flight of
fancy in check.

A short while later after they had both settled into their
respective rooms there came a loud knock at her door.

"Lady Carabelle, Lord Castena requests you downstairs
for dining. I have also arranged a bath for you should you
desire to do so although it is located within the inn itself. I
have spoken to both the owner and the on-site manager and
have been assured of your utmost privacy."

Despite her wanting to thank the Bloodsetter she kept
Lord Regam's teachings in practice and reminded herself to
keep up her act the entire time they resided in town.

"Very well I suppose. I do hope this...*place* can serve an
adequate fare."

Inwardly cringing even further, she kept reminding
herself over and over again that she didn't know who could
be listening or watching, even when she thought she was
alone. Corly lifted her head and put on what she felt was an
appropriately pompous look and followed the manservant
downstairs.

He led her through the main dining area of the inn,
already beginning to fill up with regulars and curious on-
lookers alike, and through the kitchen before they emerged
into a small room obviously used for wealthier guests and
offering complete privacy. There was even a candelabra set
upon the table as its centerpiece and Corly couldn't begin to
imagine how much of an extravagance that must be.

Arilea was there to greet them and Corly's face twisted

involuntarily.

Why is she here? I can't stand having to treat someone so nice so horrendously!

Bracing herself, Corly forced herself to keep up the act as the meal and reminder of the night thankfully passed uneventfully. The bath had been no more than luke-warm water poured into a wooden tub in the same room they had dined in, but at least the place didn't have the same level of indecency as the Bloodsetters and had plenty of privacy shutters to keep away any unwanted intrusions. Her false manservant was also in close proximity, but she tried not to think about it as she soaked. She was confident he wouldn't do anything inappropriate, but despite her efforts there still remained some of the farm girl from Breathwynd in her who worried about such things.

When she had dressed she met Lord Regam in the main dining area of the inn where he told her in a voice loud enough for everyone to hear that he had arranged for a carriage tour of the town. The other patrons didn't spare much of a glance at the announcement, but it did give rise to several whispered conversations. Corly supposed such a luxury was not common for most people so of course it would give rise to some amount of gossip. Cerventa was much bigger than the village she had been expecting, it was more of a proper town than anything, so she was actually a bit excited for this opportunity. She understood from her briefing it was to be primarily for information gathering and gaining intel on the suspected 'dissidents', but she couldn't help but feel excited all the same.

After a short wait, Corly found herself inside a single horse carriage that had pulled up to the inn just as they exited and after her manservant had joined the driver they began their 'tour' at a slow and steady pace. The interior was much more comfortable and upscale than she had anticipated. The seats were upholstered and were filled with a very comfortable material buffering her from the usual bumps and bruises carriage rides often afforded and even the floor was lined with a soft material unknown to her, but extremely pleasing to the touch. Curtains could be drawn over the windows on either side for privacy, but Regam advised against this as it would seem odd to others why a carriage tour would obscure the only avenue of viewing the town.

He kept his voice low, but informed her the driver was an accomplice from the castle placed here a few years prior. Corly nodded that she understood, but continued to remain in character.

The driver played his part well and once Regam slid open the shutter separating the driver from the occupants he began to regale them with all sorts of information about the town, its charms and most importantly its people. Several times he had an amusing anecdote about one passerby or another who all engaged in some light banter while they trundled by. It seemed the driver had ingratiated himself with the local populace quite nicely and Corly couldn't help but admire how well he had adapted to his role.

She wasn't aware of it at the time, but the driver was also secretly relaying information to Lord Regam while they conversed. Her role at this stage was simply to stay quiet and act bored while observing, which she was fine with. It had been more stressful to keep up the 'young lady" persona than she had thought so she was appreciative for the break from prying eyes.

After about forty-five minutes the carriage softly rolled to a stop and the coachman called out to someone as Corly's manservant pulled open the door for her and indicated she should take his hand and exit the carriage.

Stepping out into the cool evening air she pulled her shawl over her shoulders tightly. She was used to cooler evenings like the ones back in Breathwynd, but she had never been a fan of colder temperatures.

Corly frowned when the heady scent of ale mixed with what smelled like sweat and old straw accosted her nostrils. It took some willpower not to gag. She had been exposed to the concept of ale and liquor during her stay at the castle of course, and had even imbibed a little wine back in Breathwynd during the holiday of Wystern despite not being considered quite old enough by the standards of her village, but this felt far more pungent and raw.

"Apologies for the smell Lady Carabelle, but Lord Castena was insistent on getting a look-see at our local brewery. It is one of our best, if not the best, export of our modest town here."

Part of Lord Regam's backstory as a lord of the Jarabin

was his love of ale and spirits so this particular stop would have made sense regardless, but she knew they had stopped here for a specific reason.

The brewmaster here was the suspected leader of possible dissidents and they were here to meet the man himself at Lord Regam's request for a tour of the facilities. The hope was that Lord Regam would be able to glean any anti-monarch activity from the man, but Corly wasn't exactly sure how that would be possible. She guessed Lord Regam must have some proven methods for something like this; it would be strange if he didn't.

The coachman bowed to her slightly.

"Please accompany me a ways down the road my lady. I am sure the smell is not to a young maiden's liking and I know of a shop that, although humble, provides sweets that are sure to satisfy your palate as a dessert."

Corly exhaled a single petulant sigh.

"Very well I suppose. You! Follow along and don't lollygag behind. I will need you to serve as my packhorse if I see anything worth purchasing!"

Separating herself from Lord Regam was also part of the plan. It was ostensibly to keep up appearances as a young lady of means would never willingly tour a brewery, but she couldn't help but feel like it was because she hadn't been told quite everything. As much as feeling left out of the loop annoyed her Corly supposed it didn't really matter since she wouldn't have a clue as to what was being discussed and didn't have any inclination to enter somewhere smelling so rank in the first place.

A short walk later and she was sitting down in a hastily constructed private area within the pastry shop the coachman had recommended. The staff was noticeably panicked at their arrival and Corly apologized profusely in her head for her behavior more than once. While she patiently waited for Lord Regam to finish his business she politely sipped the lemon tea she had been served with a forced smile of disdain.

I hope Lord Regam finishes quickly. I can't keep this up much longer.

Chapter 12

Regam walked with an arrogant stride and simply nodded in greeting rather than shake the brewmaster's proffered hand. Before the girl had departed the coachman introduced the man in the stained smock as Manuel, which matched his intel. The man was wiry with hairy and spindly arms as evidenced by the exposed forearms underneath the rolled-up sleeves of a light brown tunic. Dark, matted hair and a wispy mustache under a sharply defined nose gave him a sinister look, which suited Regam's purposes just fine. The smock was reminiscent of what a blacksmith might wear, but was stained and smelled strongly of yeast and grain instead of the typical ash and steel of the forge.

Manuel's friendly smile faltered. No doubt he had hoped to win the favor of the noble he had heard about with a friendly demeanor among brethren of similar interests. Regam, however, needed to balance his feigned interest in brewing with his background of a noble rather delicately here. He was confident based on how easily Manuel was made off-balance that he could manipulate things in the direction he wanted them to go rather easily.

"Please understand I am here for the brewery only. Although, I am very interested in both the process and the finished product."

This statement allowed him to reclaim some standing in the brewer's eyes as well as hint there could be a possible benefit for the brewer if he puts up with him for the time being. No small-time brewer, or any small businessman, could resist the prospect of a noble taking an interest in their brand and should it make its way to said noble's table, it could greatly change the course of the brewery's prospects as a whole. As its head brewer it would also change things for Manuel in that he would instantly become recognizable and sought after by those both well-off and connected. It wouldn't be too far of a stretch to say owning his own brewery would become an achievable dream.

None of this would be happening of course, but Regam needed him to believe in the false hope.

Absently wiping his hands on his smock in an attempt to hide his embarrassment Manuel shifted into business mode. Regam gave the man credit for recovering so quickly when a business opportunity presented itself.

"We can begin right away, but is it ok for your fiancé to not attend?"

The man's eyes quickly flitted over towards the retreating figure of the girl and the coachman and back again, an act not lost upon Regam.

"My young fiancé is rather delicate and has no interest in the topic of brewing methods of ales and spirits. She seems to find it rather lewd. Lamentable to be sure, but what woman truly understands the value in such things?"

"Ah, that's a shame to be sure. It's quite an interesting process and we are always researching and discovering new methods and variations."

"I see. Begin the tour. I would like to return to my bride-to-be's side as quickly as I can. I am fortunate she agreed to my little excursion outside her company despite so much uncertainty in this region of the country."

"That's true I suppose, but with her manservant and coachman both accompanying her I doubt any trouble will find her."

"Well that is something I would rather not discuss out here in the open. Lead the way inside as you will."

"Will do! Please follow me."

They entered the brewery and Regam looked around at what was both a greeting area and where several items such as hand-crafted mugs and the like were displayed and available for purchase.

"You sell wares besides the ale? Interesting."

Manuel swelled with pride at the observation.

"Sure do! Hand-crafted mugs and the like, perfect for multiple drinks and easy on the missus for cleaning. Locally made too so the economy here doesn't suffer any due to imports. We're just as proud of our physical wares as we are of the ale itself!"

"Interesting. May I inspect one more closely?"

"Go right ahead. We can even place custom orders, but

that does take some time as they're made from scratch."

Regam idly inspected the various mugs and paraphernalia littering the display shelf. The clerk behind the counter bowed his head and remained silent, clearly uncomfortable with Regam's presence.

He had no interest in the wares or the clerk, but he had a part to play. After a few minutes of feigned interest, he asked to continue the tour.

"Sure thing m'lord. Please follow me."

Manuel led him through a curtain hanging to the rear of the customer receiving area and into the workshop proper. Glancing around Regam assessed the room out of habit. The room was quite spacious and had large barrels placed into three separate groups, all being monitored by brewery personnel. Each group was marked with a large 'X' and had a solid line of a different color underneath the mark. The 'X' was of a uniform color even among the three different groups, but the line underneath varied. Regam remarked off-handedly about this fact, intending to draw the brewmaster into conversation. The employees engrossed in their tasks barely even spared them a glance, which served to send Manuel into a panicked state of apology.

"Please excuse their rudeness! Brewing is a complex task that takes an intense amount of concentration in every step so they cannot spend more than a moment or two away from their station lest the whole batch suffer. You are correct though!"

Manuel was more than eager to explain and gloss over

any offense Regam might have felt at the employee's behavior. Not that he really cared, but it was amusing to see the wretch squirm all the same.

The brewmaster hastily continued his explanation. "Each group gets a different colored line to identify which stage in the malting process it contains during the steeping procedure. The first helps awaken the grain. Once this is complete the grain is moved to the barrels marked with a blue line so they can germinate. The final step is when the contents get moved to a barrel marked in red to get prepared for kilning. The 'X' denotes what batch they belong to. Its color changes each time. After that is when we actually begin the true brewing process so I am afraid there isn't much more to see here."

"How very interesting. May I see inside the barrels before we go?"

"Uh, sure, but like I said there isn't much to see."

Manuel waved aside one of the men looking over the steeping barrels and lifted the lid a crack.

"Please be quick though. We try to limit exposure to outside air as much as possible once the process starts."

Regam humored the man and only took a cursory look inside. It was more to ensure the barrel contained exactly what Manuel said it did and not something else. Anyone under suspicion from the Crown needed to be fully investigated, even if the results of said investigation were a foregone conclusion. Had he not been assigned the task of bloodswearing the girl he would have much rather gone with the more direct and brutal approach, but there were merits to be gained from this method as well.

He followed suit with the other batches before again following Manuel, this time through a wooden door the brewer unlocked with a large iron key he pulled from the oversized pocket of his smock.

The next room was much like the first, but the barrels in this area were less in number and much larger in size. One was noticeably different from the others. "Is that odd looking one perchance made of pig iron?"

"Right you are! This is where we crush the malted grain and then boil it with water brought in from the fire we keep going nonstop in the rear kitchen. We then move them to another area to be drained, cooled and fermented afterwards in order to create the finished product. There is also a trick we use where we add a bit of sweetsage to the mix, but please understand how that is utilized is kept confidential for business purposes."

"I see. I am familiar with yarrow and rosemary being utilized, but never sweetsage. I wasn't aware it grew around here."

"Well, that's the part that's a bit tricky. We have to harvest it from elsewhere and it can be a bit dangerous cause you have to travel a little too close to the Grove for most people's liking."

"I can see how that would be rather unsettling. We did see a portion of it during our travels, but not close enough to fear anything untoward occurring. There are not many who would willingly brave the undertaking of even getting close. Especially considering the distance between here and there."

"Right you are. It can really fray your nerves, that's for sure!" Manuel laughed nervously.

Regam found this particular piece of information quite relevant to his investigation. It generated concern that a business operating in this area would send employees as far as the Grove and indicated it was more of an excuse to travel without raising suspicion among the soldiers assigned to patrol the Travel Road. It was possible they may hire out contractors for the task, but Regam doubted this was the case.

"Would you care to taste the finished product?"

Regam felt the man was trying to rush through the remainder of the tour with his suggestion, but moved ahead just as well.

"Of course. Lead the way."

Manuel guided him through yet another locked door and into a storage room filled with untapped wooden kegs and led him to the farthest one to the back. He pulled a tap from a nearby shelf and carefully, but expertly adjusted it before filling a wooden serving cup and taking several experimental sips as if he had done so hundreds of times in the past.

Once he was satisfied the taste was up to standard he proffered another cup to Regam and offered up a toast.

"To the health of you and yours and to the happiness of your matrimony!"

"Of course."

Regam tilted his cup towards Manuel's but avoided making contact as a commoner would.

Manuel downed his drink in one go as Regam took a healthy sip. A bitterness typical of the region's ale was quickly offset by a light sweetness lingering on his tongue for a moment. Regam decided it was not altogether unpleasant and was somewhat surprised to find he had no qualms with the brew. Manuel glanced at him nervously, his concern about Regam's thoughts evident on his face. The brewmaster's nerves were definitely getting the better of him, but Regam had been waiting for him to mention the girl again.

Staring morosely into his cup Regam 'accidentally' sighed.

"I do hope to be able to make it all the way to the actual ceremony without any further involvement from the crown's representatives, but we can only do so much."

Manuel had already emptied his second cup, but noticeably paused at Regam's obvious lament. He looked like he had a question on his mind, but was holding himself back. Regam needed to make one more push and based on the way the brewer's eyes had lingered on the girl he knew he had him.

Regam downed his own cup as if to give himself courage and Manuel refilled it for him. "I probably shouldn't say more, but you have trusted me with most of the secrets of the process of your craft so it is a fair trade I suppose. Have you noticed the one attending to her while we have been here?

Surely you have noticed the situation is not quite up to the standards of propriety."

Manual stared at the dregs of his ale and nodded. "Yes. I assumed a noble-born young lady would have a lady-in-waiting of similar age attending to her needs. Her attendant seemed more suited as a manservant for one such as yourself."

Regam let out a loud breath. "Yes. Indeed, that was originally the case on both accounts, but the girl in question suddenly fell severely ill on the eve of our departure. The representatives of the crown who were present to officially recognize both the union and the agreement with my tribe graciously allowed the manservant they have loaned me to take her place instead. I am sure you can understand how I could not refuse and how…suspicious the circumstances could seem to be."

Manuel nodded with a look of both anger and despair on his face. "Don't want to risk angering the king, that's for sure."

"Indeed. However, I fear those officials and that manservant all have an ulterior motive, which may bode ill for all of us. As I'm sure you are aware, there are those who look less than favorably upon the Jarabin people and as such certainly have unvoiced complaints about our blessed union."

Manuel nodded, but Regam could tell the man lacked understanding so he continued as if discrimination of the Jarabin was a well-known fact. "I wholly believe there will be an attempt to sabotage our arrangement in some fashion and that the man may have been promised certain…liberties I will not give voice to. In fact I believe his patience is wearing thin and he may even act upon his desires as early as tonight based on my observations of his manner over the last few days. The lust is palpable in his eyes."

Manuel looked confused. "Then why allow them both out of your sight for something like a tour of a brewery?"

Regam shrugged. "This town had already been a part of our itinerary from the outset and my fiancé both dislikes change and enjoys her space. Not to mention she is rather clever despite her youth and would know something to be amiss had I canceled the one aspect of our trip I had insisted upon. Additionally, it could alert those plotting what may come to the fact I am suspicious of their intent and that could lead to more problems from the castle itself that I am hardly equipped to contend with. Thankfully the coachman in charge of the tour was more than understanding of my concerns for my bride-to-be's safety during the booking process and agreed to accompany her when she was not by my side, for an additional fee of course."

Manuel barked a short laugh. "Yea, he is a trustable and upright man for sure, but not above making the most of a business opportunity. There are few others like us when it comes to the crown's designs upon the common people."

Manuel glanced sidelong at him as he filled his cup for a third time and Regam offered his own in a sign of comradeship.

"That is pleasing to hear. Perhaps we could make a trade of some sort to ensure my fiancé's safety and chastity while we reside here?"

"What would that entail exactly? I am just a brewer after all, so I'm not sure what kind of aid I could provide."

"Understandable. However, as one who has devoted many years to the art of the sword your gait and balance give you away to those with a certain amount of knowledge of the craft. I would find a way of disguising that quickly lest you attract unwanted attention."

Regam had noticed rather quickly by Manuel's movements he was at least somewhat competent with the sword, not to mention if he was one of the ones traveling outside of town for supplies he would have to have at least some way of defending himself. Hinting that Manuel could give himself away to anyone looking closely was a bit of a risk, but Regam hoped the comment was interpreted as a friendly warning to simply be careful.

"Not to mention your strength of character and willingness to speak out even here against certain…imposed injustices shall we say, gives me great confidence in you. Not to mention your public profile and connections are another form of strength as well."

This was the most delicate part of the conversation. Regam had insinuated he knew there was more to the man than just a simple brewer and playing on his sympathy and acting as a comrade in their views of the crown were to lower his guard. If he pressed too hard the man would undoubtedly clam up and sever the talk they both understood they were having, but Regam counted on his reported sense of justice and the liquid courage coursing through the brewmaster in order to get him fully committed.

"If I may ask, what would you be offering?"

Regam inwardly smiled. The bait had completely hooked the prey.

"I can guarantee a direct route to my soon to be father-in-law's table and a rather…positive recommendation to those within his circle. Even my own tribe is not completely off the books as a potential buyer, but that would be for future negotiations once we have come to an accord. There is also an unwed sibling of Lady Carabelle that may or may not be in the market for a spouse in the near future, but as to how to receive a noble recommendation for engagement I cannot say."

Manuel's eyes gleamed at the insinuation his brew could grow from local to 'high-class' and imbibed by nobility in such a short amount of time. His face grew even more flushed at Regam's mention of the girl's non-existent sibling. It was an offer that no-one would be able to refuse.

If there was a unilateral trait Regam knew he could take advantage of it was the innate greed humans possessed. It was usually that or lust always pulling the noose tightly and neatly around his targets' necks. This time it was both. He again briefly lamented not being able to utilize the display of power he favored like how they had handled the old man's village, but this method did have its own feeling of satisfaction as well.

"That does sound intriguing, but what is it exactly you would like for me to do?"

Regam began to explain in detail what his 'intel' was on the manservant and what this villain had planned and when the plan would be executed. There were several minutes of back and forth between the two men until a satisfactory accord could be reached. They clasped forearms to seal the agreement as an oath; one that Regam inwardly disregarded as soon as it was made. Once the night's activities concluded Regam was more than sure the girl would be completely under his thumb and the king would be pleased that his instructions had been carried out so flawlessly.

Regam still did not like the idea of the girl being Bloodsworn, and neither did his men, but he was far past the point of return. He hoped the king would be a little more forthcoming with his own designs on the girl, but he knew not to push too heavily into something the king didn't offer of his own volition.

Manuel quickly finished the tour and led Regam out a rear exit and back around front just as the girl, coachman and manservant returned from their excursion.

"Good evening, Lady Carabelle. I hope the tea was to your liking," Manuel said with a slight bow. 'Lady Carabelle' sniffed and ignored the comment as her manservant assisted her into the carriage.

"Ahh…"

"Don't worry about it," the coachman whispered. "the

young lady is a bit distressed by the smell."

"Oh, I see."

Regam nodded a farewell to Manuel and joined his fiancé in the carriage. He withheld any mention of his agreement with the brewmaster and they all continued their respective act for the remainder of the evening.

"You should get some rest my lady. Tomorrow will prove to be both taxing and laborious. It would be best to be prepared." This phrasing had been decided upon as the designated code to inform her the main portion of their mission was to occur the following day. Little did the girl know that it would only be a few more hours before the real entertainment would begin.

Corly was exhausted, sweaty, irritable and no less stressed than usual at having to pretend to be such an obnoxious high-class noble for so long. Being alone with the coachman and manservant had put a strain on her she wasn't sure she could withstand again. She just wanted this whole thing over with.

Corly was thankful to get out of those stuffy clothes even if for only one night. They were just so hard to move around in! She was already dreading having to bundle up again into that frilly nonsense when the slightest creak of the floorboards outside caused her entire body to tense and move as if possessed.

Rolling over the bed to put it between herself and the door she landed on her feet just in time for it to explode inwards, sending shards of wood everywhere. She had already retrieved and unsheathed her sword from where it had laid hidden underneath the bed for emergencies. All of her training during her stay at the castle was immediately put to the test as a man dressed all in black leapt into the room and fluidly tossed a dagger at her with an underhand throw. A hood covered his face in shadow and there was nothing to mark who he was or where he had come from, but Corly didn't have time to dwell on it.

It was a tactic Corly had been subjected to before. Knocking the airborne blade aside, she dodged the assailant who had drawn his blade and nimbly bounded over the bed with murderous intent.

"Intruder! Help!" Corly shouted as for the first time she crossed swords with someone who was truly trying to kill her. She heard a commotion coming from the common room downstairs and assumed help would be forthcoming momentarily. She just had to stay alive until then.

The assailant grunted as they exchanged blows in the flickering of the lone candle still lighting the room, giving the entire scenario an eerie vibe. Corly's hands were slick with sweat and she could feel the unpleasant sting from places where the assailant's blade had slipped past her defenses.

There was still a lot of shouting and noise from elsewhere so she guessed this person had brought friends. Ducking a swipe aimed at her neck Corly kicked him as hard as she could in his manhood while simultaneously almost landing a solid blow to his side he was somehow still able to block. Not very elegant, but Aditsan had been adamant about adding it to her arsenal. A startled grunt indicated she inflicted a great deal of pain, but the man determinedly continued his assault.

Immediately swiping at his neck Corly was rewarded with the slightest nick, but she left herself wide open in her impatience. She winced in anticipation of the pain that was about to erupt, but instead she felt a light prick in her ribs.

She took a chance and opened her eyes to find herself staring into the eyes of the smiling Bloodsetter who had been acting the part of her manservant. Corly finally understood what was happening and an immense sense of relief washed over her to the point she almost collapsed to her knees. Lord Regam had mentioned during their travels that her training was far from complete so this must have been a continuation of the 'night attacks' she had endured a while back that had lessened in number recently. Why he chose now of all times baffled her, especially with the attention she had inevitably drawn to herself by shouting for aid, but it was too late to lament that decision; she was just glad it hadn't been an actual assassination attempt.

She supposed she should have known. It's not like anyone would want to go after a nobody like her and Lady Carabelle didn't actually exist so there shouldn't be any political enemies after her life. Corly expected Lord Regam to appear at any moment and chastise her for making a scene.

The manservant then did something totally unexpected.

"Good work, girl...no Corly. You have improved greatly

and do Aditsan's memory justice."

Corly was stunned. She had never gotten this much praise from anyone besides Aditsan and she couldn't stop a silly grin from spreading across her face. The manservant placed his hand on her head and nodded in approval. Corly's heart swelled with pride at this gesture of acceptance and acknowledgement.

That moment of joy was short lived however, as the Bloodsetter cocked his head to one side and frowned at the continued noise from downstairs.

"What's the matter? Shouldn't we let them know it was a false alarm?"

The Bloodsetter nodded. "Yes. Normally that would have been the plan, but there are unfamiliar voices mixed in with the Bloodsetters that had been arriving in secret since you retired to your room. It seems we may have been sniffed out by the dissidents Lord Regam was trying to confirm and decided to strike first while we were unaware. Stay close to me and do not leave this room, especially since you are both so lightly armed and lightly dressed."

Looking down at her sweat-soaked shift Corly suddenly felt mortified since it left nothing to the imagination. The manservant removed his hooded mantle and draped it around her as the sound of footsteps pounding down the hallway could be heard getting closer.

Tightly wrapping the mantle around her with his muscular arms, he got a little too familiar for her comfort, but she had gotten somewhat used to the ways of the

Bloodsetters so she didn't offer any resistance. Plus, she was smart enough to understand there wasn't time for complaints if they really were under attack.

Just as he had tightly covered her up he again placed a hand on either side of her head.

"You have promise. Do not disappoint Lord Regam."

"Yes!"

Corly had hoped the aforementioned Lord Regam would be the first on scene, but instead another arrived in the form of a familiar face she had seen somewhere before. The man was dressed in the light brown tunic of a commoner and before Corly could comprehend what was happening he grabbed her away from the Bloodsetter and forcibly thrust her out into the hallway where she struck her head against the wall. Her vision blurred at the force of the impact and she slumped heavily to the floor, but barely held onto consciousness.

Corly suddenly felt like something very bad was about to happen, but her tongue swelled from where she had bit it and it was difficult to form any coherent thoughts, let alone words.

She watched through hazy vision as the man began swinging his blade at the Bloodsetter. For a few moments it seemed like the Bloodsetter would easily overpower whoever this was, but he suddenly lunged towards her, ignoring the other man completely and leaving himself open to an attack from behind.

"Get out of-"

The next thing she saw was the pointed end of the other man's blade piercing through the Bloodsetter's chest and blood spurting from his mouth in a froth. Confusion reigned over Corly like a curse at the sight. Her already addled mind couldn't comprehend how somebody who seemed less skilled than her instructors just killed one of Lord Regam's Bloodsetters. It didn't make sense. *Nothing* was making sense! She had finally gotten praised by one of them and all of a sudden someone showed up and killed him right in front of her! No, it was *because* of her. If he hadn't stopped to try to get her to safety then she was sure he would still be alive. It was her fault. If only she hadn't been so slow to realize what was happening the Bloodsetter would be alive and everything would have been settled. Corly could only hazily focus on one thought. *This had to have been done by the dissidents that Lord Regam warned me about!*

Her worst nightmare about this trip had come true and now someone was dead because of her lack of ability and decisiveness. She couldn't handle it.

Despite the insanity of the last few minutes only one thing dominated Corly's consciousness. Rage. Pure, unadulterated rage at another one of the Bloodsetters who had her under his care having his life stolen from him.

Rising to her feet, she felt an odd sense of detachment as her heart grew cold. Her body moved on its own and she felt as if in a dream. The Bloodsetter had been doing nothing more than his job and performing the role he had been assigned. Corly couldn't imagine he had been pleased to be made to act as a servant to a village girl like her, but he had never once complained or shown any resentment towards her, even when alone, so why? Why did this happen?

Why do these things happen to the people I care about? Why are they all being taken from me one by one? I didn't even get to know his name!

She had been determined to get each and every Bloodsetter to give her their name like Aditsan and to earn their respect when all was said and done. She never even had the chance to ask. She would never get the chance to do so.

The Godlings were mocking her effort and determination. It was happening far too frequently to be a coincidence!

Why are you doing this? Why are you taking everyone from me? Why do innocent people have to die? I can't take this anymore!

Corly screamed in rage and rushed into the room, stumbling slightly in her stupor but still retrieving her blade from where it had fallen when she had been shoved. The man turned and began to speak "Thank the Godlings I made it in ti-", but Corly was further enraged by the triumphant look on his face and didn't care what he had to say. Quickly and efficiently she slashed his throat with a reckless lunge that should have invited a lethal counter-strike, but his guard was down since he obviously didn't see her as a threat. Later on, she would wonder how she acted so coldly and irrationally, but right now only seething anger clouded her thoughts while heightening her senses. Her entire body was hot and prickly underneath the mantle and she heaved gasps for air while looking over the two corpses at her feet.

The noise from elsewhere in the inn was muffled, as if happening at a great distance. Corly screamed again in frustration, rage and grief until Lord Regam finally arrived. Sword in hand, the head Bloodsetter warily inspected the two bodies lying in pools of expanding blood and checked for signs of life while Corly stood staring vacantly at the scene. Her entire being felt like it belonged to another and that she was watching someone else experience these events from outside her own body.

Everything felt numb. Even after killing another person for the first time she felt nothing. Just a vast emptiness. Her rage and emotion had left her with her last scream and her mind refused to accept the finality of the chaos raging around her.

Lord Regam brought her back to reality by shaking her and repeatedly calling her name. Corly almost stabbed him out of instinct until her mind registered his face.

That was the moment when she realized he was no longer in the noble garb of his alias, but in his normal Bloodsetter attire. His blood-red Makavai hung loosely from one end of his headdress and the midnight color of his tunic was an all too ready reminder of the Bloodsetter who had just been killed.

"Are you unharmed?"

Corly was barely able to nod as the adrenaline and strange sense of detachment slowly faded.

Her entire body trembled and shook as others filed into the room. The Bloodsetters who had been arriving after being on standby outside of town now had the inn on complete lockdown.

Regam grabbed her by the arm and roughly shook her back to her senses before full blown panic could set in and shouted at her.

"Look at me!"

Pain coursed through her as his hand tightened around her arm and the harshness of his voice captured her immediate attention, but her breathing continued in ragged breaths while tears fell unnoticed from her eyes.

Regam began speaking in a quieter, but firm tone. "You have done nothing wrong. Nor is there guilt to be felt about what has transpired. The shock of taking a life for the first time can be a heavy burden to bear, but you must force both your body and mind to come to grips with reality as you may have to do so again in the future."

Corly's eyes widened in panic, but Regam shook her again.

"Do not fear this! Your role in shaping the future of this country will only grow from here. In order to do so you must accept what has occurred and never forget the feeling welling up inside of you in the here and now as taking a life is never an insignificant matter. Recall what I have already told you. We spoke about if our intel was proven to be valid then taking a single life may save many others. Your actions here are not shallow, empty or meaningless. They have value. Even Nasingo would approve of your actions despite his own noble sacrifice."

It took a moment through the fog of her mind for Corly to realize Lord Regam was referring to the Bloodsetter who had been acting as her manservant all this time.

She glanced over to where his body lay, but Regam released her arm and quickly grabbed her by the face and forced her to continue to look at him.

"Mourn him if you must, but do not feel remorse. He knew the risks of this assignment and had his affairs placed in order before we departed, as did all of us. Remember his face and his name in your heart and carry them with you as we move forward to bring prosperity and peace to the inhabitants of this land. It is your responsibility to do so now."

Lord Regam held her gaze as Corly's breathing and body slowly came back under control. He shook her by the head again as her eyes began to wander around the room at all the activity.

"Listen to what you are being told! There will never be another moment in your life as monumental as this, at least for now, but do you not realize just how important tonight's events are concerning the safety and security of this country? This is what we do. This is what we must do. What *you* must do!"

Corly could tell he was trying to tell her something pretty important, but her mind was still a jumble of thoughts and fog of emotions so his words weren't quite connecting.

"I-I'm sorry. I don't really understand."

She felt horrible, both at the events of the last several minutes and because she knew from his words Lord Regam was trying to get her to understand the significance of her actions, but she just couldn't process it all at the moment.

Regam sighed and finally let go of her face. He pulled her off to the side as Bloodsetters and some very terrified looking staff filtered in and out of the room. One of them quickly mentioned the local constable was downstairs awaiting their presence before scurrying off without waiting for a reply.

Corly's face drained at the prospect of being imprisoned for the crime of murder and the harsh sentence that would surely follow.

Lord Regam must have seen the terror on her face and guessed her line of thought.

"You have nothing to fear. You acted in self-defense and in the defense of another. I myself will give testimony to not only your character but to the veracity of your account. Not to mention you will be afforded the same consideration as the rest of us as befitting of your new station."

Again Corly was confused, but Lord Regam forestalled any questions by snapping his fingers as a Bloodsetter who had been standing guard by the entrance came to his side and handed him a bundle of clothing.

"This outfit belongs to you now that you have proven yourself worthy of it. They were custom made to fit your frame prior to our departure in case of an event such as this. Normally a ceremony would accompany the first time one dons the garb, but we are pressed for time. Change quickly and then accompany me."

Corly resisted the urge to ask the dozen or so questions she suddenly had as she calmed down. She was not fond of his instructions, but she was more or less used to having to expose herself in the most embarrassing of scenarios. Not that she had been given much of a choice.

Regam wiggled his fingers at his subordinate. *Pick up Nasingo and get him out of here quickly!* The Bloodsetter hurriedly picked up Nasingo's 'corpse' and quietly left the room unnoticed amongst the chaos.

Never noticing the exchange, Corly chose the least busy corner of the room and quickly and obediently began to change into the pitch-black leggings and tunic she had been given. Supple and sturdy boots slipped comfortably over her diminutive feet and the accompanying sash pulled everything a little more tightly than she would have preferred. Only when she came down to the final piece of the ensemble did she finally realize just what it was that she had been given to wear.

The final piece was meant to be worn as a headpiece. One she had seen the other Bloodsetters don a countless number of times day in and day out. With slightly shaking hands she did her best to imitate the actions of the others whom she had always watched so closely as she wrapped it around her head and folded it in such a way that a single piece was left hanging to the side, ready to be drawn across the face at a moment's notice and colored the deep red of blood. The ritual headgear of one acknowledged as a Bloodsetter. Her very own Makavai.

As soon as she finished Lord Regam raised his hand and ordered all of the inn's staff out of the room, an order which they were all more than happy to comply with, and all of the Bloodsetters froze.

Lord Regam took on a solemn tone and he boomed out in a voice brimming with pride and strength.

"She has been bonded and bound by blood."

"She has been bonded and bound by blood!" intoned the others in unison.

"By oath. By deed. By name. She is Bloodsworn!"

"She is Bloodsworn!" the others echoed.

Corly wasn't sure how to respond, but Lord Regam motioned for her to rejoin him. Placing a hand on her shoulder he told her something she thought she would never hear in her lifetime.

"You are one of those bonded and bound by blood. One of the Bloodsworn. A Bloodsetter in body, mind and deed. You are dedicated to bringing justice and prosperity to this land and to defend it from those who have no rightful claim to its bounty. One who is ever vigilant and ready to lay down life and limb or take them as such in the course of your duties. You are the Bloodsetter Corly, but you are also whoever you need to be, wherever you are called to be it. You are one of the pillars of this nation and will be the bridge to bring it forward into the next generation...or you will die trying. Do you swear your oath on this?"

Corly was overwhelmed at such a shocking turn and at the solemnity of Lord Regam's words. The flow of events had suddenly sped up and she knew this was a pivotal moment in her life and that it was an oath she could not refuse. Taking a deep breath, she thought one last time of Village Breathwynd, Oltan, Aditsan and especially Darien. She swore to herself she would ensure none would suffer as she had and would protect those who couldn't protect themselves, even if it meant opposing someone she had loved.

"I swear it!"

At the time, Corly wasn't aware it would only be a few more months before that oath would be put to the test.

Chapter 13

Darien gasped for air and spit on the cavern floor. He grimaced at the taste of blood mixing in with the mucus and saliva.

I guess I'm still not fully recovered from melding with Koseki.

He hadn't quite felt one hundred percent since then, even when Koseki had manifested and they had spent their time together at Little Maiani's, but he had kept that from the others in order to keep them from worrying.

However, now he had a much greater worry standing in front of him. Wave after wave of rage, anger, grief and fear undulated off his longtime friend. Had things not happened as they had, the two of them likely would have become lovers, but as it was now that was a distant and painful memory.

At the moment, the person who had once been the closest in the world to him besides Oltan was not only somehow alive, but dressed as a Bloodsetter and actively trying to kill him. If Koseki was still here she would undoubtedly find the situation hilarious, but according to General Lockhart she had been taken somewhere by Hosroyu and he didn't have time to casually ask for an update even through the link.

He did get the overall impression she was fine so he let it pass for the time being. He just had to stay alive long enough to figure out what exactly in the Hells was going on.

Corly looked just as exhausted as him and he couldn't begin to imagine what had happened to her since their village had been decimated, but she wasn't in the mood for conversation, that was for sure.

The moment her Makavai had been ripped free Darien had momentarily frozen in shock at seeing Corly's tearful visage marred by anger and injury. Unfortunately, she had taken that opportunity to try to skewer him through the heart and he had only made it through that situation alive thanks to the reflexes and instincts he had honed learning from Jack, Tartas and others from the Order of the Fist.

Blood seeped from the wound across the bridge of her nose while he felt the initial injury from when she had stabbed him healing and already crusting over. He could also feel blood already clotting and healing the other, smaller wounds she had inflicted during their exchanges.

Darien was unsure what to do in this situation. Had it been a normal Bloodsetter he would have fought his hardest to survive long enough to escape from here, even if it meant killing him. He had resolved himself to having to do so a long time ago during his stay within the Order, but neither escaping or harming Corly felt like the correct option with her standing there right in front of him.

"Corly. What...How...?"

The words tumbled out in a confused stutter, but the only answer he received was an ear-splitting screech rivaling that of the Movai as she launched into another frenzy of slashes. Fortunately, her pattern was the high-low combination often favored by the Bloodsetters he had learned to counter from Jack and Tartas so he was easily able to avoid further harm for the moment.

Holding back from returning any of his own strikes, despite having ample opportunity to do so, he tried to think of how to stop her long enough to figure out what happened to her and why she was trying to murder him. The biggest, and most obvious question was how she managed to survive and why she was acting like a murderous Bloodsetter. They were the people responsible for burning most of their village to the ground and slaughtering their friends and families; if anything, she should be trying to escape with him!

Inhaling deeply, Corly grunted and made as if to attack him again. This time he was able to conjure up a semblance of a plan, one that would only really buy some time to talk, but he hoped it would be enough.

When she began her next series of attacks he parried her blade and ducked low in order to drive the point of his elbow deep into the pressure point directly above the stomach and just below the sternum. Doing so immediately drove all of the air out of Corly's lungs and she sank to her knees with a panicked gasp.

Moving quickly before she could recover Darien knocked

her blade away and placed the edge of his own against her neck. He did so not to threaten her, but to keep her in one place long enough to ask what in the Hells had happened to her.

"Why in the Hells are you trying to kill me?! Why are you dressed like that? How did you make it out of Breathwynd alive? What happened to you?!"

Trying to catch his breath, all his questions came out in a jumbled rush. Corly remained silent and glared at him with anger smoldering in her eyes. The rapidly changing mists of color swirling and writhing around her hadn't lessened any, but the momentary respite allowed him to deal with it a little better and they became less of a problem.

Tears formed at the corners of his eyes when he looked down at Corly. He was so relieved to find she was alive that he wanted nothing more than to cry, embrace her and tell her how happy he was to see her. The words died in his throat as she viscerally growled at him and finally gave an answer.

"Aren't you going to kill me and feed off of me like you did to everyone else? Go ahead! You're an absolute monster for everything you've done! My parents! Mistress Wavely! Master Beldhar! They all loved you and look at what you did to them! Everyone in the village…even Aditsan…"

Darien didn't know what Corly was talking about or who Aditsan was, but the rest of what she was saying baffled him.

"What are you even talking about? Feed off you? What

does that even mean?"

"SHUT UP! You can't deceive me! I know all about you and what you really are, what you always have been! You used everyone in the village like fodder and treated us like fools! And when you knew his majesty had found Oltan you decided to destroy everything and everyone before trying to erase all signs that you had ever been there at all!"

"What? That's not what happened at all? Who in the Hells told you something so ridiculous and why would you ever believe them?"

Corly didn't hear him. She was spewing out all her pent-up rage, grief and frustration and Darien was too busy trying to alleviate the effects of the mists while trying to protect both of them from the falling debris to properly concentrate.

"You didn't get everybody though! Lord Regam found me and saved my life. They took me in and gave me a new home and taught me so many things, more than Oltan could ever teach! I promised I would avenge everybody with my own hands and now you're mocking me!"

Corly slightly leaned into his blade and a trickle of blood ran down her slender neck.

"I can tell what's behind those wretched eyes of yours! You're an abomination! I can't believe I was naive enough to follow you around all those years trying to get your attention and thinking you were so gentle and kind. I can't believe...I...loved you."

Corly dissolved into a mess of sobs and any response or

words of comfort he could think of caught in his throat. His emotions were a warring mix of relief at finding her alive, confusion about what she was accusing him of and anger at those who had so thoroughly deceived her. Because his mind couldn't focus properly he just ended up repeating himself, which proved to be a mistake.

"What in the Hells are you even talking about! None of that is true!"

"It is!" Corly choked out between sobs. "You've been hiding in the village all this time, you and Oltan! Just waiting long enough for you to feed on everyone's auras and use it for yourselves! I know everything!"

Darien still had no clue what she was ranting about, but it was clear someone had filled her head with malicious lies and poisoned her against him. He would never forgive those who were responsible for turning his closest friend against him, but the desperate look of anger and fear on Corly's face made him decide he should try to get a little more information out of her, at least before she went back to trying to unalive him.

"Corly, I…"

"Stop! I don't want to hear any more! Just kill me already!"

Darien's emotions boiled over and he finally snapped in anger and started a rant of his own.

"Will you shut the Hells up and actually listen for once! Godlings above, you never let me finish anything I'm saying!"

"You shut up! I don't want to listen to anything you have to say, you lizard bastard!"

"I...I'm not a lizard!" Darien bellowed so loudly the cavern shuddered so hard even more fragments of rock and sediment rained down around them.

Corly stumbled onto her backside at the force of Darien's voice and tears continued to mix with the blood seeping from her wound.

Darien quickly moved to place his blade against her neck again, sure that she would start attacking given the chance and took several breaths to calm himself. He wasn't sure why, but he had never felt so insulted in his entire life.

Steeling himself, Darien spoke quickly and quietly through gritted teeth in the hopes of not giving Corly another chance to interrupt.

"First of all, I am not a lizard. I want to make that clear, ok? Secondly, I haven't always been like this. It only happened a few months ago after I met Koseki and her mother in the Grove. And Godlings above, I had nothing to do with what happened back in the village. I was locked in the library thanks to Oltan and didn't make it out until everything was over. Do you know what that was like? Finding the village completely destroyed and seeing everyone I've ever known lying lifeless on the ground? Even Beatty! Do you know what they did to her? I don't even want to say it! Now I suddenly find you're alive and are not only trying to kill me but are working with the people responsible for what happened to Village Breathwynd in the first place!"

"That's not true! They saved my life!"

"It is true! I've seen what they are capable of.
Destroying, pillaging, wasting resources and killing innocent
people! Remember that stranger who appeared in the
village just before we were attacked? Who do you think
gave the rest of the Bloodsetters the go ahead to invade the
village? Are you daft?"

Darien's emotions were starting to get the better of him
and his training from the Order of the Fist wasn't helping as
the stress of the situation was causing him to unravel.

"You're lying! He was there to stop you!"

"No, I am not! I don't know why they spared you, but
they are the bad ones, not me and Oltan. Do you even
understand how many people they've killed? How many
times they have tried to kill me? How terrified, angry and
alone I was until General Lockhart and the others found
me? I even went into the Grove alone! Do you even
understand how wracked with grief and guilt I was after
losing everyone…after losing you?"

Corly fell back with a twisted look on her face and finally
broke down completely, all thoughts of battle and bloodlust
forgotten as she sobbed and screamed "no, no, no…" over
and over again.

"I don't know what you've been told or what you've been
through, but I promise you that the Bloodsetters are the ones
who destroyed our home and Bamaul is not only responsible,
but is not the rightful king of Katama by any means. I will
tell you this as many times as I have to. You have been lied

to this entire time!"

Corly had been lightly rocking back and forth while Darien had been shouting at her and she suddenly reared her head back and screeched so loud Darien thought he might have burst an eardrum.

Shouting something unintelligible, Corly suddenly lunged forward in an attempt to tackle Darien to the ground.

Quick reflexes saved him and he was able to dodge in time. As she lunged past, Darien made a snap decision. He quickly and with more force than was probably necessary used the hilt of his short blade to strike Corly sharply on the side of the head and she immediately slumped heavily to the ground. Sinking to his knees in exhaustion Darien heaved a deep sigh, coughing as he waved away the dust in the air. His decision was to let his future self handle things where Corly was concerned, but he couldn't just leave her there. He had no way of telling how long the chamber would remain stable and if the falling debris was any indication it wouldn't be long before the whole place collapsed.

Gritting his teeth he lifted Corly onto his shoulder, thanking the Godlings above she hadn't grown any since the last he had seen her. He felt his most recent wound she had inflicted on him rip open, but he took a slow breath and waited for it to begin healing again before making his way quickly and carefully to where Lockhart and the others had gone. Maybe one of them would be able to do a better job at convincing Corly she had been wildly deceived.

He prayed to whatever Godling might be listening that

they could settle the issue peacefully without Corly doing any more stabbing. There was no telling just what she would do when she woke up and found herself surrounded by people she considered enemies.

Just gonna hope for the best I guess.

Deciding to focus on the task at hand Darien hustled into the tunnel the others had disappeared into. The cavern receding behind him was becoming more and more unstable by the moment and he wasn't sure how much longer they could have spent in there before it came crashing down on top of them. He got his answer as a violent shudder accompanied by a loud groaning signaled the cavern finally caving in on itself. A billow of dust followed after him and he was hit by a blast of air that threatened to send him tumbling, but thankfully he had made it far enough he was able to withstand the pressure.

Coughing again at the dust Darien tried to put thoughts about how close they had come to being buried alive out of his mind and pushed on into the darkened tunnel. Thanks to his dragon eyes he could see just fine, but Corly's remark from earlier still rankled him.

"Definitely not a lizard," he grumbled.

"What is this about a lizard?"

Following markings scratched into the wall left behind by one of the others, probably Squirrel, Darien had rounded a sharp corner and almost ran straight into the last person he wanted to see at the moment, Liana.

"I see you have acquired a new toy to play with," she

sighed as she turned away and began to head back into the tunnel. "Come now. If I don't return with you in tow soon that very scary leader of yours will undoubtedly become upset with me and we can't have that now, can we? I *do* wonder what he will say about the latest female you have collected, but we'll just have to wait and see about that now won't we?"

Darien's ears burned at Liana's insinuation, but he couldn't deny the fact he always seemed to find himself in troublesome situations where women were concerned.

Wochisa is the only one I'm in love with though.

He briefly wondered how the daughter of the Jarabin chief was doing and what she had been up to the last few months, but he had more pressing things to worry about at the moment.

The tunnel around them creaked and groaned in unison with the collapsed cavern behind them. Darien tried to hurry as the sounds ringing in his ears made him more than a little uneasy, but hauling Corly along and his healing wounds weren't very helpful in that endeavor. Dust and debris floated all around them, occasionally accompanied by another ominous creak or shudder.

Sighing at his luck Darien wished he could stop for a moment to catch his breath. Both he and Liana continued in silence for a short while before she inevitably began to pick at him.

"By the way, that is a *spectacular* trophy you have acquired. I do wonder just how much longer you can refrain from eliminating your enemies. The rest of the world is not as forgiving or naive as you and inevitably one of them will come back to haunt you."

Darien only grunted. What Liana was saying made sense in a way, but there was no chance he was going to kill undoubtedly his best friend, especially since she was woefully misinformed about a multitude of issues. Not that Liana would understand or even care why he would save someone who appeared to be just another Bloodsetter, but that could wait for later.

"Can we move a bit faster? I doubt this area is gonna last much longer and I'd rather not get buried alive here."

Liana arched one of her thin, delicate eyebrows at him, but only let out another sigh. "I suppose. Although I assume you are aware such a thing would pose no real threat to either you or I?"

"Sure! But she wouldn't fare so well and I'm not about to let her get killed after spending so much time trying to talk some sense into her! She isn't just some random Bloodsetter, she's from Village Breathwynd and I'm not letting anything happen to her until I figure out what in the Hells is going on with her! So let's get a move on already!"

Liana exhaled in exasperation, but began to glide along the earthen floor into the depths of the tunnel, her feet barely even touching the ground.

Seeing in the tunnel with his dragon eyes was no issue for him, but it was the first time he had noticed such a strange anomaly about Liana, aside from the multiple auras she possessed and her ability to converse with both Koseki and Hosroyu using him as an intermediary.

Following Liana further into the tunnels he tried to shake off his shock and annoyance. Thankfully it wasn't much longer before they caught up to Lockhart and the others.

The rest of their group had seemingly chosen this spot due to it being stocked with a moderate amount of equipment and provisions. How the General would know about such a place Darien wasn't sure, but he had learned the hard way asking unnecessary questions was a waste of time where the General was concerned.

Gently placing the unconscious Corly on the ground Darien sat heavily against an earthen wall. He took in his current surroundings; lit only by a taper slowly burning in a small brass chamberstick fitting within the palm of Squirrel's hand. The light wasn't an issue for him, but he was sure the others needed it to see any further than the end of their own nose.

"Don't worry much about it. It doesn't produce enough smoke or fire to be a problem for our lungs, right?"

Squirrel must have noticed Darien's quizzical look despite the lack of light as he answered the foremost question in Darien's mind. Normally one wouldn't dare create any amount of fire or smoke in a closed space like this because it would inevitably make one unable to breathe pretty quickly, but Lockhart must have approved it if no-one was opposing its use.

"Who is the girl?"

General Lockhart's question snapped Darien to his senses. Leave it to General Lockhart to not even give him a moment's rest. The tone of his voice indicated the General was less than pleased at Corly's presence, but for once Darien was prepared with an answer.

"She's from Village Breathwynd like me. I don't know why she is acting on the behalf of the Bloodsetters, but her name is-"

"Corly..."

For the first time Darien noticed there was another person who had been added to their group from when they had first arrived at the Castle of the King. The man was emaciated, filthy and haggard as a beggar, but there was no mistaking the rasp in the voice that he had listened to every day of his life until Village Breathwynd had been attacked.

Darien's eyes widened and if he wasn't so tired he would have jumped to his feet at the realization of who had spoken finally sunk in.

"Oltan! Is that really you? How...How are you alive? What happened to you? What..."

"That is enough for now," Lockhart broke in. "Once we're done doing what we can for Oltan and for my ankle we are moving on, and quickly. These tunnels were our salvation this time, but now that Bamaul knows about them, what was once our trump card is now forever useless to us as we will never be able to utilize them again. I intend for that fact to be symmetrical when all is said and done."

Darien didn't know what 'symmetrical' meant, but the

sense of joy and relief he felt at seeing Oltan alive was so palpable mists of purple and violet sprang up around him and he had to concentrate to subdue them.

Oltan wheezed a short rasping laugh. "I bet the boy doesn't understand what symmetrical even means, but know that young Philip here was once almost as thick-headed as you lad so there is hope for you yet."

Oltan's words came out in belabored breaths, but his smile was evident to Darien's dragon eyes even within the dimness of the tunnel.

"Ahem. Leaving the old man's senility aside we need to get moving now that you're here. Since the girl is known and of some importance to both of you, you will give me the full story later. Jack, how much longer?"

Jack, who had been concocting some sort of splint out of cloth and pieces of wood salvaged from the supplies, muttered a jovial reply.

"You do be right as rain in a mite, good General. Nurse Jackie here do be fixin' ya up real nice."

"Shut up and just answer the man without being Nurse Jack-Ass for once," quipped Geru as he inspected several crates stacked haphazardly nearby while Tartas merely grinned. Jack cackled at the admonishment, but he did quickly finish his ministrations on the General's ankle not long after.

Darien noticed the excitable fellow named Gelas quietly sitting nearby with his arms wrapped around his knees and staring off at nothing. Wily stood close by his strange friend, but oddly offered nothing more to the conversation. Liana, as usual, chose to ignore the lot of them and was quietly conversing with her retainers Marco and Mari apart from the rest.

Darien took a bit of solace in the normal banter between Jack and Geru amid the myriad chaos unfolding around them, but the General put an end to that quick enough.

"If you two are done let us get moving. Geru, Tartas, are there any usable supplies still here?"

"None worth mentioning." It was the olive-skinned Geru who answered. "Weapons haven't been maintained or replaced in Godlings know how long and the rations are all rotten. I don't think anyone from our side would have dared get this close to the castle when we were preparing to use the tunnels for our assault. These must be relics of several years ago."

General Lockhart fell silent for a moment with a frown before giving instructions, his voice betraying none of the considerable pain he must be enduring.

"We have a temporary destination, although it feels like unnecessary backtracking, we don't have much choice. According to Oltan these tunnels can eventually get us most of the way to where we were headed before we encountered Little Maiani, but I have granted his request for a small detour."

No-one asked what the detour was or why Oltan thought it was important and instead only looked expectantly at their leader for further instructions.

"We will check what stores we can along the way while we can, but once we reach our temporary location I have been given an assurance we will be able to collapse the majority of the tunnels leading there behind us."

"The ones we intend to use later on will still be sound enough for us to do so, right?" Squirrel asked.

Lockhart nodded. "That seems to be the case. Darien, you will tell me about this girl you are so concerned about along the way. You mentioned she is from your village, correct?"

"Yes." Explaining Corly would take some time, especially since he still wasn't sure what had happened to her and she had been accusing him of some pretty outrageous things back in the cavern. Resigning himself to endure another one of General Lockhart's interrogations Darien started trying to put his thoughts in order for the journey ahead.

Gently and carefully lifting Corly's limp form over his shoulder Darien absently gave voice to the unspoken question on everyone's mind.

"Where are we stopping anyway?"

Instead of Lockhart, it was Oltan who answered with a wheeze. "My boy, we are headed home for a spell."

"What!?"

"These tunnels run through most of Katama. One such path will lead us to a very familiar place, the library. We will be stopping at Village Breathwynd."

Darien was stunned. Not only was he once again going to stop by the place he had grown up, but another aspect of the library unknown to him had been revealed. He was sure Oltan would tell him more eventually, but for now they just had to make it there and hope Corly didn't try to kill him in the meantime.

Darien adjusted Corly a bit on his shoulder and took a deep breath.

"Alright. Let's go."

Here ends Volume III of the Dragonsouled Chronicles